ONLY HUMAN

Diane Chandler

blackbird

First published in Great Britain in 2020 by Blackbird Digital Books

A CIP catalogue record for this book is available at the British Library
ISBN-9781916426856

Printed and bound in Great Britain by Clays Ltd, Elcograf S.p.A.

for Mum and Dad

On the whole, humans want to be good, but not too good, and not quite all the time

George Orwell

1

What were the odds that I would spot them that day from the top of the 94 bus? Sitting up front like a child to bagsy the best view, enjoying the warmth of the year's first sunshine on my face. Ironic that I was en route to buy him a birthday gift too, one of his favourite polo shirts. My husband, down on the pavement, in the secret shadow of a pub doorway, tenderly kissing another woman. The way it had wrenched them when they'd pulled apart, the way it had punched me in the gut. And it was I who had felt criminal, loping off the bus, stomach on slow spin, and into a furtive black cab home.

That evening, Ollie had been hosting a wine tasting at the shop, Sophie was sleeping over with a friend, and so I sat in the darkening kitchen tormenting myself – that look between them. Play, misery, rewind, play. When he was finally home, my face must have glowed white in the gloom. At first, he'd thought I was ill and sat down concerned by my side, a caring hand at my shoulder, while my belly roiled on; all out of vomit, it offered only limp spasms.

'What's her name?' I said, quite calmly.

'Who?'

'You shit.'

Ollie flinched, his own face drained of colour, but still he said nothing, still he must have hoped.

1

'I saw you,' I said. 'On the way to Westfield.'

He grasped my hand. 'She's just a friend.'

A dizziness took hold then. At some point, I was going to have to stand and stomp off, but my body was denying me that triumph.

'Kiss all your friends like that, do you?'

He was nicked. A plaintive sigh and he released my shoulder, slumped into his chair.

'How long's it been going on?'

He hung his head, it was a good minute before he spoke.

'Christmas.'

'Since *Christmas*?'

My mind hurtled back through the months; snatches of days, events in our diaries, Ollie's business trips. Nearly five months and I'd not had an inkling – how had he pulled that off?

I really did try to leave the room. Had I been in a film, I would have risen with dignity and glided, turning at the door with a damning, 'Finish it now or you'll lose me.' Truth is that I didn't dare challenge him like that. Truth is that a tear bobbled onto the rim of my eye and, against my vehement command, slid down my cheek. I watched it plop onto my shirt. It was he who had stood and left the room.

A wave had smashed me off my feet. I found myself tumbling, rolling and spiralling. Where was the surface? Where were the depths? What would I do if he left me?

It never occurred to me to leave him.

Nearly two weeks on and I was still reeling. Any hopes he may have harboured at finding himself still in our bed were skewed; it was crucial that Sophie remained oblivious, and so there we slept, back-to-back, stony-to-sheepish. Some mornings he'd attempt a sickening hand to my shoulder as we passed in the kitchen, a lopsided smile, grotesque in its meekness. While I sustained the ice treatment.

Why had he done it? We were still having sex, weren't we? – true it was same old, same old – but what ancient marriage had not slid into the comfort of a fleeting missionary every now and then? What was he not getting from the marriage? From me? My own shortcomings unfurled before my eyes like a magician's handkerchief, endless and garish, but I remained frozen by shock, by fear. Unable to confront him again.

'I hate seeing you like this,' said Scarlett as I sank into her sofa, cowed like a rescue dog. 'You've got to have it out with him. Don't let the bastard off scot-free without telling you everything.'

Sound advice. Scar was one of my dearest friends, and the only person I'd confided in, but whenever I sought to muster that anger I found only vulnerability, my once exuberant confidence shattered. She too must have been stunned by the depth and speed of my unravelling, a ship's cable whipping from its spool. The fury did bubble, finding release at odd times – and on unlikely victims – but I had not yet gathered the courage to unleash it upon him. In case he did indeed tell me everything?

Instead, I'd been scrabbling to fortify myself, to restore the old Anna, so that I might cope with whatever the consequences of that *everything* would be. And the way forward, as I saw it then, was to flee backwards to a time when Ollie and I had been equals, to unearth my corporate self. I might now be a product of the school gate, but I used to *be* somebody.

So, after a spontaneous email to a former colleague, I was sitting once again in a slick meeting room at my old firm, a city investment bank. But what was I thinking? Sixteen years since

I'd left, much longer since I'd last been interviewed, and the nerves were tap-dancing inside my chest, breaths coming in staccato bursts. Was I really up to this? At least, outwardly, the Max Mara suit was bestowing some of the old swagger. Black wool with a soft chalk stripe, and classic I thought, plus the fact that it fitted me again after the recent weight loss – every cloud and that.

'*Nice*,' Sophie had said that morning. 'Don't let the fashion police see you, Mum.'

'I need to impress on them that I was once a professional woman. Can't wear anything too funky.'

That sing-song voice I now assume to appease my tricky teenage daughter.

'*Funky?*'

That eye roll she'd recently perfected.

I cast her from my mind, thoughts of Ollie too, and fixed a smile for the man across the desk, middle-aged, white, alpha – all that privilege in one human being – and then for his sidekick, a young Asian woman. My email had fallen upon good times. They now had this diversity scheme, a drive to recruit women returners, to harness the experience and perspective that evaporates once we leave to have our kids. Not an opening at my previous level, of course, but still.

'Research suggests that women are better at spotting opportunities, at inspiring others, even that they are more strategic than men.'

From his smug tenor, I knew that he believed otherwise, and already I disliked the man; flashes from my past, of a thousand other chauvinists.

'Oh, I'm very strategic,' I said, with a firm nod.

Even if, at home, I was being buffeted like a dingy in a perfect storm.

His eyes narrowed, did he sense that?

'So, can you flesh out the qualities you would bring to this position?'

Qualities? The word flitted, my mind unable to pin it down. I rummaged for those lines I'd rehearsed in the mirror, lamenting how the face above the suit was now more crêpe de chine than porcelain, shaking my hair forwards to hide what it could.

Qualities, qualities... How do you vocalise the expanse of life you've encased yourself, *infused* yourself with, during all those years at home as a wife and mother? And make it count? Not those weekend mornings I'd dragged Sophie out of bed to engage in every activity under the sun. Not those playground drop-offs spiked with testosterone-pumped women. Nor those evenings of playing wifey at wine events, or poring over recipes with ingredients I'd never heard of.

No, I knew he was after the soft skills I'd apparently acquired in that role of *homemaker* which would see me well back in the corporate world. And, thankfully, they came to me just in time – the critical thinking, the time management, the resilience. I held forth at length, added a joke too, well that was my intention, one that might capture a skill he would appreciate.

'And I chaired the PTA at my daughter's primary school,' I said. 'Put me in a room full of tiger mums and I'll emerge alive and kicking!'

A slow nod, just the one, but no smile – I guess the tiger mum bit was lost on him. (Of course, I was one of those pushy mothers myself, most of us seemed to be these days, even if as a tribe we'd be shocked to be considered such.)

As the man made a few notes, my clammy palms found the rough wool of my skirt with a surreptitious clench; so nervous, but did I really want to subject myself to this life again?

'How would you feel about getting up to speed on the new technologies, which will have transformed themselves twice over since your day?'

Helpless. But that was ageism – even if I must have been one of the oldest potential returners.

As if in tacit agreement, the sidekick uncrossed and re-crossed her legs; a silent signal, and he did clock it.

'I mean, change has been especially rapid in our business,' he added, shifting in his seat, a hint of weakness which bolstered me – and also brought a sudden memory.

As a young graduate I'd once been advised to imagine all interviewers sitting naked in the bath, a rubber duck floating between their legs. So that's what I did. Stripped him off, paunch and all, steering that duck clear from his stub of a modesty, and my shoulders sank a little.

'Well,' I said, with a deep breath and a more relaxed smile, 'I understand that these days emotional intelligence is just as valuable as technical ability.'

And I happily added two more qualities to my list: empathy and intuition. Not that I'd intuited my husband's affair, had I?

A flicker of smile. Steepled fingertips. And then he floored me.

'An impressive track record while you were with us.'

'Thank you.'

I felt myself flush, surprised tears springing in gratitude.

Because, yes, I'd been bloody good at my job, had been valued, on other people's radar. And yet here I was, Anna Bond, in my mid-forties, in the prime of life, and floundering. The female term for a cuckold, I'd read, is a cuckqueen, and that felt perfectly apt.

On the Tube home, I stared through the pages of the *Evening Standard*. They'd said they'd be in touch but, whatever their decision, I'd known. Even as I'd sat gazing at the abstract swirls of colour on the walls in reception, as I'd been led through the open plan, with its splash of screens and the stench of callow greed. Let's face it, I'd known even as I'd dressed that morning. I had moved on. The corporate world which had once given me meaning would no longer rouse me, and if offered the job I wouldn't take it; there would have to be some other route back to me. The interview, however, had fortified me – I was still in there somewhere. Perhaps the way forward was philanthropic, some form of charity work, even if the thought of sorting fusty second hand clothes or stuffing envelopes left me cold.

I nearly missed my stop. Dashed to the closing doors and out onto the ground I loved. Chiswick, my one constant. Down on the pavements of Turnham Green Terrace, the heatwave which was to smile upon the nation that summer was already warming itself up, and the yeasty scent of Fuller's Brewery steeped the air, a deep breath of it heightening my sense of home.

Hanging back, I glanced in at Ollie's shop on the other side of the road, its frontage painted in Plummet Grey, the lettering a deep charcoal, *Oliver Bond Esq. Purveyor of Fine Wines*. He stood planted at the oak desk, frowning down at his phone, one hairy arm outstretched, hand resting on the layers of tissue paper. Pillar of the community, so he always joked. Still a thick crown of hair, still sandy too, and cut to perfection by the guy opposite – all the local businesses enjoyed the fruits of barter and Burgundy was a heady commodity.

A woman entered and Ollie looked up with that winning smile. Expecting the sight of his face to bring misery, I found instead that it stirred a surge of defiance. *An impressive track record*, the man had said. Who was this bastard to have an affair on me? He fetched down a bottle from the wooden shelves, holding it with reverence, stroking it. Not unlike he once used to hold and stroke me. Did I still love him? I had no idea. We just were. Anna and Ollie a solid couple, married now for nearly twenty years. A slide into marital oblivion so steady that the moment when I'd no longer caught my breath, when my insides had no longer flipped was indiscernible.

'Leave him,' Scar had said. Simple words for such a terrifying act of dismantlement.

I crossed over to the deli in search of something quick for dinner.

At my front door I assumed that cape of super-motherhood which smothered all fragility of my own. I'd been slipping it on since Sophie was born, and it now draped itself automatically in her presence.

In our hallway I found a bike propped against the wall, heard her chatting to someone in the kitchen and smiled with relief, it was easier these days when we were not alone, just the two of us. Cocking my head to gauge which of her friends she'd brought back from school, I was pulled up short. A male voice, rich and deep, suffused with a particular joyous-come-cheeky resonance, which I recognised from my own youth. They were flirting. I wandered through to them.

The boy was sitting at the island opposite my daughter, and he didn't look up immediately. Between them sat our pet tortoise, Horace, whom the boy was feeding, leaf by leaf. Cocky then. Finally, he glanced at me, his eyes a startling pewter grey, luminous with his laughter, with enthrallment.

'Hi,' I said, bearing down on Sophie with a quizzical smile,

8

unable to hide my initial shock.

'Hi Mum. This is Jack.'

Her tone towards me was warmer than usual, right from the start I was aware of that. Her smile shone half euphorically, half sheepishly, and our eyes remained locked while the impulses leapt between our synapses – why didn't you tell me? Why should I? And then I looked away, softly rueful of her inevitable slide towards independence. She'd been pulling away for some time now and this was a further step. For a moment I felt completely alone, abandoned by husband and daughter, the two truths of my life.

The boy stood up from the bar stool, causing it to rock on its legs, and I pretended not to notice the face Sophie pulled at him, mocking his stumble, but was heartened to see that she held such power.

'Hello.' I strolled over and held out my hand.

'Nice to meet you, Mrs Bond.' A chunk of dirty-blond hair flopped onto his forehead as if by remote control. 'You have a lovely house.'

'Thank you, Jack. Cup of tea?'

'Awesome, thank you.'

I turned to fill the kettle. Her first boyfriend. But this was not a boy, he must have been six-foot tall, his chest was as broad as Ollie's, his wrists were muscled for Christ's sake! As I unloaded my bag of food into the fridge, I could feel the energy dancing between them and finally I swung around, arms folded.

'What are you up to, then?'

'Revising together. History. We're in the same set.'

'The rise of Hitler.' It was Jack who spoke, his smile disarming. 'And the causes thereof.'

Thereof. Clearly from an educated family.

'Sounds like a plan. Biscuit?'

9

I took the tin over, it felt good to have a prop.

'Awesome, thank you.' He dug out two chocolate digestives and slipped one whole into his mouth.

Again, I contemplated Horace, now abandoned on the island to feed himself, and I shared a further lingering look with Sophie. My hygiene rules were strict, no tortoise on eating surfaces, but we both knew I wouldn't nag. I wandered back to pour the teas.

'How was the interview, Mum?'

I turned with a bright smile but her own eyes were on Jack, her radiant face carefully framed by a mass of blonde, and my heart leapt out in protection – take it slowly Sophie.

'Great,' I said, watching the boy as I placed his mug of tea down. His smile oozed filmic confidence. 'If wanky bankers float your boat.'

'Mum!'

I was pleased to see him blush; not *so* cocky then. 'Hope your father doesn't work in the City?'

'No, er, he's a garden designer.'

'Creative, I like that. Anyway, been a long day, I'm off for a bath. Nice to meet you, Jack.'

I slunk from the kitchen, mug in hand and stopped on the first stair to catch Sophie's words.

'Parents, hey?'

I waited, leaned into the banister.

'She's mad,' said Jack.

I'd intended to soak off the interview but instead I was fending off thoughts like missiles. Ollie. Why had he had the affair? I was going to challenge him while that post-interview defiance was still fresh; the Max Mara suit alone had restored a bundle of confidence. But I had been counting on a return to my old firm as the way forward, it would have allowed me to walk away from my marriage – if that was the path I chose – or to cope if he were to leave me. I saw again that woman in the doorway, the look between them. What was I going to do now? Where next would I search for that elusive someone I used to be?

And now there was Jack. This stranger lounging in my kitchen, a boy-man whose presence hung in the air. The space he took up was disturbing, a mass of limbs and flesh, a trace of earthy aftershave too, whereas most teenage boys smelt of baked beans.

The bath water had cooled so I topped it up with hot and plunged beneath the foam of raspberry bubbles (I still bought Sophie's childhood favourite) wallowing until my breath burst. Sweeping back up, I scooped a palmful of froth, squeezed until the bubbles had vanished and reached for another. What had just happened in my kitchen? Well it seemed that, totally out of the blue, a rite of passage was underway for my daughter, an emotion in her eyes I'd not yet seen. Had I warned her enough about sex? About the privilege of her own body? What if Jack were to coerce her into it? You can't tell a teenager not to do it, I myself was younger than she is now, but somehow, at fifteen, I seemed older than my daughter, more street-wise.

A gale of laughter from below and I sank again beneath the water, losing myself in its cocoon. Mad, he'd called me. And I knew that mad was teenage slang for cool – it didn't mean loopy or unhinged.

By the end of that summer, however, I would be unable to fathom quite what I had become.

2

The following morning, Saturday, I sat at the island with a coffee and my laptop, waiting for Sophie to leave the house so that I could have it out with Ollie. She was off to Chiswick library to revise with her mates. To take my mind off the matter, I sat idly Googling vacancies at Save the Children. For a charity it was an unexpectedly slick outfit and I came across a job in finance that suited my investment background, but I remained unconvinced that an office in any shape was the way forward. Unless it was one where I'd start my own business – now that idea thrilled me, even if I had no inkling of what I would do.

My daughter bounded into the kitchen and flung the fridge open in search of her favourites, dried mangoes. I've always ensured a steady, military, supply.

'Off then, Mum.' She fed a heap into a Tupperware and smacked on the lid.

'You'll get something more substantial to eat too, won't you?'

A jerk of her head and she busied herself packing her mini rucksack.

'What subject today?'

'Maths.'

And how I'd endeavoured to step in and help on that one. All to no avail.

'Don't forget, it's output not input at this stage. Past papers are key.'

I withered beneath the dead eye she dealt me.

'I've got this.' She yanked on the rucksack and left the kitchen.

'Bye, then.'

The front door slammed, shaking the house, and with it the wings of my heart; back to normal after yesterday's thaw while Jack was there.

The moment my daughter had begun to slip away from me I cannot pinpoint. She'd always seemed happy with my drive for extra-curriculars, the piano lessons, the dance, the swimming, all of it. Even the tennis, driving around England for tournaments – until the day she broke down and begged me to stop. I could still see her beside me, windscreen wipers battling with the M1, believing she was crying because the match might be rained off, not because she was sick of all that tennis.

Tiger mum? We all deny it, but I was a whacking great five hundred pound Bengali, paws all over my daughter. I'd realised long ago that I had diverted the energy devoted to my career into her, a seamless switch of points. She became my project. All those times I'd banned TV for a week when her exam grades were not among the highest, refused the odd sleepover, even vetoed her wish to take art GCSE. An A* was tough to achieve in art, they said, and A*s were the prize.

Despite my follies we had once been close, Sophie and I, but she'd suddenly whipped herself away. And in the face of her withdrawal I have clung on. Shoot the arrow, they say, but I have not even bought the bow, let alone loaded it.

I heard the stairs creak with Ollie's tread. I'd woken determined to ambush an unprepared moment before he left for the shop, but Sophie's disdain had gnawed at that resolve. My hands shook as he pootled into the kitchen, rolling the sleeve of his pastel shirt to conjure the laid back look of a wine merchant.

'Back to the salt mines.' His affable bluster and again that spaniel smile, gauging my mood.

'I wish you bloody well would.'

The words fell out, and he paused mid-roll, eyes widening in surprise, but then continued with the other sleeve.

My chest surged. 'What was her name?'

He gave himself several moments to collect his thoughts before unfurling a sigh, arms dropping to his side.

'Kathy Hunter,' he said quietly, his eyes finally meeting mine.

'Huh! By name and by nature.'

And who would call themselves Kathy not Kath at our age?

'Where did you meet her?'

Again, he played for time. 'Wine Fair. She worked for Majestic.'

'Classy.' I paused. 'A whole five fucking months? How did you manage that without me knowing?'

'I'm sorry.' His eyes dropped to the floor.

'You coward. What lies did you spin me? All those buying trips abroad? The wine-tastings? What were you really up to, huh?'

He shook his head. 'I –'

'Would have been longer if I hadn't caught you at it, wouldn't it? Five bogus months. Has our whole marriage been a sham too?'

'No.' He looked up at me then. 'And it was more like four, I just…'

'You just what? Couldn't keep your little prick in your

14

trousers?'

That was cruel, but he took the sting, his eyes levelled on mine.

'I'm sorry. It's over. It would have been over, I was going to end it.'

Really? I thought again of his tender kiss in that clandestine pub doorway, of that look between them.

'I didn't love her. It was just... sex.'

'What's wrong with sex with me?'

'It was a fling, she meant nothing to me.' He looked genuinely contrite, but then he was a master of the service industry. 'I'm sorry.'

'Well maybe sorry isn't enough.'

His palms flew up in surrender. 'I told you, I ended it there and then. What more do I have to do?'

I glowered at him, stunned by all that had happened in my life when I'd had no notion of what he was up to. All those times we'd been having sex when he was shagging another woman. How had I not known? I had been oblivious and I felt stupid. Duped.

And yet at that moment we were on the brink. What more *did* I want him to do? Our eyes met in a flash of recognition, an age-old analysis, the one of the other. And I was too scared. Thumping my laptop shut, I reached for my coffee, stone cold now, and feigned a sip.

My climbdown was palpable.

'Do you want me to leave?' he asked, knowing then that I did not.

I said nothing, but he was right, I didn't want him to leave. Because I was in no place to sustain myself emotionally, because I couldn't bear the thought of Sophie choosing him over me, because I loved the very bones of the home I had made for us all. And because it seemed that I still loved him. At least I thought I did, I was so buried in the marriage I didn't know the difference anymore.

'Why did you do it?' I snapped, sensing both his relief and my diminishing power.

So much so that he chanced it then. 'You allowed me a long leash.'

'Long leash? Pathetic! What, are you a dog or something?'

A smile broke onto his face then, no doubt he hoped I'd return it, humour having been endemic to our marriage, but my mood was volcanic and the smile vanished.

'I mean...'

'Are you saying it's *my* fault?'

'Well you tell me? Why do *you* think I did it?'

Clever move, Ollie could always reverse the question, and stupidly I rose to it.

'I have no idea. But I will not allow you to pin *your* infidelity on me. Have the balls to take responsibility for your own sordid actions.'

'I don't know, Anna. You'd changed. Seemed distant, less attentive, somehow.'

A grain of truth there which required deflection.

'And what about Sophie?' I cried. 'What if it had been her who'd seen you snogging in that sleazy doorway? You've betrayed her too.'

'I'm not married to Sophie.'

'Well you *are* married to me. And I would never do that to you!'

I dropped down from the stool, livid at his skill in taking the advantage, the silent power I'd held for the past couple of weeks dissipated. I've never carried myself with a stoop like so many tall women do, and I puffed myself up to full height, causing him to step back as I loomed – but I think we both knew that my ferocious beast was more of a terrified cornered one.

'Pathetic!' I cried again. 'Long leash, bullshit!'

The doorbell rang, stunning us into silence, and Ollie scuttled down the hallway with me in half-hearted pursuit. Picking up his briefcase, he opened the door.

Jack stood on the path with his bike. My heart lifted to see the boy back.

'Hello.' He smiled disarmingly.

'Yes?' Ollie barked, still planted in the doorway, while I hovered behind.

'Er, I'm a friend of Sophie's. She said I could leave my bike in your hallway.'

'I'm not having a bloody big bike in my hallway.'

Ollie stomped down onto the path and around Jack, who shrank back. My husband muttered his way to the gate, flinging it shut behind him, while I opened the front door wider with a warm smile.

'It's fine, Jack, bring it in.'

The boy had blushed a confused crimson. 'Just that it might get stolen outside the library.'

'No problem, don't mind him, come on in.'

He wheeled the bike inside and carefully set a handle bar against the wall, where a collection of dark smudges caught my eye; clearly he'd already been to the house several times.

'Thank you, Mrs Bond,' he said. And then he couldn't escape fast enough, poor lad.

Closing the front door, I sank my brow to its cooling panes. Fire within there was still aplenty, but that had been an inferno rather than the pithy burst of flames I'd intended, and I was now squarely on the back foot. I glanced at the bike, that evening at least Sophie for one would be in better humour.

With a fresh coffee I wandered out into the garden, where our tortoise, Horace, the only pet I was not scared of, or allergic to, was eating his way through the purple rain daisies I'd just planted. I sat down at our garden table and watched him.

'What's happened to our family, Horace?'

Had we just come close to mention of a separation? Divorce? Never before in nearly twenty years of marriage, and so blindingly shocking that I knew for certain I didn't want to go there. Neither did he though – we had both shied back. Perhaps he too dreaded that Sophie might choose me over him (after all, that would be the traditional outcome), perhaps the prospect of a tumultuous break up distressed him as it did me, but neither of those was a sterling reason to stay. It could be that he still loved me. Huh, the cheating bastard.

Long leash? What a load of bollocks. More like a chance he'd jumped at. Majestic? *Kathy* Hunter? Judging by the memory of her, all double-D and dark roots, I bet she'd thrown herself at him. Admittedly, that look between them, it hadn't seemed like *just sex* but then Ollie was an accomplished actor, it went with his job. So it could have been a fling, as he'd claimed. A whim he'd indulged, an opportunity for exciting sex with someone new.

I sipped my coffee. He was right though, I had been less attentive. Not that this was grounds for infidelity, but I had barely focused on him for a while now. During the affair had he ever been dreamy over dinner? Not that I'd noticed. Ever been unexpectedly absent beyond his habitual buying trips abroad? Not that I'd noticed. I had stopped noticing, because I had been absorbed in my own future.

Panicking would be a more apt description. What was I going to do once Sophie left home? It was only two years off, and already I was barely needed, her peers were far more important than me, her forays into London unreported. She'd royally rebuffed my endeavours to help organise her final year of GCSEs, and I knew that barren times lay ahead so I had been out seeking self-enrichment. Evening classes on the history of London, talks on melting ice caps, the desperate hunt for a new project – all of that long before I'd applied for the job with my old firm.

Maybe I had taken my eye off the family, off our marriage. Less time on Sophie inevitably entailed less on Ollie. And it's true that I'd no longer joined him for his wine evenings, hadn't thought it mattered to him. House could do with a spring clean too. And with it our sex life. I mean, I wouldn't mind a fling either, wild sex with someone new, how *exhilarating*, but marriage was a contract, and I would never accept that it was my fault he had broken it.

I would never break it myself, would I?

3

On Monday morning I met Scarlett for breakfast as usual. Odd that *I* look forward to *her* day off, but then every day is a day off for me, as Sophie once told me – that's what you get when you give it all up for your offspring. Scar had suggested it was time for me to brave High Road Brasserie again rather than hide out on her sofa, and I was conscious of having recently become a drain rather than the radiator I used to be around her, sucking life and not exuding it, so I'd agreed. Even if I had savoured her home; the expensive fig candles always lit, the BAFTAs on her mantelpiece, the nude sculptures (one of which was apparently of her – Ollie once said, if so then she was scrawny).

We sat near the window, on a velvet bench seat they tended to reserve for us.

'Not seduced by your old firm, then?' Scar sipped her coffee.

I shook my head. 'Banking's not for me anymore. But feels good to have landed the job, and they did mention my *impressive track record* from all those years ago. Yay! Hold that thought.'

'You *are* impressive, Anna. You're an awesome woman.'

'Not feeling awesome right now.'

'You've just taken on your crappy husband, haven't you?'

I shrugged my gratitude, I'd spent the first half hour holding forth about the spat, and she smiled, her soft brown eyes drawing me in like the warmth of an open fire. Eyes which were always perfectly pencil-lined, with a flick too. Some years ago I'd found myself copying the red lowlights of her hair, seeking the deftness of her layers, the sincerest form of flattery and all that. I dared to hope that her trademark heeled boots which brought her to my height were a similar accolade.

We had met on day one of our kids' primary school. Her Nicky in shorts, my Sophie in summer dress, all lined up to be led away from we mothers who anxiously flanked them.

'Knock, knock,' came Nicky's reedy voice from behind.

And Sophie had turned around to him, plaits swinging. 'Who's there?'

'Nicholas.'

'Nicholas who?'

'Knickerless girls shouldn't climb trees.'

Full of giggles, Sophie had clamped a hand to her mouth and swung back to face the front, while Scar and I had struggled to stifle our own laughter, eyes meeting in a flash of mock shock, an instant bond. I loved the idea that her home embraced such naughtiness – knock knock jokes in our house were innocuous – and I loved her nickname with its whiff of mafioso, (Sophie, her initiation to death having been through *The Lion King*, was less keen).

Soon we were caught up in that mutual balm of play dates, wine dates, and ultimately dinner dates with the guys. At some point Scar had returned to her career in TV production, while I continued to stand at the school gate – because my own mother hadn't (well didn't we all wish to reverse poor parenting, whatever we believed it to be?). And I had clung vicariously to my friend's company, one who still worked, in an exciting realm too, not those other mums like me who didn't.

21

A friend called Scar.

The waitress served our breakfasts and she tucked in, but the sight of poached eggs made me queasy. I was still losing weight.

'What about a new hobby? My neighbour keeps chickens.' That roguish smile of hers was back.

'Think I'd rather learn to knit.'

'Then you'd need a rocking chair, Grandma.'

We both laughed.

'Actually, I'm wondering about charity work. Until I stumble upon the big passion, whatever that might be.'

'Cool. They'd snap you up, any of the biggies like Oxfam or Cancer Research. With your background.'

'Mm. Was thinking something more hands on. At the coal face, with real people rather than head office.'

She nodded. 'You go girl.'

I smiled, mindful of hogging the conversation yet again. 'So how's Nick?'

'He's good. Least I think so. Mid-GCSEs. I'm relieved he's boarding in all honesty, at least *they* handle the stress of him not revising.'

It was my turn to smile gently. Her husband Alex had shunted their son off to board at the tender age of eight, a point which continued to be moot so many years on. She'd even had an affair over it, had shared all the details with me, which I still found shocking – also slightly titillating. Now they went to edgy concerts, ran marathons together. Their way back into the marriage, she'd said. Sexual substitutes, I wondered.

'He'll always be able to wing it, won't he, Nick?' I said. 'Brain like his, probably doesn't need to work too much.'

'And he has an incentive. Alex has offered a hundred pounds per A*. Ludicrous if you ask me. But that's my twat of a husband for you. What about Sophie?'

'First exam today.'

'Bet she'll sweep up too.'

I reached for my coffee. Somehow, I hadn't revealed anything to my closest friend about Sophie's recent trickiness.

'And she's got a boyfriend,' I said.

'Ooh, tell all.' She pushed her empty plate away.

'Only he's not really a boy, more like a man, if I'm honest. Six foot tall, tanned, all ribbed.'

'Ripped, you mean?'

'Whatever. He's got this aura about him too. Called Jack.'

Her eyes narrowed with a glint. 'You fancy him, don't you?'

'Don't be crazy, he's sixteen! That'd make me a bit creepy.'

'Oh I don't know, some of Nick's mates are so mature. Sometimes I find it... well, unsettling. I swear they even flirt with me.'

I nodded. 'It was that fire between them, took me back. You know, lost youth or something?'

'I know it well.'

She gestured to the waiter for more coffee, catching sight of a TV news presenter across the room, with whom she exchanged waves.

'Sophie's first boyfriend, eh?' She said, turning back to me.

'Yep, slipping through my fingers. Just hope she doesn't do anything stupid.'

'Got to happen sometime.'

Scar flashed her eyes and I laughed. Nick was no longer a virgin and she found my qualms odd – but it was different for boys.

'She's *fifteen*,' I said. 'And I don't want her to feel rushed into it, that's all.'

'Hi Mum.' Sophie slammed the front door.

'Hi darling.'

We always get off to a good start, but the meta messages are woven even in those banal greetings, and I flashed a smile as she entered the kitchen, calculating her mood. She made straight for her wall chart and drew a diagonal line through the maths box.

'How was it?'

'Fine.' She flicked on the kettle, back to me.

A lacklustre response. My chest surged with the urge to know more; I can't stand down, even though I really do strive.

'Manage to answer it all?'

'Well… the last page was impossible, but nobody could do it, everyone was saying so afterwards.'

'Lot of marks in a whole page, Sophie.'

I winced at her stiffening back.

'Yeah, well, if I don't get an A* then you'll just have to live with it.' She poured water onto her herbal tea bag and jabbed a spoon.

'Whatever you get, I'll be proud of you.'

Too late, I'd lost her. She wrenched the lid off the biscuit tin.

'You going to have a breather? Relax a bit?'

'Geography tomorrow. Gotta revise for that.'

'OK. Let's talk over dinner with Dad, shall we?'

Without responding, my daughter left the kitchen and took the stairs to her sanctuary. Where was the new boyfriend when needed? She'd softened towards me again on Saturday when they'd returned together from the library.

I made my own cup of tea and sat down at the island, again me and my chattering mind for company. After considering, now for the umpteenth time, whether to Google Kathy Hunter,

24

I resolved again not to demean myself. I picked up a brochure for an event on Women Returners I was half planning to attend and a sticker fell out of it. *I am Enough,* it read. The instructions said to stick it up onto the bathroom mirror, repeat the mantra each morning and take inspiration.

'I am enough,' I said aloud. Huh. 'Clearly not, Anna.'

I chucked the sticker aside and flicked through to the section on business start-ups. Imagine, a business of my own. One canny woman featured had wheedled a whole new career out of her passion for the environment, but I had not the faintest idea what my passion would be. Ask yourself not what you want to do, but rather, what problems you want to solve, was her advice. So, what problems did I want to solve? Well, currently, a big sandy hairy one called Ollie. I smacked the brochure shut and my mind chattered on.

Soon after 7pm I called Sophie down to help me prepare dinner.

'I'm sure you'll have done really well, Soph.' I failed to catch her eye with a smile as I set her up with a chopping board for salad.

'That one's behind me now. Got to think forwards.'

Of course. In my efforts to summon the appropriate words I was often ending up the lesser of us and I wondered when it was that my child had become more strategic than me.

'You're absolutely right.' I attempted a nonchalant stroll to her chart and added a line to form a cross through the maths box.

Working the marker pen back and forth, I saw myself through Sophie's eyes – how awkward, how lame. I turned and nodded at the cucumber she was chopping.

'Oh, you're cutting it into discs, are you?'

Sophie dropped her knife onto the board. 'As you can

plainly see!'

'Sorry, that's great, keep going.'

Just that I would dice it.

The door slammed, Ollie's briefcase landed on the hall floor, and I braced myself. We'd been evading each other since the fight that weekend. Knowing he was safe, he was now playing the long game, I could tell, giving me time to soften as he always would after a row. After all, why would he invite a discussion about the state of our marriage when he could simply wait it out? Indeed, as it was dawning on me, why would I?

'Hello lovely.' He strode into the kitchen and threw his arms about Sophie. 'You smash it?'

'Hope so. You know how much I hate maths though.' Her nose scrunched in a way it never did for me. 'I'm chucking it behind me, like you'd tell me to, onwards to the next one.'

'Onwards and upwards.' Ollie pulled a Usain Bolt pose, his paunch straining at the jeans, and let out one of his fake guffaws. 'All the best people hate maths.'

I used to love maths.

'Hi darling.' He slid a hand around my back and, for the benefit of our daughter, kissed my cheek.

'Dinner's nearly ready,' I said, slapping three fillet steaks down for seasoning.

The meal was eased both by the bottle of Malbec and by the manufactured genial conversation we currently reserve for Sophie's presence. No further mention was made of the maths exam and Ollie held forth about a new corporate client, while I told them Scar's latest news; it was an art we'd recently perfected.

Sophie's plate was far from empty when her phone rang. Defiant of our rules, she reached for it, and I caught sight of the caller. Jack. I smiled to myself, something about this boy's presence would bring balance, a respite of some sort, I knew it.

'Mind if I take this?' She was up and off, while I, normally a stickler, simply shrugged at Ollie.

'Hi,' we heard her say as she took to the stairs, in a voice rich and odd enough for him to frown.

'Who's that?' he asked.

'That's Jack,' I said brightly, pleased to see him frown.

We lapsed into silence. And with Sophie's absence, so an elephant walked into the kitchen, ears flapping, trunk searching. Our marriage.

Was it that I wanted to stay or that I did not want to leave?

4

'Mum, have you seen Jack?'

'He's in the garden with Dad.'

I gestured towards the two of them, backs to us, both pretending to admire the ceanothus bush now in glorious cobalt bloom. Sophie hurried to the open patio doors and hovered there.

'What's he doing to him?'

'Just wanted a chat.'

Instilling the fear of God, more like.

It was the last Sunday of May half-term. More joint revision, Sophie had said, now well into the gruelling GCSEs, so I'd invited Jack, nonchalantly, to stay on for our usual roast. At their most recent encounter earlier that week, four now in total, Ollie had again ignored him. It was becoming embarrassing, so thankfully he was finally talking to the boy.

'Help Horace in, Soph.' I nodded to our tortoise struggling to clamber over the threshold from patio to kitchen.

Sophie bent to lift him inside and he set off towards me at the hob where I was stirring gravy. Stepping over him, Sophie did likewise.

'You can't let Dad at him like that!'

I smiled at my daughter, enjoying this conspiratorial behaviour; once again, in Jack's presence, she'd lightened towards me.

'Don't worry, I'll protect him for you.'

To soften it for my husband, I should have added that he was simply surprised to be faced with the first boyfriend in the house, that he needed time to get his head around it, but I didn't want to detract from our moment. Nor did I wish to be loyal to Ollie.

After that one eruption in the kitchen, we had settled into a pattern of perfunctory communication which, almost one month on from the affair, was becoming the new norm. Whenever I walked into a room where Ollie sat, that elephant would plod in after me, and so my husband would walk out, before the beast could hunker down. And I admit to the same evasive behaviour. While we did not talk of our marriage, I was nonetheless absorbed by the matter, even if my mind chattered through boundless scenarios without ever settling. To stay would mean rekindling it, and I smarted too keenly for that right now, but the prospect of dismantling it remained terrifying.

People joke about splitting the music collection, but surely taking apart a marriage was more akin to rending a human being? Physically, tearing at flesh, chipping at bone, down to that tiniest of all inside the ear. Emotionally, gouging the heart, stripping the thinnest capillaries. And spiritually. How did you even begin there? Ripping out the soul, the messiest business of all.

Ollie and Jack turned and began to walk back up the garden path, the boy with a clear urgency to his step. I watched my husband, his pale flesh pinched by the sleeves of his polo shirt, and then Jack, his own arms smooth and tanned with a bulb of muscle. And I was ambushed by a memory. A one-night-stand with a Greek man on the island of Paros. I must have been

29

nineteen, hadn't even known his name, and whenever I came across the one photo I'd taken of him this fact heightened the sumptuous memory. I shook it off and threw Jack a warm smile as they stepped into the kitchen, an irate Ollie making for his wine cellar.

'Oh my God, Dad,' Sophie said to his retreating back, 'I nip to the loo and come back to find you boring the pants off Jack.'

The boy lingered by the patio door, gently wringing his hands, a sight which tweaked my heart. I was still cautious about him and such moments of vulnerability were reassuring.

'Would you feed Horace for me, Jack?'

'Sure.' He took the spinach leaves I offered.

Sophie picked up the tortoise which had just reached my side and flew him back towards the patio doors. 'Come on Horace, din-dins,' she sang, clearly proud to show off a family ritual to Jack, and set our pet down in his feeding corner of the kitchen.

I watched them as Jack knelt and began feeding him torn bits of leaves, with a stroke of his shell after each one.

'You don't stroke a tortoise.' said Sophie, nudging him off balance.

'What do you do then?' Jack beamed at her. 'Tickle him under his chin?'

She fell about laughing as he slipped a finger beneath Horace's head, and I smiled at her dramatics, at the innocence of their chatter.

Ollie, however, was now rattling around the kitchen, yanking a drawer for the corkscrew, overly clinking glasses. Sunday was his day of recuperation. A man who existed as a social butterfly for six days a week, but who on the seventh day rested. He would barely notice Sophie and me drifting alongside him, but was miffed by this intrusion and I rolled my eyes at his back.

'So what's up next week, Soph?' he asked, ignoring Jack as we began the meal.

'We've both got history on Tuesday.'

'You ready for it?' He refused to allow Jack eye contact, how churlish.

Sophie noticed this too and turned to the boy. 'Think we are, don't you?'

'Yep.'

Yep. Not a diminutive yes, but a flippant yep. Good on you Jack, don't let this bastard grind you down.

Ollie nodded and fell silent, intent on his food.

'More spuds, Jack?' I piled two onto his plate.

He waited until his mouth was empty. 'Thanks Mrs Bond. Your roast potatoes are *almost* as good as my mum's.'

I smiled, enjoying the way he played me, blatant but it did the trick.

'I respect your loyalty, Jack. And please, call me Anna, or I'll feel like a fossil.'

He blushed, an endearing smudge of red at each cheek.

'Mum's roasties are the best,' Sophie said, helping herself to another one, a rare compliment which cheered me, even if we were supposed to be holding back on our carbs.

'I cooked them once,' said Jack. 'For Mother's Day, think I was about ten. I let the lamb rest, like it said to, and there was football on telly, so I forgot all about the roast potatoes in the oven.'

'Oops,' I said.

'Set the smoke alarm off and came out like black rocks. Dad said they'd be carcinogenic, but Mum still ate them.'

'Aw... You'd still eat them if I'd burnt them, wouldn't you, Dad?'

31

'I'd get my chisel out,' said Ollie. And our eyes met in laughter, before we both glanced away in surprise; it had been a while.

A lull and then, 'What team do you support, lad?' His voice was brusque but he was finally making an effort.

'Chelsea. We live in Fulham'

'And what's wrong with Fulham, if you live in Fulham?'

'Dad supports them, but I prefer the Blues.'

'I'm a Man U boy myself.' Ollie swigged his wine, eyebrows raised in challenge.

'A glory hunter!' The boy's grin was cheeky.

'What's that?' asked Sophie

'One of those pretend fans who don't live in Manchester,' I said, smiling at Jack.

'But I'm a die-hard fan, me.' Ollie pulled out a Mancunian accent I'd rarely heard. 'Didsbury born and bred. Shadow of Old Trafford.'

'Do you miss the Fergie days?' asked Jack, more gently; such intuition from a teenager.

Ollie allowed him a nod. 'You sorry we snaffled Mourinho?'

'Yes and No. Bet we'll trounce you again next season.'

Even Ollie was unable to hide a smile then, it was as if the boy couldn't stop himself, too bright to hide the mischief.

I laughed. 'Are you a second child Jack?'

He nodded. 'Older brother.'

'Thought so.'

I shared a conspiratorial glance with Ollie, a second child as was I, and again the moment caught us both unawares. It had been months since we had last colluded, and I looked away while he reached for the bottle to top up Jack's glass.

'Thank you,' he said. 'My parents only allow me a bottle of cider at the weekend, even though I'm sixteen. Nearly seventeen.'

I frowned at Ollie, we too only allowed Sophie one weekly glass of wine, but he shrugged and refilled his own, along with mine.

An awkward silence fell. From the corner of my eye I caught the pair of them sneak a sideways smile before bowing their heads. My daughter's first boyfriend. Weird, really, that we three had inhabited this house alone for so long. The Three Musketeers, The Three Bears, even Snap, Crackle and Pop on one intrepid holiday to Costa Rica. Her friends often stayed for meals, but never before had a boy made our table up to a four.

'Sophie tells me you play tennis?' I said finally, stamping a motherly seal.

He nodded 'Won my match this morning. Yes!'

He pulled a victory punch at Sophie, who smiled and took a coy bite of her chicken.

I went on. 'We should all have a game sometime. We've always needed a fourth, haven't we, family?'

'Mu-um.' Sophie rolled her eyes at me.

'Awesome. Might even let you win.'

Jack nudged her and she punched him on the arm.

'Fine, you're on. Mum and I stick you two. Walkover, eh Mum?'

'Absolutely!' I was loving this, the first time she'd sided with me over Ollie for a long time. 'You've yet to see mother and daughter in full combat gear.'

'Get your exams over first, Soph,' said Ollie.

We all three looked at him, and another hush descended on the meal.

'So, your dad's in garden design?' I said after a while. 'And what about your mum?'

'Oh, she does charity work, volunteers for an organisation

called Old Friends. They do befriending of old people and stuff.'

'Sounds interesting. What exactly does that involve?'

'She visits this old lady once a week, keeps her company. Mum loves it, and the lady does too, they've become really good friends.'

'I'm liking that idea.'

'Sounds right up your street,' said Ollie, a comment which made me bristle. Did he really judge that to be the extent of my capacity?

'So, when you say *old* lady, how old is she?'

'In her eighties, still fit though. I met her once, when Mum took her swimming at our health club. Her teeth fell out in the pool.'

Sophie laughed. 'Her false teeth?'

'Didn't she take them out before she got in?'

'Forgot. So I had to dive for them. In the end I stood on them. Urgh' He paddled his feet on the floor.

'Gross,' said Sophie.

'Indeed.'

There was I telling Sophie to slow down, yet I myself was beguiled by this kid. Even Ollie found his tale amusing, and there were moments of genuine hearty laughter around our kitchen table which it had not witnessed for a long time.

Looking back, I do think the boy knew how to engineer a good belly laugh.

When Jack had gone, we all seemed aware that something lighter had fluttered across our Sunday lunch, even settling on occasion. Humming happily, Sinatra, but out of tune as ever, Ollie retreated into the living room with the Sunday papers, Sophie took to the stairs for more revision, and, after clearing up, I slipped into our study which gave off the hallway.

The website for Old Friends engrossed me. Soft-lens photos of elderly men and women, their arms linked with younger versions, everyone smiling benignly. I began to read. *... befriending for older members of the local community... respite from loneliness ... help them lead fulfilling lives.*

Gazing into the watery eyes of one old man, I thought of my father. A kind and gentle man who had never been allowed to grow old, killed in a car accident along with my sister when I was four. I barely remembered him, his woolly smell on occasion, but one constant image remained with me, of his soft hazel eyes smiling down. Of the game where he'd bounce me up and down on his knees, then open them to drop me through, swiftly catching me before I hit the floor. Horsey, we called it.

Right up my street, Ollie had said. Naturally, he would consider this voluntary work a safe option, nothing that would stretch my wings, and so it probably would be but I was intrigued. I printed off the application form. On a whim then, I searched for Jack's mother, hoping she might be mentioned in one of their newsletters. Indeed there she was, Candice Mattison, sitting on a bench with an elderly lady, expensive jeans, silk shirt – and unmistakeably Jack's mother. I vaguely recognised her from the odd school event, but we'd never spoken.

That evening, while my daughter lay in the bath, face mask on, I sat contentedly on the sofa with one last glass of wine, watching six white BBC horses pull a coach across a windy moor. Scar said they used the same ones for all period dramas. Her name would be on the credits, but I was only half-watching, musing again about that Greek man. A languorous coffee by a port bathed in amber sunshine and then our goodbyes, both of us instinctively knowing not to swap addresses. I'd often wondered what had become of him. Ollie and I had met and fallen in love several years later.

Ollie, the man I had married. Lunch had been mostly amicable – a word normally paired with divorce, yet there we were seated together at our table. Could we proceed as such going forward? Without tackling the state of our marriage, bumbling along *amicably* forever. The notion had its attractions.

I heard the study door open. Lately he's chosen Sunday nights to do the books – I guess he's devised his own avoidance tactics – but that evening he finished them earlier than normal and moseyed into the living room. We chose to smile at each other.

'You open another bottle?'

'Felt somehow necessary.'

'I'll join you.'

Returning with a glass, he sank onto the sofa beside me.

'So, what do you think?' I asked.

'Seems like a nice lad. Long as he doesn't try to make a move.'

'What did you say to him in the garden?'

'Only that I'd kill him if he laid a hand on my daughter.'

'Good.'

'Scary dads didn't put me off, mind. Gorgeous girl like Sophie, legs up to her chin. What's stopping him?'

'Well, hopefully *she* will.'

'Absolutely. Sophie knows what's what.'

I nodded. 'And I do like him. Something about his presence, self-possessed but not self-obsessed. Seems kind, very bright. Obviously from a good family.'

'Don't think we're talking marriage here, Anna.'

We both laughed. And I realised that we were enjoying a conversation about a subject neutral to our state of conflict, about Jack. However faintly, something had shifted that day.

'I mean, I do realise he's only polite in front of us. They all do it, Sophie too. Half the cunning of these teenagers is in their disarming smile.'

'I'll have tabs on him.' Ollie pointed two fingers at his eyes and speared an imaginary Jack.

And then my husband rested a palm on my thigh, as he once would have done frequently. The physical contact took me aback and I froze, instantly on my guard, was he inveigling himself in? After a further moment he squeezed my thigh, an outrageous act of intimacy. Surely he didn't expect sex? I shoved his hand off.

'You don't think I'm going to let you back in that easily, do you?'

'Sorry. Hands in the air.' He raised them theatrically.

'And I know that you're thinking this charity lark will keep me chained to the kitchen sink which is where you want me to be, but –'

He smacked his own thighs as if making to stand and leave. 'Here we go.'

'But I can tell you right now that it's a stop gap and I will still be looking for a new career.'

'I don't want to chain you to any sink, Anna. I just want you back.'

He did throw me with that, but I motored on. 'What you want is a Stepford Wife. All gym, nails and Ottolenghi.'

He eyed me, weighing up my words for humour, and risked a cock of the head. 'I'm not a *veggie*.'

His bid to harness the wit which had once been pervasive to our marriage brought an unwanted smile to my face, and he clocked it.

'Gordon Ramsay, maybe,' he added.

I bit back the smile. Many moons ago his gentle teasing had endeared me, and I realised that a fondness still maintained. He was joking about the little woman even – his way of acknowledging the crux of the matter?

'Ottolenghi does meat too,' I said wryly.

We may both have been playing at this, but it was a first step. Stand-off was exhausting and this rapprochement welcome, so why not let myself be drawn along? Acceptance it was not, more of an accommodation, a behaviour which I could sustain until a point where the hurt might subside and my feelings for him become clear. I would stay largely because I did not want to go. No pull, no push, but neutrality. For the moment anyway. Perhaps he felt the same way.

'You're still on probation, you know.'

'I do know.'

I reached for my glass and decided to leave it there, my power crackling. The TV credits rolled and with them Scarlett's name. Lots to tell her in the morning.

5

Fred Wildsmith's home was tucked away in a backwater of Chiswick, behind the park where I used to push Sophie on the swings every morning when she was a toddler. On the walk there, I went over my hours of training at Old Friends. They'd snapped me up immediately, coached me in something called, 'Active Listening', had me acting out self-conscious role plays, trained me in safeguarding, and then they'd offered me a match with an elderly widower. He was lonely, my designated manager said, had recently lost several of his peers, had been referred to Old Friends by his GP – and he was potentially a vulnerable adult. The required DBS safeguarding checks had come through quickly given that, while no longer head of her PTA, I was still an active volunteer at Sophie's secondary school, and I was armed with a new certificate.

Again, I mulled over my reasons for taking this on. Because he reminded me of my father, whom I missed more than ever at this difficult time in my life? Or was it because voluntary work would boost my confidence and ease me towards a proper job? Whatever, I had been impressed by the professionalism of my new manager, a Polish woman half my age, whose passion for her work I envied, and I too would be professional about it.

His street was unprepossessing, salmon pink curtains, neat

privet gardens, the green recycling boxes already out on the pavement with barely a bottle between them. I stood across the road observing his home, a semi-detached with a mock Tudor gable, and gazed at the windows as if into the depths of a murky river. Eighty-five they'd said he was. How hard could it be to manage an old man? Find something about his home to compliment and I'd be off.

A sudden movement at the upstairs window, not unlike the flip of a fish in dark water, startled me then. He'd been watching me too, awaiting my arrival, and had stood back. Already some history between us and we hadn't even met. With a deep breath, drawing the comfort of Fuller's brewery into my lungs, I crossed over and made my way up his path, heartened to see two empty red wine bottles in his recycling box. Fixing a smile, confident but warm, I rang the bell.

Despite a frantic and terrifying yapping (they hadn't mentioned a dog) he kept me waiting.

'Hello,' I said, once the door finally opened. 'I'm Anna.'

He stood in the gloom, sucking frog-like at a hefty pipe. A tan mop of dog lodged itself at his knees, a black button nose, eyes obscured by fur. I balked at its long pink tongue and teeth, already visualising them at my shins, and glanced back up at the man. What struck me first was his own abundant crop of hair, steel grey, above a tanned, weathered face that seemed much younger than eighty-five. He was tall and broad, albeit his shoulders now slightly bowed, but he must have been a catch in his youth. Oddly, he wore two V neck sweaters despite the hot day, wisps of grey hairs curling at his neck.

'It's lovely to meet you.' I extended a hand.

He looked at it. 'You'd better come in then.'

Still barking, the mutt retreated, gliding backwards across the floor as I stepped inside; could this living waterfall actually see me from behind its coat? The house reeked of tobacco, a sickly sweet stench, and I curled my nose as the man traipsed me into his living room. An enormous wooden mantel clock, the shape of Napoleon's hat, struck the hour with four hearty chimes – we were to become well acquainted, this monster and I.

'Ah, I'm just on time,' I said, not as confidently as I'd intended.

The man shuffled, rather than walked, across the room to a winged armchair, while I took a nifty glance around. A sunken settee (too old-fashioned to be called a sofa) covered in swampy green cord, a standard lamp with a fringed shade, and a brown carpet patterned with swirls of orange into blue. What could I possibly compliment as an opening gambit? I sat down on the settee, preparing for loose springs and itchy horsehair, but it was deceptively comfortable.

'It's lovely to meet you, Mr Wildsmith,' I said again.

He nodded and pulled on the pipe. What now?

'Nice dog,' I said. 'What's his name?'

'Dougal.'

I smiled. 'As in, *The Magic Roundabout*?'

'Wife named him. He's a Lhasa Apso. As was Dougal.'

'He's the spitting image.'

Too soon to mention his dead wife, of course.

'Is it that charity that's sent you?'

'Old Friends, yes.'

'Have you come to clean?' A sudden twinkle lit those walnut eyes.

'No, Mr Wildsmith.' I cocked my head. 'I think you know that.'

'They said they'd send someone to help.'

Tread carefully now, Anna.

'They told me you liked doing crosswords. Wondered if we might give one a go together?'

'I see.' He contemplated me, and I him, something of a stand-off. 'I've a fancy I might have one I can help you with. Shall I put the kettle on?'

'Thank you, I'd love a cuppa.'

With a heave-ho the man pushed himself out of the chair and shuffled, dog first, out to the hall and into his kitchen. My shoulders slumped. What had I let myself in for? Two hours of this *every* week? I'd only been there for five minutes, and this was supposed to be easing my life not adding to its burden.

I stood up and wandered about the room. It was certainly tidy, vacuumed recently even, and in one corner sat neat piles of *The Economist*, all of them well-thumbed. Brexit! That was something we could talk about, even though he was probably a Leaver, one of those old codgers who blamed it all on the immigrants. On his bookcase sat a framed photograph, clearly of him, a much younger version, standing beside what appeared to be his wife and daughter, both attractive women. As for his books, a few novels I'd read myself, but mostly thick volumes on international relations, treaties and conventions. Nonetheless, all conversational fodder to be stored for future use.

His clock chimed the quarter hour, making me jump and guiltily shove a book back in its place. He'd been gone for ten minutes.

I ventured to the hall and frowned at the kitchen door. 'Mr Wildsmith?' I pushed it open. 'May I come in?'

The room was empty. Two mugs sat ready on the counter, and a kettle, an old-fashioned hob contraption with a lidded spout, was pouring out angry steam. I turned off the gas and gingerly looked out into the back garden. The man was pruning his roses.

'Er, shall I make the tea?' I called.

'What?' Was that genuine astonishment as he swung around? 'Oh yes, love, please that'd be nice.'

Love? Well I think we'd call that progress, but had he actually forgotten about me, or was this some bizarre initiative test?

I wrapped a tea towel around my hand against steam burns, poured water into the mugs, and looked around for the fridge. The kitchen was pristine. I'd half expected a heap of dirty dishes I could usefully have offered to wash during my first visit, but everything was orderly and his fridge neatly stocked, the milk fresh.

Out in the garden I made for a small wrought iron table and set the tray down beside his newspaper (*The Guardian* – so maybe not a Brexiteer after all). With a tentative glance at the dog, now flopped out on the grass like a caramel sheepskin rug, I sank back, taking in the mass of blooms which lent a magical feel to his garden. We were now well into the heatwave that was such a balm to most, and the sun was high, the sky a baby blue.

'What a fabulous garden, Mr Wildsmith. Do you manage all this yourself?'

He grunted, back square on to me, and continued nicking rose stems. They'd told me this first meeting was only an ice-breaker, that I wouldn't have to stay long, but it would be more of a ball-breaker, or even a deal-breaker if I didn't manage to win him over.

'So many different varieties of rose,' I went on brightly. 'And they seem so well established.'

'You must treat them well. 'Course soil's good too, which helps.'

'Wish I had your green fingers, I'm hopeless in the garden.'

At that he finally turned around to me and broke into a smile, dazzling, spontaneous, and wholly without guile. Laying down his pipe and secateurs, he settled himself at the table.

'Let's take a look at your crossword then.'

I smiled to myself and folded his newspaper open at the quick crossword.

'OK. One across. To challenge. Ship's rigging. Six letters.'

'Tackle.' Spoken without a beat.

'Quick work.' I began to write the word in pencil.

'What's that pencil for? Get it down in pen, love.'

'But what if – ?'

'Take life by the horns.' He pulled a pen from his pocket and slapped it down.

'OK.' I wrote lightly, my perfectionism railing.

We spent a truly enjoyable half-hour completing the crossword, no mistakes, no crossings out, a light banter running between us. Even when I knew the answer first I allowed him to voice it. Ha, I can do this, I thought, mentally preparing myself to leave once we'd guessed the last clue.

'Right, that's our warm-up,' he said, 'now for the proper crossword.'

'The cryptic one? Oh I never really got the hang of those.'

'There's always a pattern. As in life. I'll give you a few minutes to get your brain into gear.'

He reached for his pipe and began to clean it, turfing out the old tobacco onto the lawn. I contemplated the dog, now watching me hopefully, and its tail began to wag. Oh shit, I thought, as it got to its feet and glided over, resting its head on my knee.

'He doesn't bite, does he?'

The man chuckled. 'Did Dougal?'

I placed a tentative finger on its head. 'Just that I was bitten

44

by a dog when I was a kid.'

'Only thing he does with his teeth, love, is smile.'

As if on cue Dougal's tongue lolloped out and his mouth widened, so I added a second finger, stroking his crown, surprised by the silkiness of his fur.

'So, Mr Wildsmith,' I ventured finally.

'Call me Fred.'

'Fred. And I'm Anna' I gestured at his garden. 'You've clearly lived here a long time?'

Get him talking, they'd said at Old Friends – ask open questions, nothing that can be answered with a simple yes or no.

'I have.'

That was basically a yes. I tried again.

'I noticed the heavy tomes in your bookcase. Was your career an international one?'

'It was.'

So lame, Anna.

'For the United Nations,' he added, helping me out.

'Wow.'

'Wow, indeed.' He eyed me, knocking the empty pipe against his chair.

'I know nothing about diplomacy, I used to work in banking.'

He nodded, as if weighing me up and finding me wanting. Well you would wouldn't you? What was it again? Advertising, estate agents and bankers, the most despised professions.

'I mean, I gave it up years ago.' I shook my head in apology. 'You know, I had a child and then got caught up in family life, and before you know it sixteen years have gone by…'

I thought again of the hollow atmosphere at home; Sophie, all awkward shoulders, shirking as if from an itchy sweater,

Ollie and I mildly reaching for conversation of the lowest common denominator. Except when Jack was around. The house felt warmer then.

Fred was watching me, filling his pipe with fresh tobacco, and his eyes softened, the surrounding skin creasing into thick folds.

'Parenting is the most important job of all,' he said.

'Yeah.' I dismissed the glib comment with a flick of my hand.

'I'm serious, Anna. If you get it right. Not all of us do. And I speak from experience.'

'Oh, *I've* not got it right, not by a long shot.'

I laughed, sniffing back an astonishing tear. I could so readily have gone on, could have poured it all out to this kindly old man, but this was supposed to be about him, not me. So I thought of another question.

'What did you do at the UN?'

He re-lit his pipe, puffing at it, holding the moment. 'International Aid Programmes, but I'll tell you about them another time.'

'I'll look forward to that, Fred.'

'Now, I've a fancy that we've got half an hour of sunshine before it leaves the garden, enough time to crack this cryptic crossword.'

That evening I returned home from a stand-up comedy night with Scar at the George IV pub on the High Road. Jack's bike was in the hallway.

In the kitchen, Ollie sat at the island scrolling his I-pad, glass of wine at his side, and he glanced up, a tentative smile in place which I returned brightly. Bright with guilt, as it happens, because after the gig I had flirted with one of the comedians.

46

This flirtation I had by no means initiated, had simply been jostling at the bar for another bottle of wine, albeit having picked the spot by his side, but when he'd turned to me I had certainly risen to the occasion. A younger man, a fit body, a dirty comedic mind which had brought bubbles of throaty laughter from me and Scar.

'Wanna shout a starving artist a beer?' His Aussie drawl was languid.

'Live in a garret, do you?'

'Na, dungeon in Shepherd's Bush.'

'A sex dungeon?'

Where had that come from? I'd shocked myself.

'Could be.' That glint in his eye, it clawed my insides.

Those eyes had then dipped overtly to my cleavage and as I'd bought him a beer I'd slipped open another button on my shirt. So long since I had felt at all sensuous. Scar told me his eyes had trailed me back to our table, but by then I was ignoring him, the panic, the fear, the reality, whatever.

'Would you ever have an affair?' she'd asked.

'I think one in the family's enough, don't you?'

'Ooh I think your shit of a husband would have it coming to him if you indulged.'

I smiled, shook my head.

'I'd do it again. If I could get away with it,' she said. 'I suspect Alex has fun with his young ingenues.'

Her husband was creative director of a small but well-known London theatre, and an extremely attractive man – physically and mentally.

'Think I'll stick with what I've got, Scar. We're both trying to make a go of it again now.'

Were we, though? Or were we making a show of making a go at it?

47

I mulled this over, sunny smile for Ollie still in place. He would probably be expecting me to turn and head for the living room, but I decided to brazen it out and join him at the island. Why should I have felt guilty? It's not as if I'd even kissed the guy, whereas Ollie had *shagged* another woman. A mere few minutes of flirtation, that's all. But I was still buzzing.

'Where are they?' I asked.

'Upstairs.'

I cocked an ear at the ceiling, Jack had now become a fixture.

'Gave him the old shufty.' Ollie threw me a sideways dead eye and I laughed.

'Well that ought to do it.' I perched on a stool opposite him while he fetched me a glass and poured the last of the bottle between us.

'St Emilion. Arrived today, snaffled a case for the cellar.' He chinked his glass to mine. 'Good night?'

'Fair to middling,' I shrugged the corners of my mouth. 'Seen funnier.'

'And how did it go with the old geezer?'

'He's not a geezer.' A prickle of defensiveness towards Fred. 'Mid-eighties, so old yes, but sharp as a knife. Used to work for the UN.'

'Impressive.'

'We did crosswords, even the bloody cryptic one.'

'Give us a clue then.' He folded his arms and leant forward conspiratorially, his relief that I was engaging with him palpable.

'OK, What's this one? His job is upsetting the classroom.'

He frowned in concentration, while I sipped my wine, watching him count with flicks of his fingers. As a couple, we'd always loved to lock intellectual horns, and the moment took me back to the day we'd first fallen for each other.

It was on one of those corporate teambuilding events, an overnight castaway experience in the wilds of Wales, soon after I'd been promoted into his division at the bank. Twelve of us were raced out to sea one morning, six men and six women, an exhilarating rib ride to the Gower peninsula. It was the height of summer, so not that wild, but the wind did buffet as we offloaded supplies on the deserted beach. Given a map and survival kit by the 'natives' awaiting us, we then had to find our way to the camping ground, where we would be expected to set up shelter, build fires and secure food until we were 'rescued' the following day.

Ollie and I had both considered ourselves natural leaders and we clashed in our efforts to rise supreme. He was first to suggest that we build shelter from the abundant ferns and bracken on our hike to the camp site. Niggled by his foresight, I then attempted to split us into two teams, each consisting of three males and three females.

'That way, there'll be complementary qualities and skills on each team,' I insisted.

'However, we will be sleeping two to a shelter. And in your scenario, each team would have one guy and one gal cosying up together.'

As we stood squabbling, a rabbit scurried out of the undergrowth and past our feet. One of the guys lurched and dived on the animal, grasped it and broke its neck. A fleeting moment which brought a stunned silence to the whole group. Instinctively, Ollie and I exchanged glances, both of us shocked and sickened by the man's gusto. An instant connection, I think we both knew then. Afterwards I backed down, allowing him to command the group. Had we gone with my plan, of course, we could have spent the night together in that shelter of feathery ferns. As it was, he had smuggled in a hip flask of whiskey, and when our bush kill was eaten and darkness finally fell, with a simple flick of the eyes we found ourselves picking our way through the woods. In a small clearing far from the others, we flopped down onto the carpet of bracken and became animals of the forest.

We had once loved each other very much. Could we find that in us again? Could I climb back into my marriage, or would the hurt and the shattered trust prove too momentous? This sparring, along with the humour, his sensitivity, they were all elements of our marriage that I'd missed, but somehow the act of stripping our union back to those components, highlighting them for appreciation, seemed indicative of a relationship which was broken. We'd always scoffed, Ollie and I, at those couples who have their marriage blessed after so many years together – renewing their vows twenty years on. Must be something wrong to resort to such a public showcase, we'd say, yet my deconstruction of our own marriage felt as if it stemmed from the same sense of desperation.

'Got it!' He slapped the work surface. 'Schoolmaster. It's an anagram. Upsetting means you shuffle the letters in *the classroom* around.'

'It does. Well done.' I paused. '*Fred* knew it too. I had no idea myself.'

A mollifying nod to his prowess, I'd always backed down, ever since that camp in Wales, exponentially so since he'd been the breadwinner. But that night I felt the stronger for it. *Lead from the back and let others believe they are in front* – a quote by Nelson Mandela on one of our fridge magnets. Could I play my husband? He had shown such cruel guile, its impact still caustic, and perhaps there should be some cunning on my part too.

Ollie took a self-satisfied glug of his wine, detecting none of this, while a hefty thump came from Sophie's bedroom.

I rolled my eyes at the ceiling. 'Hope that wasn't someone falling out of bed.'

'Better not be.' Ollie rolled his eyes back, he was loving the way I'd thawed.

Her door opened and the pair of them came hurtling down the stairs, Jack in mock pursuit of his girlfriend. Barefoot, she raced into the kitchen, swerved around the island in a cartoon skid, and flung herself at Ollie.

'Stop him, Dad, he's tickling me.'

Jack came to a halt by the kitchen door, and hovered there. From the safety of her father's side, my daughter taunted him, while he caught his breath, his body lifting and sinking. He sounded like a man coming back down to earth after sex. Bloody well better not be. He wouldn't dare try it while Ollie was in the house, but it was now clear that one of my pep talks for Sophie was required.

Finally, the boy stepped across the threshold to my side, his bare arms almost brushing mine, and his presence was disturbing, the air steeped with earthy aftershave – that or pheromones. I glanced at Sophie's shining eyes and was bowled over by the maelstrom of her happiness. Poised for life, she was gazing forwards, straining at what would be, while I was gazing backwards, yearning for what had been. We seemed to be steamers crossing mid-ocean – even if I was the only one waving. I wrestled with the rising emotion.

'I'm off then, Soph,' said Jack.

She sidled round to him, hands out in self-protection, and squealed as he took one last dig at her ribs. All very innocuous, but nonetheless.

'Night Mr and Mrs B.'

'Night Jack,' we replied in unison.

After the front door had closed and Sophie had called out goodnight, I realised that Ollie was contemplating me. Had he been smoking a cigar, he would have taken a deep drag, tipped his head and blown the smoke out seductively. I held his eyes with mine. Yes, I was aroused after flirting with the comedian, but right then I felt only intrigue for the shift between us. The emboldening of Anna, as if through some sudden super power – Popeye's spinach? Peter Parker's radioactive spider? Whatever, if there was such a thing as a power-ometer I was sliding up it.

'Night Ollie.' I tipped myself from my stool and slipped off to bed.

6

'Choose colour please.' The Asian woman swept her hand across the racks of polish.

I picked out a vibrant purple. 'What do you reckon, Soph? Change from my usual reds?'

'Purple's in,' she said, reaching for a psychedelic orange. 'Neon too. This one's a bit young for you, though.'

'Cheeky.' I nudged her hip with mine, she nudged back tipping me off balance.

We sat in the window of the nail bar waiting for the two pedicure chairs to free up, and I silently rehearsed the words I'd planned once we were ensconced in the deep fake leather, nowhere to hide. All the Vietnamese women who worked there understood only a smattering of English, I knew that.

When we were called, Sophie grabbed a handful of magazines, so I took a copy of *Hello* and followed her to the back of the salon. Up on the wall, MTV was playing videos, songs I recognised given that Capital Radio was now a fixture at home, when she was around anyway.

'Ooh I like this one.' I hummed along to the opening riffs as we settled, feet in the water.

My daughter threw me a sideways smile. 'Mu-um.'

'You used to love it when we sang and danced around the house together. Can't you remember *Tikkabilla* on children's

TV?'

'Yeah, like when I was three.'

I dipped my head with a smile. 'Two, actually.'

A pang of guilt at her bright smile; such guile in warming her up.

The woman tapped my leg, a prompt to remove one foot from the water so she could remove the old polish. OK, you've got about forty minutes, I thought, make sure you pace it right. Still, I lingered over *Hello,* thoughts swirling. Scar always asked why it mattered, had made me feel prim, prudish even.

'Who are you to determine when she pops her cherry?' she said, such an ugly expression. 'It's her life not yours.'

'I'm her mother!' I cried.

Haughtily enough to swamp any feelings that I was simply unable to let my daughter grow up. The idea that Sophie might lose her virginity before she was mature enough filled me with fear. Jack was a warm, funny and kind boy, but he was also cocky, and if he did coerce her into bed before she had real feelings for him she might end up regretting it forever. And if I didn't say something so might I. Exams were now over and the previous evening they'd been hidden away again in her bedroom, watching Netflix, she'd said. Hovering at her door, I'd found comfort in the crashing chords of an action movie, as had Ollie when reporting back to him – he was fully behind me on this.

My mind chattered on. The women had clipped and buffed us, and were onto our calf massages before I plucked up the courage, no going back.

'The massage is the bit I love best, don't you, Soph?'

'Mmm.' She beamed at me. 'Thanks for bringing me, Mum.'

'So… Jack seems a nice lad.'

She flicked a page of her trashy mag. 'Yeah.'

'You're spending quite a bit of time with him.'

'He's cool.'

I glanced up at the TV screen. They were now showing a replay of *Love Island*, the young men and women sitting around in a horseshoe as night fell. Sophie began to watch too, the beautiful people all dressed up and languid, glass of wine in hand, and I saw the perfect opportunity to preach without awkward eye contact.

'You remember that chat we had? Last year?'

No need to remind her of which one, that too had been excruciating.

'Ye-es.' She frowned.

'Well. Look, Soph, I know you're sensible and you wouldn't do anything silly, but I wanted to reinforce a couple of things.'

Silence.

'Just…well your body is precious.'

'Oh my God!' A furtive glance at the women lined up opposite for manicures, and she began zipping through the magazine.

Heart quickening, I picked up pace. 'Don't give it away lightly. And don't ever, *ever* let any boy coerce you into it.'

'Will you shut the fuck up?'

Both Vietnamese women glanced up, that was one word they did comprehend. The manicure line-up also straightened, pretending not to have heard. I too was shocked but I wasn't going to pull her up, I was in a speed wobble. I lowered my voice to a whisper.

'I only want you to be careful, that's all. Please. I'm not telling you *not* to. Just never do anything you don't want to do.'

'What is this? Entrapment? Is that why you've brought me here? 'Ooh let's go and have a pedi together, Soph,' Wait till I'm stuck here with you then ply me with another of your

55

moralistic spiels?'

Absolutely that.

We lapsed into silence and the women began to apply our polish. The *Love Island* candidates, though fully clothed, appeared now to be acting out sexual positions. I watched one couple arrange themselves in the sixty-nine and felt myself blush, mortified to be watching this bizarre game of charades alongside my daughter.

'It's not the moral thing, Sophie –'

She let out a strangled cry, but I hurtled on.

'Look, I was up to stuff at your age too. It's just that I want you to be absolutely sure. 'Cos once it's done it's done. There'll never be a first time again.'

She shook her head furiously, eyes glittering. 'Have you *finished*? I'm not stupid, I know all that, now will you shut up? Please?'

'Sorry if I embarrassed you, but it's my job Soph. I love you so much and I don't want you to get hurt.'

She snatched at magazine pages, head shaking, but soon we were both again drawn to the TV where a couple were enacting another sexual position for their friends to guess.

'Scissors!' cried one of the lads.

Not sure that one existed in my day. Maybe Scar was right, I was a prude. My eyes dropped again to *Hello*, while Sophie snapped her mag shut and threw it down.

'Great colour.' I nodded at her toes.

'Yours too,' she said.

I was relieved to have finally aired my qualms, and did feel reassured that she was behaving with maturity, but Sophie was still cross with me the next morning when we four were to play our first tennis match.

'Wanna get down with the kids, Mum?' Her caustic remark at breakfast about my eagerness.

Guess I did. But then, after we'd signed Jack in at the Hogarth Health Club, it was she who brought up the old family joke of our tennis trios as we led him outside into the fierce sunshine. A beautiful Sunday, heralding the week which would mark the longest day.

'We've always been Sharapova, Seles and Becker,' she said.

'So who am I today?' asked Jack.

'You can be Nadal.'

Yep, that'll do, I thought, turning to catch Sophie plant a kiss on his bare shoulder.

On court, I flipped open the sun cream with a smile at Ollie. 'Shall I do your neck?'

'Thanks.' He smiled back.

I was making a good job of managing him, of remaining in my marriage without total immersion, and for the moment, until it became clear what I wanted to do next, I would continue to exist as such – I suspected oodles of marriages out there were also muddling through every day. Who knows? Perhaps Ollie was playing the same game, covering his own deliberations with this amiability. And the fact that we had once been in love, smitten at the start, left me hopeful that with time I might be able to climb back in fully, I'd just have to ride it out.

He turned his back and I smoothed the cream onto his flesh, conscious of our first skin-on-skin contact since the affair but, having primed myself for some inkling of desire, sadly I found only that his neck seemed bulkier these days; all that wine.

Sophie and I won our first game easily by playing on Ollie, who was never one to shine at the net, and as we changed ends she gave me an ostentatious high five, so Jack turned to slap one on Ollie too.

'So, Mr Bond,' he said with the voice of a James Bond baddie. 'Would you like to serve?'

'You want me to talk?' Ollie rose to his humour; naturally it was not the first time…

'No Mr Bond, I want you to die.'

We all laughed, and Jack blushed.

'Sorry Mr B, no offence.'

'None taken, lad.' Ollie clapped him on the back, by then he too was largely won over. 'Got the whole box set if you fancy a watch sometime? Crack open a beer?'

'Awesome.' Jack beamed.

More at the prospect of the beers, surely? I mean, what sixteen-year-old wants to watch a film with his girlfriend's middle-aged father? I guess Jack was charming him as he did me – and indeed the prospect of him lounging around our house was energising.

'Best you serve first.' Ollie ambled to the net and clutched his racquet.

I steeled myself as Jack threw up the ball to serve, but somehow my return spun down the tramline past Ollie and bounced off at an angle. Meanwhile, Jack was hurtling across the court. A spectacular reach and he lost his balance, skidding face down onto the Astroturf.

'Jack!' Sophie dropped her racquet and sprinted around the net.

I strode after her, while Ollie looked on, a concerned hand at his mouth. By the time Sophie reached the boy he was up on his feet dusting himself off, both knees daubed with bright blood.

'I've got plasters.' I rushed to my sports bag but Jack stood brushing at the grazes, smearing blood onto his tennis whites.

'Come on, let's sort you out,' I said.

'I'm fine, Mrs B, don't fuss, please.'

'Better let her, Jack, she loves to cluck,' said Sophie.

He smiled then and walked over to me. 'Top shot, by the way.'

He raised a foot onto the bench. Antiseptic spray poised, I was drawn to his tanned thigh, to the fine hairs trailing up into his shorts. Get a grip, Anna, he's sixteen, and he's your daughter's boyfriend. I blasted antiseptic at his knee.

'Ouch,' he laughed. 'That hurts more than falling over.'

Back on court, he played as if unhindered by pain, but we took it easy on him. We drew one set each, and even though Jack was by far the best player on court it didn't occur to me that he may have contrived this score. When I look back now, however, I reckon that was well within his gift.

'I could murder a beer,' Ollie said as we packed away our racquets and the next players arrived on court, two attractive guys around my age.

One of them threw me a flirtatious smile. 'Nice forehand.'

'Thanks.' I blushed, and felt Ollie's proprietorial hand at my back.

We made our way to the shady patio and a free table, where Sophie flopped down and crossed those long legs of hers, and I surreptitiously angled my chair so that I could watch the men play.

'Need a hand Mr B?' Jack's bloodied leg was now rusty.

'No son, I'm fine.'

Son? That was a first.

Ollie crunched across the gravel to the clubhouse and I snatched a few glimpses at the man who had flirted with me. I seemed all of a sudden to be visible again. Twice now in a matter of weeks and, curiously, when I'd been feeling so deflated.

'You're pretty useful, aren't you?' said Sophie,

'You too.' Jack went to rest a hand on her thigh but pulled back as I turned around.

'Which club do you play at?' I asked him.

'Hurlingham.'

Where else? Clearly garden design was *the* career move these days.

'Do your parents play?'

'No, I got into it at school when I was ten.'

'Sophie was barely four.'

'Yeah.' Jack held my eyes with his. 'She said.'

I glanced at Sophie, had she told him about my mania?

'She used to play all the tournaments,' I said, testing him. 'We travelled all over, didn't we, Soph?'

'Yeah.' She gave a slow, deliberate nod. 'We did.'

So she had told him, so they were already that close.

Ollie had emerged and placed the tray of drinks down. 'Did what?'

I smiled. 'Drive the length and breadth of England for tennis.'

'Mum's always done a lot for you, hasn't she, Soph?' He winked at me then, the first time he'd colluded with me over our daughter for months.

'It's really paid off too,' said Jack.

'Guess so.' Sophie allowed me one of her special sideways smiles. And that warmed my very bones.

'Let's play again soon,' I said.

Did I wanna get down with the kids? Well it was later that evening that Ollie suggested we buy Jack a new tennis racquet for his seventeenth birthday – which, incidentally, was still three months off.

7

'Have you got the postcode?' I brought up the Satnav.

Sophie read it out. 'Jack's at the station already.'

'Good, we'll scoop him up and drive through Richmond Park.'

'Thanks for taking us, Mum.' She threw me a smile.

'Pleasure.' I flashed her one back.

We set off in the courtesy car provided by the garage while they repaired mine after a minor scuffle. An automatic, which I'd never driven before, it staggered down the road to the junction, where I slammed on the brake, mistaking it for the clutch. We pitched forwards.

'Mum!'

'Oops.'

She laughed. 'There's only two pedals! How hard can it be?'

'Instinct,' I said, laughing with her. 'Primal reflex to hit the clutch with my left foot, even if there is no clutch. You'll understand one day, if ever I pay for driving lessons, which given that impertinent remark is looking unlikely.'

'Ooh primal, eh?'

I was feeling cheeky myself. 'Yep. Like when a boy wants to make hanky-panky with a girl. That's primal too.'

'Mu-um.'

'Don't Mum me. You be careful tonight, they've told us at

61

school all about parties.'

She threw her arms up. 'What's this? *Another* pep talk?'

She was right – and we were getting on so well too.

At a red light, again I stamped on the brake, my intention to change gear, and the car stopped dead catapulting her to the dashboard.

'Have you gone mad?'

'Sorry. Did it again.'

She turned on the radio and Capital blared out some indistinguishable rock music. Far too loud to talk over, but I had her captive and could not resist.

'I don't even know the parents tonight. I mean, normally, I would have emailed them...'

'Well they're gonna be there, so you don't need to worry.'

'Good.' I paused. 'And I *do* trust you.'

'Green.' She nodded at the lights. 'Yeah, well I'm not stupid, am I? I'm the product of your meticulous mothering. Tiger, helicopter, submarine, the lot.'

Submarine? I didn't even know what that was.

Camila Cabello's *Havana* came on the radio, serendipitously a song that I loved, so I began to sing along and soon we were belting out the lyrics together, swaying as one. We were again in companionable mood by the time we reached Richmond station, where I brought the car to an abrupt halt, a black cab sounding its horn from behind. Jack waved and jogged towards us.

'And you're sure there'll be no alcohol?'

Thought I'd slip that in before he reached the car.

'Oh my God, you're impossible.' She smiled at him as he opened the door.

'Hi Jack.' I too turned to smile and the car began to drift backwards.

'Whoa.' He stumbled, one hand on the door. 'Put it in park, Mrs B.'

I slid the gear stick in place, while he slung his tennis bag onto the back seat and jumped in, bringing a palpable shift in dynamics to the car.

'Looking very smart tonight, Mrs B.'

'Thank you Jack. We've got friends coming round for dinner.'

Not that I'd needed to slip on the silk dress for the drive.

'I'd hold onto your seat, Mum's driving like a lunatic,' said Sophie.

With exaggerated care I set off again, listening in to their chatter. Youthful, playful and quite innocent, even if they were also texting furiously – I did wonder if at each other. We entered Richmond Park, where I cut the air con and opened the windows onto the stunning evening, above us a vast sky drifting with raspberry ripple, around us the deer grazing on savannah grasses.

'Oh, look at the fawns,' I said brightly.

'Cute,' said Sophie.

'Aah,' said Jack.

The pair of them began to sing along to some rap number and I fell into my role of silent chauffeur, enjoying the entertainment. We left the park and reached the outskirts of Kingston.

'So are these friends of yours tonight, Jack?'

'From school. Soph knows them too, don't you?'

'Yeah.' Her voice dwindled.

'Don't worry, Mrs B, these guys know how to throw a party.'

Do they now?

The Satnav called for a left turn but I took it late, cutting in front of a cyclist who kicked the car and swore at me as I swung around the corner.

'Mum!'

'The Highway Code says no undertaking. He should have waited.'

'Think it's changed,' said Jack softly, and in the rear-view mirror I caught him turning down his mouth. 'But I can see your point,' he added.

Clever boy, managing me like that. Looking back, that's clear.

I pulled into the gravelled driveway of a double fronted house. A grey cat, too furry to be so grumpy, regarded me from the windowsill, but there was no sign of a party.

'Is this it?'

'Bianca's house, we're gonna get ready here.'

'OK. You'll book an Uber home together, won't you? In by eleven-thirty.'

'Eleven thirty? But we're miles away.'

'Midnight then, but not a minute after. Understood?'

'Thanks, Mum. Bye.'

She swished out of the car and Jack scrambled after her.

'Thank you Mrs B. OK if I pick up my tennis gear when I drop Soph home?'

'Sure.'

They approached the front door without a backwards glance, but I turned off the radio to catch their chatter as I began to manoeuvre out of the drive.

'Kiss-ass,' she said. '*Looking very smart tonight…*'

I watched Jack laugh and pinch her bum. Then the front door opened, and I was relieved to see Bianca who pulled Sophie inside.

You lost *your* virginity at fifteen, Anna Bond, I told myself silently as I set off for home. So what is the difference? It had been over a month now since she'd first brought him home, and they were clearly very fond of each other. That's all I wanted wasn't it? For her first time to be right.

In Richmond Park I pulled into a car park and found *Eternal Flame* by the Bangles on Spotify. Volume high, I sat back, and the bewitching memories of that distant Anna sashayed forth. My first kiss at thirteen. The love bite at fourteen. And, at fifteen, sex with Matt McGarvey of 5B. In his bed, parents out, on a balmy summer's evening akin to the one I was gazing up into. Nothing sordid, simply the exquisite bliss of the very first time with a guy I adored. The memory was intoxicating.

Most days now, vibrant swirls of my own adolescence were washing over me, sweeping me back to the long ago and faraway. Even my dreams were laced with vivid forays into the past. As if the genie was out of the bottle.

'Keys in,' said Alex, tossing his into the bowl on the hall table where mine always sat. He wore his signature red leather jacket, butter soft, and his hair was meticulously tufted with gel.

Normally I indulged his joke with a roll of the eyes, but that evening, still dreamy, there was I planting a kiss a tad too close to his lips. Scar followed her husband in and I hugged her to me, savouring her perfume, Chanel Allure. She too wore a plunge neck dress, funny how we both scrubbed up for our dinner parties, whereas jeans and a shirt served us well at all other times.

I led them into the kitchen where a beaming Ollie waited, jovial buffer in place, boarding school personified. Public school public face, I'd always joked. This was our first dinner party since his affair and I'd returned from dropping Sophie to find the table set, candles lit, edgy music, and had thanked him with a kiss on the cheek. My first one and it felt comfortable enough.

He took the champagne bottle offered by Alex and they man-hugged with much use of the word *mate*, and the odd impromptu guffaw from Ollie. Over the years they had grown into each other, jocularly, despite Alex's total disinterest in Ollie's go to topic of sport. Scar, I watched for any signs of anger on my behalf but she pecked his cheek as always, a professional woman with no wish to incite.

'Where's Sophie tonight?' she asked as we began our starters of crab and avocado, and I explained about Bianca's.

'They'll have been frontloading,' said Alex, with the ironic smile he pulls off when he's got one over.

'Surely not?'

'Vodka! No alcohol at the party – well that's what she told you. So they'll drink themselves stupid beforehand.'

'Shut up Alex,' Scarlett jumped in

'But Sophie's not like that. And she hates vodka, doesn't she, Ol?'

He was opening a bottle of red and sniffed the cork with a shrug. 'Never drunk more than a good glass of wine or two.'

'They'll be glamming up together,' said Scar. 'We used to at their age, didn't we?'

'Yeah.' I shucked my head in thanks.

'Anyway, we don't know what Nick gets up to, do we?' she added.

'Nope,' said Alex. 'Housemaster's job not ours, however.'

Ollie and I shared a fleeting glance, still in genuine collusion when it came to other parents shirking their responsibility, and I caught Scar and Alex exchanging a look of their own; because doesn't every parent secretly consider themselves superior? The tenor of our evening, however, already not its usual frivolous

66

self, threatened to curdle, so I attempted to lighten it.

'I mean, I drank too at their age, used to brazen it out at the Red Lion with my *one* Martini and lemonade.'

'Cinzano in my case.' Scar smiled her encouragement and I smiled back.

'Clearly more classy than me. But Sophie does seem so much *younger* than I was at fifteen.'

'That old chestnut,' said Alex. 'Fifteen's the new eighteen, didn't you know?'

I gazed at him and fell into a silent fret; maybe I should have prepared her with a vodka session at home so she'd know how little it took.

'First time I got trolleyed was on five pints of lager and black.' Ollie blustered into the lull. 'Village pub. Summer I spent with my best pal from boarding school. Reckon I was fourteen. How about you, mate?'

'Probably ten. At the house in Cannes.'

'Trumped us all Alex.' I stood to clear plates with a mocking, '*At the house in Cannes.*'

He flashed a smile at me and, though niggled by his goading, I couldn't help but smile too, again musing how it might be, a quickie with this rogue of a man. As a minor celebrity, he was occasionally on the telly talking about the experimental plays he showcased, and I could well believe that he did have sex with his young actors, as Scar suspected. He ran a youth programme each summer, which I'd always considered odd given that he'd sent his own son away to board, but he was often quoted by rising stars as having been instrumental.

'Scrummy, thanks Anna' said Scar, passing their plates, while Ollie leaned back for me to remove his.

'So what are you all up to workwise?' I asked, foisting a change of subject as I carried them to the sink.

The three of them remained seated, nobody stood to help, they never did. Each of them had forged two decades of enriching career out of their lives, growing, maturing, flourishing to their full potentials, while my role among them was that of nurturer. Scar and Alex never cooked for us, rather they would whisk us off to the Groucho Club, apparently immune to its deafening music. Their annual party on the eve of Christmas Eve was always a wild affair, their living room peppered with famous faces. Ollie claimed to encounter these in the shop daily, but I admit to relishing the exhilaration of small talk with a guy off *East Enders*.

While I served up the main course, as usual they discussed these careers of theirs. They all counted thousands of followers on Twitter while I had about ten, and I suspected they deemed it kind to air their latest coups while I was otherwise occupied, lest I felt bored, or envious – or inferior even? Whatever, I knew they would not be interested in my new venture, an old man called Fred.

I'd visited him twice now and found his company intriguing – more than that, it was comforting, enriching. And I had also finally signed myself up to a course on business start-ups that summer, so I could well soon have a new enterprise of my own to discuss at dinner parties. Having already spent hours sitting at the island, mind mapping ideas for what trade that business might ply (most of them fanciful) I was ever hopeful that some nugget would eventually gleam through.

I tuned back in to hear Ollie holding forth.

'So this guy came in with a wine scanner on his phone, you know the type.'

'I do, mate,' said Alex.

'Wanker. I'm not having a bloody know-all in my shop.'

'So how did you handle him?'

'Asked him very politely…'

'But in no uncertain terms…'

'To fuck off.'

Ollie and Alex clinked glasses. His lease and business rates were astronomical, Brexit loomed, and with it anxiety for the wine trade, but he would not suffer upstarts even if it lost him custom.

By the time I'd dished up, their animation over the workplace was fizzling out and they each turned their focus on the rack of lamb and gratin dauphinoise.

'You've surpassed yourself, darling,' said Ollie.

'Thank you. Darling.' I sat down, shoulders tightening. 'Fetch me my phone, would you? Hall table?'

After a momentary glance my way he slowly stood and went in search of it.

There was nothing from Sophie, so I sent a text. *All good?*

'No message,' I said to no one in particular, 'but she's with Jack.'

'That'll be OK then.' Alex raised those teasing eyes to mine.

'Alex.' Scar frowned.

'You're not helping here…'

'No, mate, you're really not.' Ollie too was annoyed. 'Sophie knows what's what.'

'And Jack's a good kid,' I added.

Awkwardly then we reached for more innocuous dinner party fodder of books, films and box sets, but Alex was in mischievous mode and I could tell he was biding his time. Finally, plate empty, he bit his lip at me provocatively.

'So while we're on first alcohol, how about first sex?' A snake-like emphasis on the sibilants.

'On the brain, Alex?'

'Already know how old you were, Scarsie.' He nudged his

wife.

'I was sixteen,' she said, in no mood to be passed over.

'You must have been a peach.'

Alex tweaked her now less than peachy forty-something cheek and I caught my friend's momentary fury in her lips.

Other people's husbands. They always seemed appealing, fascinating even, but deep down you knew that they were just as tricky as yours. I glanced at Ollie, happily pouring the wine and seemingly oblivious to the tension between the couple, and I wondered if he was as good as it gets. Fundamentally, we had always worked well together, a neat fit – he might patronise but he had never sniped at me like that. Then again, he had shagged another woman.

It had been almost two months now and we had still been shambling along, no more spats, but my distress had been displaced by an emotion I was finding hard to pin down. Placidness? Disinterest even? We were largely on a comfortable plane, but the shift had been undeniable. Would I ever love him again as before? Did I want to? For the moment I remained happily skimming the surface of my marriage.

'I was fifteen,' said Ollie, and I knew where this was going. 'I was staying at this hotel in Devon with my parents, and so was she, all alone on a rambling holiday, walking the coastal paths.' He paused. 'She was forty.'

'Forty?' said Alex. 'You dark horse, why have you never told us that, mate?'

Ollie gave a smug smile. 'Anyway, one night at dinner she winked at me. I thought it must have been at someone else, but it came again. Then she jerked her head at the ceiling.'

He sipped his wine, holding the moment, Alex and Scar a rapt audience.

'So I told Mum and Dad I was going outside to take photos

of the sunset, and I followed her up the stairs. Can you imagine it? The first time with such an experienced woman? Thought I'd gone to heaven and died.'

'Died and gone to heaven,' I corrected sharply; he must have known that this tale of sex with another woman was inappropriate.

'No heaven came first, I can assure you.' Evading my eyes, Ollie threw a stage wink at Scar, who laughed.

'Crazy woman,' she said. 'Theoretically, she could have been hauled up for child abuse.'

'Don't think she realised. I was very well endowed for a teenager.'

'Were you now?' Scar raised her eyebrows at me, so I played along with a comedic nod.

My friend. She really was a Scar rather than a Scarlett. On Monday mornings she maintained her vicious assassination of Ollie and his affair, and here she was bantering with him as ever. But then there was I imagining having sex with *her* husband! The two-faced beast, was that how we women negotiated life?

We shared a furtive smile; still complicit then.

'I wasn't legal, either,' I said. 'But I really was much more streetwise than my daughter, we all were back then. We cocoon our kids nowadays, don't we?'

'Mm.' Scar's eyes fell to her plate.

'*You* do! 'Alex spoke the words his wife had spared me. 'If you were both so young why are you so uptight about Sophie having sex?'

'Because I'm clearly a prude,' I said, before he could, any desire for a quickie with Alex rapidly evaporating.

'And she should do as you *say* and not as you *do*,' he added.

Ollie saved me with another of his guffaws. 'My daughter

won't be having sex at *least* until she's thirty.'

Conscious of the hovering spite, we all laughed a little too hard at that, but Scar deftly changed the subject and began talking about a school mum who was an extra on one of her productions. It had been a bizarre conversation and we were probably all wondering at the turn the evening had taken, normally our dinners were peppered with warmth and laughter.

Once we were back on a benign footing, I stood to prepare the cheese.

'Where is this party, Anna?' Ollie asked as I unwrapped a slab of Brie.

'Somewhere in Kingston. Don't know the actual address.'

'Let's find out.'

I swung around. 'You've put a tracker on her phone?'

'Find my phone, its already on it. No big deal.'

I set the cheese plate on the table and settled down to focus while Ollie brought up his screen.

'Hmm,' he said, 'take a look at this.'

I peered at it, frowning to get my bearings. The tiny outline of an I-phone peered back at me, this must have been Sophie. But there was no Richmond Park. A river yes, but no swathe of greenery, only streets upon streets, grey upon grey.

Finally the letters leapt out and formed words. Soho, W1.

8

'Brave little blighters, aren't they?'

We stood side by side at Fred's patio window, sipping our tea.

'That one there, he flies down every afternoon to visit me, you could time him like clockwork. He sits waiting on the shed roof until I've put the raisins out for him, then down he hops.'

I contemplated the blackbird jabbing at the juicy fruit on Fred's beautifully mown lawn. At my feet sat Dougal, ears cocked, whimpering at the sight of this unattainable wind-up toy. It was a ritual I hadn't witnessed before, even though I arrived each week at the same time, but Fred seemed sure of it. Just as he'd asked me to take out his recycling the previous week but it was already out. Just as, on my arrival that day, he'd been surprised to see me – was it Wednesday?

'Look he's eyeing me up,' he said. 'I've a fancy that he's saying thank you.'

'Think he is, Fred.'

While I feigned interest in the scene, my mind was still reeling at the events of Saturday night. Despite robust efforts to clear it while at Fred's, the rabble blustered back in.

'What the hell do you think you're up to?' I'd screamed down the phone at Sophie. 'You get back home right now. Book an Uber. You hear me?'

She'd been sheepish but still I'd ranted on, my voice spiked with the language of my own mother's outrage when I myself was fifteen. 'You scheming minx! You're in so much trouble, Sophie Bond. And make sure Jack brings you home safely.'

When she'd arrived at the front door some time later, leaving Jack hovering by the cab door, my daughter was contrite to the point of tears.

'Sorry, Mum, they all wanted to go to this club.'

'This *club*? This club is where they found a tab of that drug, Ecstasy, on the floor after a *child's* birthday party! This club is a well-known haunt of date rapists. This *club*…'

While my screeches reverberated, Ollie hung back in the hallway, half on my side half on hers, and Alex and Scar lingered in stunned silence.

'You're grounded,' I cried finally, slamming the door on Jack. 'Grounded for the next week, Jack's banned too. And I'm not sure there'll be a sixteenth birthday party in this house anymore either.'

'Penny for them?' Fred was peering into my face, a benign smile fixed on his own.

I shook the thoughts off. 'Sorry Fred, I was engrossed in the blackbird.'

Luckily it was still working through its snack. At Old Friends they'd imbued on me always to appear interested, to focus during the whole two hours. That's how I would build maximum trust, that's how an elderly person would feel valued. And it was only my third visit.

'Anything you want to get off your chest, Anna? I'm here for you.'

Who was befriending whom here?

'Good job you're there for *him*,' I said brightly, feeling

myself blush – I hadn't fooled him; funny how often we think ourselves cleverer than others. 'Shall we sit in the garden? Gorgeous day out there.'

'Well, I don't like to disturb him when he's filling his boots.'

So we sipped our tea and watched on, while I tried to imagine what Fred experienced from a glossy blackbird pecking at a heap of raisins. A symbol of the simple life we should all embrace? Communion with nature? Or was it the comfort of company?

'Do you believe in fate, Fred?'

'I do. It's treated me well, by and large.'

'When my daughter was tiny I thought I could make the world safe for her. Kept her hands clean, dressed her warmly, always strapped her in her pushchair, you know.'

I glanced sideways, that soft noisette smile of his.

'Then, one day, our fridge door fell off. Dropped like a tombstone to the floor. Missed Sophie by an inch. She was barely walking, could have killed her.' I paused. 'That was fate, you see, warning me not to believe myself omnipotent. And now it's mocking me again. My daughter's ready to fly, Fred. She's already up there, flitting and fizzing, and…'

'It's not among the particular stars you would wish upon?'

I nodded. 'But I have to let her go, Fred, don't I? I have to let her soar.'

He reached for my hand, his skin parchment dry, and squeezed. 'You've done your best, love. I can feel that you have.'

'I've tried. But I know I've pushed her, I've overdone it a bit. Sometimes it was as if I was kneading her like dough, forming and re-forming to get her right.' I swallowed. 'So wrong of me.'

A cotton handkerchief appeared, crisply folded. I took it

gratefully and blew my nose.

'Thank you. I'll wash this.' I stuffed the hanky into my jeans pocket and flashed a winning smile. 'I'm so sorry, Fred. You have this kind face and I… Well, why don't you tell me your news. What have *you* been up to?'

With a final look, so gentle, so knowing, he decided not to press. 'As a matter of fact, I marched for *The People's Vote* on Saturday.'

'The Brexit March?' I'd spent the afternoon cooking.

'Would you like a sticker?' He placed his mug on the sideboard, and took a reel of yellow from a drawer.

'Here you go, *Bollocks to Brexit.*' He peeled one off and slapped it onto my arm. 'You mustn't give in.'

'Thank you, I'll wear it with pride. Who did you go with?' Loneliness was Fred's big issue, they'd said.

'My Thursday club. Old chaps like me, we meet in the pub every Thursday and talk rubbish. Age is a great leveller, doesn't matter what your background has been. 'Course, mere handful of us left now, but we made it down Whitehall, speeches and all.'

'Go Fred!' I raised my fist.

'Power to the people.' He raised his own, eyes twinkling. Then he patted his pockets and began to search around him. 'Have you seen my pipe, Anna?'

I smiled, mustering the fondness of a daughter for her scatty dad. 'It's on the sideboard.' It always was.

He took the pipe and shuffled through the dividing door to his living room. When I reached for his forgotten coffee mug, I noticed that his landline phone was skewed and emitting a low beep.

'Phone off the hook, Fred?' I slipped it back on.

'Blessed nuisance calls, I play them at their own game. They can't hang up until I do, must cost them a pretty fortune!'

'Smart move.' I smiled to myself at his guile.

The clock monster struck the half hour. With each quarter it added jangles, culminating with a flourish of deafening bells on the hour, which I found utterly depressing – I'd hate to have been there at noon. That was unlikely, however, because Fred had requested afternoon visits, timed perhaps for that lull between his after-lunch snooze and the moment it would be respectable to turn on the television.

'Crossword, love? I've saved it for you.'

'Was hoping you'd ask.'

By then he'd sat himself down, so with a wistful glance at the glorious day outside I joined him, swapped his mug for the newspaper and sank into a chair.

'OK, one across.'

''Course it's not been a bad life.'

Intrigued, I rested the paper on my lap. 'I'd love to hear about it, Fred.'

He pulled on his pipe, seemingly lost in the past and wondering where to start.

'I met my wife before I was twenty,' he said finally. 'The fifties was a time of hope, of renewal, after all the strife. That's her there, together with our daughter, Beth.'

I glanced at the photo on his bookcase. 'They both look very pretty.'

'Grace was a beauty. We met at a dance hall, she wore a red dress cinched at the waist, and we hit it off right away. She was nineteen too. 'Course there was no such thing as a teenager back then. In our day we were children and then we were adults.'

Fred told me about his life. Born in 1932, his father had been a bank manager and his mother a teacher. After his engagement to Grace, he had gone up to Cambridge to read history, had rubbed shoulders with the likes of Burgess and Maclean, and after graduation found himself searching for an opportunity to do good.

'The fledgling UN was a symbol of optimism, you see. So I built myself a career in overseas aid with their development programme, UNDP. Forty years of service. Always with Grace by my side.'

'You lived abroad all that time?'

'We did. Vietnam, Yugoslavia, various African countries. And HQ in New York, of course, that was my final posting before I retired. Then the Soviet Union collapsed and they were after experienced people for government advisers, so I was called back.' He popped at his pipe. 'Fascinating times, Anna, the end of communism, not seen the likes of it since. The global village, that was our mantra. And we're about to bugger it all up with Brexit.'

That evening, after preparing an elaborate chicken salad and allowing Sophie to eat in front of the TV (normally verboten in our house) I met Scar for a quick drink in the sumptuous lounge at Villa di Geggiano on the High Road. We'd missed our Monday morning coffee that week, and naturally our dinner parties were a different beast, what with the men there, so a catch-up was not an unusual request, but I knew that she was after the lowdown on Sophie. I, however, was bursting to talk about Fred.

'He's had such a purposeful life,' I began, having agreed to a bottle over a glass. 'He reminds me of David Attenborough, so decent. As if he's lived only a respectful life, never lied, or stolen, or been cruel to a living thing in his eighty plus years on earth.'

She narrowed her eyes playfully. '*You've* never stolen anything, have you?'

Scar was in no mood for my solemn tales about an old man called Fred, but with an impatient shake of the head I held forth regardless.

'He belongs to a bygone era, to a world that was moral.'

'You need a proper job, Anna, this old age thing is contagious.'

That smarted.

'Don't *you* worry about the world our kids are having to embrace? I mean, there's porn for starters.'

'Why porn suddenly? Sophie went to a nightclub, that's all.'

'Oh, something Fred said. About never seeing his wife naked for the first year.'

My friend pulled off an exasperated shrug. 'So *how* is Sophie?'

I sighed, gave in. 'Cooped up. But I'm softening already, I know I went a tad over the top.'

She livened. 'A tad.'

I grinned, she was after frivolity and I was again being a downer. 'Still holding Jack's tennis gear hostage. See if he's got the balls to come get it.'

'Bet he has another racquet.'

We both laughed.

'Don't spoil it for me.'

I waggled my glass at her and she chinked hers against it; this was the banter she wanted.

'Good looking lad, isn't he?' she said.

'He's a good lad all round. It was youthful exuberance, the teenage brain needs to take risks, can't help it. Did you know that?'

'I did. Constant in Nick's case. If they catch him smoking

weed he'll be thrown out, but he swears he only ever indulges at home. Alex supplies him.'

'Alex supplies his son with drugs?'

'He can be a tosser at times. As you saw on Saturday night.'

I sipped my wine and realised that I was nodding.

'I know I've got to let go of her. The term tiger mum was invented for me, wasn't it?'

Scar shucked her head, a kindness that meant, *Yes, but...*

I smiled. 'You probably won't remember this, but back in Year Three, Sophie won the annual art prize, for a papier-mâché clown she'd made.'

'Funnily enough, I can. Bulbous red nose, scary eyes?'

I frowned at her recall. 'Well it was me who made it. It was all my work, and I passed it off as hers.'

'Yeah, we all knew that.'

I gazed at her. 'You *knew*?'

She shrugged.

'You and who else?'

'All the mums in Year Three.'

'So why didn't you say anything?'

'Seemed important to you. You weren't the only one, you know. I used to do Nick's English for him... metaphors, personification. We all want our kids to impress.'

'It was more than that for me though. I missed my job. You all went tripping off from the playground in high heels to yours, but where was I? Once all-powerful, all-colourful me? Left to dwindle after drop-off at coffee mornings with bitchy Lucy Marshall.'

'You chaired the PTA, Anna.'

'Planner of school fair and head of second-hand uniform sales.'

She laughed along with me.

'You did a fabulous job. Nobody else would have been able to corral that gaggle of women like you.'

'Gaggle is the word,' I said. 'But do you remember when I instigated that ridiculous rule to reduce the kids' sugar intake? Only sugar-free lollipops as a reward for speaking in assemblies? And only two puddings a week at lunch?'

'I do.' Scar reached for her wine. 'But we were all behind you.'

'And then, when they started secondary school, every single one of them hit the shops on the way home and stuffed their faces with sweets, shovelling them in as they walked up the garden path.'

Scar coughed on her wine and I laughed too. She reached across the table for my hand and squeezed it. 'You really need to get back to work, Anna.'

'I know. It's driving me crazy, Sophie too. I need diversion, but what *am* I going to do with the rest of my life, Scar?'

'Something magical.'

Something magical. The words resonated on my walk home.

In the hallway I found Jack's bike propped against the wall, adding a new smudge which made me smile. He was ensconced on our sofa with Ollie and Sophie, watching *Live and Let Die*; four days since the party and my heart sang to see him back. All three looked up hesitantly to gauge my reaction, pausing the film at the funeral procession through New Orleans.

'Hello Jack.'

'I swung by for my tennis gear, Mrs B, hope that's OK?'

'Sure.' I smiled and sank into an armchair, tucking my feet beneath me. 'This is my favourite bit.'

When the film had finished it was gone midnight. We all yawned and stretched, wondering who would speak first, and Jack sprung to his feet.

81

'See you tomorrow night then, son,' said Ollie as the boy left the room.

'Awesome, thank you.'

I threw Ollie a quizzical look.

'World Cup,' he said. 'Belgium. We've invited Jack to watch it with us.'

My heart sang louder; they'd pulled him back into the fold without me losing face over my outburst.

9

The heatwave sweltered on into July and, along with the whole of the country, our family became more carefree. To avoid the football frenzy, Scar and Alex had escaped to their place in Cannes. I'd been pondering her words about everyone knowing I'd passed my work off as Sophie's, and the fact that she'd held this from me all those years ago, and I was bothered – to the point where she'd featured in several troubled dreams. I was ready for a few weeks of absence from my friend.

While she had evaded it, we gorged on the football. Whenever England were to play, Jack would watch the match with us. I vaguely wondered why he chose our home over his own, after all his father was an avid football fan too, but he said his dad had a big job on out in the sticks, that he'd find a pub showing the game. Ollie did ply him with beer, which must have been a factor, as we knew his own parents were stricter. Whatever, I was delighted to have him among us, and by the later stages we all claimed that he would jinx England if he were to watch them elsewhere. So we four sat together, match after match, the kids spilling onto the floor, and we cheered and screamed England onto the semi-finals.

On that day, the match against Croatia, London was buzzing. Bathed in heat and optimism, strangers smiled at strangers. Finally, I had attended my first business start-up workshop – gleaning so much about how to do it, but not *what* to do – and had found the Tube already deserted as I rushed home for the start of the game. The family were settled, beers for the *boys*, as I'd come to call them, and I poured a glass of wine for me and Sophie. When England scored within the first five minutes, Ollie and Jack were up on their feet, punching the air, arms around shoulders, belting out *Football's Coming Home*, and we girls were quick to follow, dancing and singing.

This was the life. Every family should have a Jack. He had broadened us, infused our trio with renewed joy, brought me and Sophie closer. The previous week, she and I had spent a glorious day at Wimbledon – centre court, strawberries, Pimms, Serena Williams, the lot. So when Croatia scored, taking us into extra time, and then won the match, our World Cup viewing reached a gloomy end. But after he'd left for home, Sophie asked if Jack could come on holiday with us, and both Ollie and I happily agreed. We clinked glasses over the prospect when she'd gone to bed. Oh to prolong this quality family time – never mind Harry Kane's golden touch, what about Jack Mattison's?

July was a special month for Fred and me too. I'd been wanting to get him out of the house for a treat and the opportunity arose to watch the RAF centenary flypast at a swish law firm where an old university friend of mine worked. My Polish manager at Old Friends sanctioned it readily, albeit after I'd completed a risk assessment of the outing.

In the lift up, we were joined by a swarm of male lawyers, partners judging by their confidence and distinguished grey hairs. Breathing in the aftershave of one man whose back was an inch from my chest, I glanced up at the mirrored ceiling, and our eyes met; he'd also looked up, and we shared a hint of a smile. Then I caught Fred smiling at me too, clocking the mild flirtation.

The top floor meeting room boasted a picture window, where Fred sat in his smart grey suit popping at an unlit pipe and drinking in St Paul's Cathedral, unaware that as the room filled some of the staff were drinking him in too.

'Let's stand,' he said, as it was about to begin.

A young lawyer made his way to Fred's side. 'Were you in the war, yourself, Sir?'

Fred cast him a sideways glance, slow and measured. 'How old do you think I am, lad?'

'Sorry.' He reddened. 'Of course, stupid of me.'

'National service, 1950, Bassingbourn,' said Fred, eyes fixed on the window. 'It was my father who flew the Spitfires.'

There's always that moment at the beginning of any event which sparks a special awe, the first firework of the night, the parade drumroll, the MGM lion. When the first helicopter appeared in the distance our silence was audible. Fred stood to attention, and I swear that each person in that room did likewise, spellbound at the Hurricanes and Spitfires sailing past our eyes. Destination Buckingham Palace, but their performance seemed for us alone. Chinooks I recognised from Vietnam War films, Lancaster Bombers from the Christmas afternoons of my childhood, and the futuristic craft from endless news bulletins on Iraq. Finally, the Red Arrows brought forth a nostalgic sigh, their patriotic plumes of red, white and blue perfect chalky trails which our eyes clung to as they dissipated.

When the sky was once again an empty blue, the hubbub bubbled, but I waited a few moments before glancing at Fred. His eyes were bright with emotion.

'Gallantry,' was all he said.

Goose bumps swept my flesh. Had I brushed other arms, I would have felt their own hairs prickling, their own respect stirring. Gallantry, a quality obsolete in us all.

Afterwards, Fred took me for lunch to a brasserie he'd once known off Piccadilly, which fortuitously still existed. The morning had visibly taken its toll, physically and emotionally, so I helped him down from the black cab, linked arms with him, and we entered the restaurant as an old-fashioned couple. The dark wood panels, brass rails and green shades were welcoming, as was the cool air. Fred made a show of sliding me in at our table and I smiled a music hall nod of thanks.

'Does this place have special memories?' I asked.

'It does.'

'Of your wife?'

His shrug caught me off guard.

'Nice tie,' I said quickly.

He flipped it. 'I rather like it, do you?'

'Airforce blue, very fitting.'

'Took myself off to Peter Jones.'

I was pleased to hear he'd made such a journey alone. He was always telling me how he *used* to swim in the Serpentine, *used* to attend lectures at the Royal Geographical Society.

He fumbled for his glasses and peered into his menu. 'Let's see if they still cook a mean steak au poivre.'

After ordering for us both, including a bottle of heavy red Cabernet Sauvignon, he pushed his reading glasses up onto his forehead, where they sat below his sunglasses already propped there. Both pairs were balanced precariously, tufting his hair out at angles, but this was not the moment.

'Thank you again, Anna. That was special.'

'So are you, Fred.' It didn't sound in the least corny. 'And your father too by the sounds of it. He flew Spitfires?'

'One of the Few. One of the oldest too, but he came home again. Lived to the ripe old age of ninety.'

'My dad died the week before his fortieth birthday.' I hadn't intended this to slip out, but the memories sallied forth.

'I'm so sorry, love.'

'Car accident, when I was four. He used to run a plastics company. Back in the sixties they were all the rage, you know?'

'I do know.'

'Ironic really that now they've become so sinister, plastics.'

The waiter arrived with our wine and fussed over the cork, allowing Fred to taste it before pouring for us both.

'Anyway,' I said, though I really should have let Fred talk about himself, 'Dad was an only child so Mum inherited the business, but she spiralled into depression and ended up selling it.'

'Is your mother still alive?'

'Lives in Australia. I mean, she set me up financially, with shares and stuff, but she couldn't hack life here after Dad died. Theirs was the big love story, you see. At least she waited until I started uni.'

I'd always joked with Ollie that I'd brought myself up, that when she wasn't balling me out she was comatose in her bedroom – that's how I recall my teenage years. We'd softened over time, but it had been a while since I'd last Skyped her. Or her me.

'Dad was a kind man. You remind me of him.'

He cocked his head with the softest of smiles. 'I'll stick with you, love.'

I took an emotional draught of wine. 'You know, whenever I search for myself online, the only mention of me is on his *Wikipedia* page.'

'You search for yourself online? Whatever for?'

'I live in hope.'

'Of what, Anna?'

'Oh, whatever… You're in there, you know? Frederick Wildsmith. All those papers you wrote on international development.'

'Am I now?'

'I'll show you sometime.'

As he contemplated me with those soothing eyes, our food arrived and he took up his cutlery, so I followed suit.

'Fill your boots,' he said with a nod at my steak.

I realised then that Fred was a man who enjoyed eating in silence, head down, as if into a nosebag. Once again, I wondered who was befriending whom.

10

And then, one evening in late July, when the heatwave had taken such a hold that I could never imagine it being cold again, I decided to join Ollie on one of his corporate events. Life was generally placid and, nearly three months on, I was making a renewed effort to stand by his side.

The local wine society were to hold their annual black tie dinner at the Orangery in Kew Gardens. Ollie supplied the wine for their monthly meetings and often gave the expert's talk about its provenance. All guests were to enter through the Victoria Gate and take a leisurely stroll to the venue.

'Fancy a detour through the Rhododendron Dell?' Ollie took my hand as we walked beside the lake and the Glasshouse. 'Spot of bush craft?'

I smiled at his reference to those team building days in Wales but allowed him only a platonic chuckle. On one of the recent hot summer nights I had succumbed. It had been so long since I'd had sex and my dreams were now kaleidoscopic, bombarding me nightly with erotic urgency, but I had abandoned the deed some moments in, claiming it was still too soon. The image of him with another woman was indelible.

We strolled along the Broad Walk, now alive with purple meadow flowers, and stepped off the path to visit the Hive. A visual symbol of the role bees play in feeding the planet, and the challenges facing them today, so the leaflet said. I gazed up into the mesh, bewitched by the pale flickering of lights, a thousand LED bulbs triggered by movement in an actual beehive somewhere in the gardens.

'Incredible,' I murmured, all those bees buzzing to mate with the queen. 'Who'd have thought to create something like this?'

'Absolutely,' he said.

And I knew that he was bored, so on we walked.

The Orangery was bathed in the peachy glow of evening and had been set up to spectacular effect; round tables, golden chairs and stiff white linen, while the gardens had been quirkily mined for the exotic floral centrepieces, scoops of orange, spikes of magenta. As we mingled over a flute of champagne, I enjoyed the appreciative glances at my new dress of emerald silk, chosen to reflect the venue, and I relaxed into the occasion. Reaching for a second glass from a passing tray, I followed Ollie to our table.

We took our seats alongside the chair of the wine society and his wife, whom I barely knew, and Ollie immediately turned to charm an attractive woman in a low-cut dress. Briefly I listened in to his chatter which bordered on flirtation, and wondered if that's how he'd begun it with that woman, Kathy Hunter. My mood tensed, I downed my champagne and focused on the chairman to my left.

I was nattering on about holidays when I first saw him. A hand slid by my head and placed a small plate on the table before me.

'Thank you,' I said, glancing up.

The eye contact startled us both. Minute jolts of the head and our connection lingered. His eyes were wolf grey and mesmerising.

'You look nice,' I found myself saying.

His face opened into a smile. 'Thank you. You also.' His accent was East European.

'I mean your get-up.' I nodded at the long white apron over black trousers, smart shirt and bow tie, which all the waiters wore.

'My *get-up*?'

I was flustered then. 'Your uniform.'

'Thank you.' He moved around my back to place a plate before Ollie. My husband, I was relieved to see, was still flirting with the woman on his right.

I knew my face was flushed as I continued my conversation about my host's plans for the Amalfi Coast in late summer.

'You must go to Capri,' I said. 'Take the boat tour to the Blue Grotto, it's incredible, really, something that has stayed with me.'

I watched the man circle our table with his plates, nothing spectacular about his face, mousy hair even, but those eyes. Again they met mine and he held my gaze as he continued his round. When he left to fetch more plates, I sat up straighter to catch sight of his back, a body which was lean but not skinny, a round bottom which I was visualising naked. He must have been a good ten years younger than me.

Returning with another stack he smiled, at his cheeks two sudden wisps of vulnerable red, and I caught my breath, managing a brief smile before dipping my eyes like some winsome virgin.

'Capri itself is an odd place, full of ostentatious shops,' I gabbled on, chest thumping, 'but the boat trip alone is worth it.'

I wasn't even sure if the man was still listening and didn't dare chance a glance at him. Surely he must have clocked what was happening here? For distraction I contemplated the food on my plate; a mound of burrata cheese, a ring of tomatoes, a slice of avocado, a smattering of torn basil. I began to eat, scanning the room, stretching my neck, but the kitchen was behind me, and with it the waiting staff. Beside me, our host appeared to be responding, but I heard nothing of his words.

'What's up with you?' said Ollie. 'You look like a meerkat.'

'Nothing, just awfully hot in here isn't it?'

'Can't you socialise?'

'What, like you are?'

Guilt snapping.

Out they came again, ploughing the room. I watched him clear the plates of our hosts, then I sensed him behind me. Lifting my empty plate he brushed my bare arm with his, and I was drawn to the rolled back sleeve, to the lily-white flesh peppered with fine blond hairs, a stark contrast to the sandy hirsute arms of my husband. Emboldened, I glanced up and behind me.

'Was good?' His eyes were searching my thoughts.

'Delicious.'

I know you, I thought. I've never met you, but I know just who you are.

The blink I allowed him was slow and measured, but I was in a funk. As if some small beast, furry and furious, was scurrying inside me and zigzagging my thighs – a sensation I had not experienced in so many years, had thought dead to me. Unfathomable.

Having cleared our starters he left the table, dirty plates in hand, and disappeared into the kitchen, so I stood, excused myself, to nobody in particular, and headed for the ladies toilets. Inside the cubicle, suffused by heat and chaos, I slumped onto the closed lid and fanned my cheeks, pressing the cool clasp of my handbag against them to quash any visible signs of fire.

'You stupid cow, get a grip,' I whispered. 'He's a complete stranger.'

It was a few minutes before I left the room; by then they must have already served up the main course. Still flushed, still disorientated, I swung the door open.

There he stood in the corridor, back to the wall, arms folded, and I sprang backwards. We considered each other. Nothing was said but I shook my head while he nodded. Slowly, then, he pushed himself off the wall, took me by the wrist and pulled me towards the door which led out into the gardens.

'No,' I laughed, hauling him back as if he were a dog straining on its leash. 'Are you mad?'

He turned, an enigmatic smile, and he pressed me gently back against the wall, took my face in his hands and kissed me. A brief meeting of tongues and I pushed him off. This was crazy, what if somebody came through that door? We watched each other, chests heaving, his eyes trawling mine. Again he kissed me, and this time I succumbed with a rough desperation, biting his lip, spurred on by the taste of iron.

'Jesus Christ,' I whispered, drawing back.

'In fact, my name is Gabryel.'

I smiled. 'Close enough.'

His eyes were questioning.

'Anna. It's Anna.'

'Hello Anna.'

The door from the main room began to open and I pushed him off me as an elderly woman walked through it. He stepped back quickly and turned for the garden door, while I followed her into the ladies.

'Crafty fag outside,' I laughed, with a quick glance over my shoulder to see him leave the building.

Again I sank onto a closed toilet lid, and I began to shake. A glance at my watch confirmed that I'd been gone nearly ten minutes, so I hastily reapplied my make-up, gazing at myself in the mirror. What had just happened?

'Darling, we were getting worried about you.' Back at the table, Ollie threw me an intense fake smile which said, where the hell have you been?

Socialising, I didn't say.

'Sorry, I felt faint, needed some fresh air. I'm fine now, bit chilly even.'

A smile of apology at our host and his wife and I slid on my jacket.

Within moments the waiters surged out to clear the main course. I had shifted the beef around my plate, secreting vegetables like a small child, and when his arm slid past me to whisk it away I focused on the pale flesh, head reeling. What madness had transpired?

Each time he passed our table I felt his eyes on my face, but not until coffee was I able to meet them again. We held each other's gaze, a serious contemplation the one of the other, before he allowed me the sliver of a smile: our secret.

After the dinner, Ollie and I wandered back through the gardens, each of us keeping our own counsel. Perhaps he was still cross about my absence, or guilty about his own flirting, but our silence was welcome. I should have been ashamed of myself, I had never kissed another man since meeting Ollie, and yet I felt no shame. The Hive was flickering in the night sky, all those bees shagging, and I felt as if a leaden cloak had been cast from me, leaving me with a lighter step, every nerve in my body exposed. Freed to revel.

Behind us a noisy gaggle approached, male voices, and I knew it was him. That language didn't sound Polish, though, more of a Latin tinge to it, I thought, as I glanced over my shoulder, my breath coming in snatches. He'd changed into jeans and a white collarless shirt, in his hand the bulbous case of a musical instrument.

'Tom Tom Club,' he said to his friend as they came level.

'Tom Tom Club?' the man echoed, a fleeting glance my way. 'Soho?'

That night I was unable to sleep. Wired to the moon, imagining how it might have been if I'd followed him outside. I closed my eyes and played out the delicious scene. The gardens were deserted, closed to the public, the tinkling of cutlery still audible as he half dragged me across the lawn to a slim path between a thicket of trees. The prospect of being caught horrified and thrilled me, a danger which drove me on. With a tight grasp of my wrist, he led me in, pushed me against a tree, and slung his apron at the ground. I slid off my knickers, hoisted my dress. Those wolf-like eyes did not leave mine as he hauled me up and onto him, as I caught my legs around his waist. I cried out. He slid his hand across my mouth. 'Shh,' he laughed. Afterwards, we stood panting, heads bowed, brow to brow, my body encased in his shirt sleeves, and I felt nothing but perfection.

The Tom Tom Club, in Soho. I could already feel its dark depths.

11

'What do you two want to eat?'

Jack and Sophie were thundering down the stairs. He had such a heavy step, that boy, hit the ground with the self-assuredness that was now part and parcel of our home. Not sure what the old house made of him, having been used to a light touch for eons, even Ollie held himself with a certain grace as he moved about the world.

The pair swanned into the kitchen, Sophie first, in her skimpy skirt, tanned midriff on display, then Jack in his Drake T-shirt. The glow of their attraction engulfed me, creating another of those frissons: Gabryel.

'Steak?' I said. 'Or I could fry some chicken? With chips?' These days I was stuffing the fridge in anticipation of Jack's visits, and was stunned by the inroads he made, steadily chewing his way through like *The Hungry Caterpillar*.

'Steak please, Mrs B.' He spoke without deference to Sophie.

'Cool,' she said, slipping onto a stool at the island, where she began picking coquettishly at her hair, sifting the recently dyed platinum blonde ends – ombré they called it. 'You out again tonight, Mum?'

'No.' I slapped four fillet steaks on a board, already marking out the largest for Jack. 'Tomorrow. That woman I used to work with got the wrong night and the concert's actually on tomorrow.'

The lies flowed out of me like bubbles blown by a child.

'Oh.' No curiosity from my teenage daughter.

I slid a tray of chips into the oven and busied myself seasoning the meat. For once, the fact that she was wrapped up in her own self-centred life suited me well. I had surprised myself with the absence of guilt, but this outrageous situation was an out-of-body experience, as if it was not happening to me, and at most I felt a sense of unease. I'd never lied to my daughter before, apart from telling her I was never going to die, back when she first felt the fear. Apart from telling her our first pet tortoise had escaped to join his family in the park. And, naturally, all those times I'd told her she was right and her teachers harsh. How could this subterfuge be so ready? The former colleague's name was going to be Gabby, if ever she or Ollie asked.

The previous evening, having covered all my tracks, clearing the history after triumphantly Googling the Tom Tom Club and fabricating a concert at another venue, Ronnie Scott's, I'd arrived to find that Gabryel was not playing. Ollie had been hanging out after work with his Chiswick crowd at Hack and Veldt deli, so I'd aroused no suspicion when slipping out of the house, sporting my best jeans and silk shirt. Chest heaving, sick with nerves and anticipation, I'd slid into the darkened club. And then Gabryel had not been there.

'Is Gabryel not on tonight?' A casual request of the barman as I'd bought an awkward glass of rosé.

'Gabryel?' he'd cried above the thumping bass. 'Sax player?'

'Yeah.' Sax player, that brought a smile to my lips.

'Nah, he does Tuesdays and Fridays.'

Such disappointment, a shard of glass scratching my soul.

I'd gulped the wine and fled, with a last stray glance at the young clientele, all of them a long way off forty-five.

It was now Thursday. So the following night I would be concocting another lie and Tubing it into Soho once again. But my confidence had been shaken, my bravado hammered. He really had been so much younger than me. What if he did this kind of thing all the time?

'Anything particular I need to bring next week, Mrs B?' Jack broke into my thoughts.

Forcing the flurries down deep inside, I conjured up sunshine and surf – we were all three excited to be taking Jack along to our place in La Rochelle. As some kind of prop, I'd realised, and wondered if Ollie and Sophie had too.

'No news and no shoes.' I smiled. 'I finally spoke to your mum about it.'

'Oh? She didn't say.' He began setting the table.

'Well I thought she should know something about the family who are whisking her son off to France.'

Well I'd wanted an excuse to suss her out.

'We have three bedrooms,' I'd assured her, and had felt her smile; did she know something I did not?

'May I contribute to the cost?' That languid voice – all slim fingers and polished nails.

'Not at all.' I'd studied my own nails, their fresh polish now chipped.

The front door slammed, the thud of briefcase on the hall floor, and Ollie ambled through to the kitchen. My ready smile for him was free of guilt and full of guile.

'Hi darling.' A kiss on the lips for me. Limp in comparison to Gabryel's.

'Beer?' I tipped the tops off two bottles and offered one to Jack, whose face lit up as he took it, clinking with Ollie.

'Two more days at the salt mines.' Ollie heaved himself up onto a bar stool with the youngsters. 'Pack your tennis gear, Jack, we've got racquets out there. Body boards too.'

'We'll probably chill at the pool most days, Dad.' Sophie swung her hair.

'Me too, Soph, me too.'

I smiled to myself, that was not how she was visualising it. And what about me? How did I see this holiday panning out? I loved our house in France, had planned to immerse myself in various books on business, but my mind was blocked by Gabryel and was now unlikely to find the necessary concentration. I was desperate to see him again and if I failed in that mission it would be the end of this little escapade; he'd sent me a clear message, and a no show on my part would make him think I wanted nothing more. While, in fact, I wanted so much more.

I slid the steaks into the buttered pan, the rush of steam in synch with the surge charging through my body.

It was another hot one when I arrived at Fred's to drive him out to Syon Park Garden Centre the next morning. I rang the bell with a dreamy smile, indulging yet again my fantasy of wild sex with Gabryel in Kew Gardens. But it was an agitated Fred who opened his door, phone to ear.

'You've had me on hold for five minutes,' he bellowed. 'Four times I've called about it and I want the blessed thing mended before somebody trips up.'

Stunned, I followed him inside. Dougal lay curled up on the living room carpet, compliant and well out of Fred's way.

'Do you want me to break my neck on it? No, *you* listen to me, you jobsworth, you treat us old folk with total disrespect. I shall expect to see it repaired soonest or I shall take the matter higher.'

He strode to his sideboard and slammed the phone back onto its cradle.

'Strike a light!'

The closest I'd ever heard Fred come to swearing.

Ignoring my presence, he marched through to the kitchen. I followed, hovering back, and watched him fill a glass of water, before opening a tin and dropping several blister packs of drugs onto the work surface. He began to pop the pills, gulping water between each one, while I stood mutely wondering what to say. This was my first morning visit and I'd stumbled across two new aspects of the man: anger and drugs. The thought struck me that perhaps he hid his true colours during those two hours of an afternoon I normally spent with him, when his eyes were soft and his mood gentle. Of course, at his age he would be on medication, statins no doubt, and possibly blood pressure pills, but this array seemed excessive.

'Can I make you a coffee, Fred?'

'I should like that, yes.' He drew himself to his full height, sighed heavily and slung the drugs back into the tin, pressing the lid on firmly.

'You take a seat in the garden.' I mustered a sympathetic smile. 'I'll bring it out to you.'

'Thanks, love.' He stepped out of the back door.

I set his ancient kettle on the hob – it would take an age to boil – laid out the coffee mugs and took milk from his fridge. Then my eyes fell on the tin. A quick glance into the garden, where he was filling his pipe, and I darted back, opened the lid and took out the packets, one by one. I noted the name of each drug on my phone and slipped them back into the tin. The kettle was still far from completing its mission and I sank back against the counter and sighed, guilty for not spending more time with Fred.

He must really be lonely. His daughter, Beth, lived in France and barely ever visited, so he'd said. I'd begun to consider myself a mainstay in his life, but suddenly my effort seemed paltry – it occurred to me to increase my weekly two-hour visits, informally and on the sly from Old Friends. But then, of course, I was about to go on holiday for a fortnight and fully neglect him.

Out in the garden, I set down the tray, sat beside him and blew on my coffee.

'Everything OK, Fred?'

'Everything's fine, love. Thanks for this.' His hands shook as he sipped.

'Was that the Council?'

He nodded. 'Paving slab out front.'

I'd tripped on it myself, why hadn't I offered to sort it for him?

'I hate those officious phone calls too, they stress me out.'

'And stress is the one thing I'm supposed to give a wide berth to. Pretty dress.'

He'd changed the subject without a ripple.

'Thank you. I'll call the Council for you, if you like?'

'Don't want to put you out, love. And I need to feel useful, you mustn't give in. So, what I'm after today is something for my patio pots.'

Another seamless transition, but I made a mental note to call the Council anyway.

'Anything in particular?'

'Let's see what they have to show me, shall we?'

On the drive to the garden centre, our chatter remained amiable, and by the time we reached Syon Park, my friend appeared to be restored to the Fred I knew – and let's face it was beginning to love a little. I took charge of the trolley while he added plants with the zeal of a child filling his stripy bag in a sweet shop: peonies, petunias, roses, a clematis, more roses.

'Where will you put it all, Fred?' I asked, then wished I hadn't, this was his treat.

Finally we headed for the café, parking the overloaded trolley at a table in the shade.

'You're looking bright and bushy today,' he said as we shuffled to the tills with our tray of sandwiches, elderflower pressé and cake.

'Am I not always, then?' I was quick, but the heat rose in my cheeks.

'Always well turned out. Just a certain 'je ne sais quoi' about you today.'

'Didn't know you spoke French?'

'Un petit peu. And today you 'ave zee cheeks of a rose. Anything to report?'

'Told you, I'm off on holiday tomorrow.'

Overly brusque, Anna.

'Ah yes.'

He glanced pointedly at my fingers drumming against the tray and I stilled them.

Back outside, we ate our lunch in silence, as he preferred, and it suited me too. His scrutiny had unleashed my imagination – in precisely ten hours I would be seeing Gabryel, indeed, I might be having sex with him. Where would we do it? Backstage? Up an alleyway? How sordid. How thrilling.

'Those peonies are gorgeous, all pink and fluffy,' I said, wrenching myself back to the present.

'Angel Cheeks. Grace's favourite, her wedding bouquet was smothered in them, and I had to sport a peony buttonhole. Great big flouncy thing. She had the whole spray dried and framed for our bedroom wall too.'

'I'd love to see that sometime.'

'I've a fancy that I'll pot them outside the patio window. That way I'll think of her each time they catch my eye.'

'That's a lovely gesture.' I smiled and he smiled too.

'How long have you been married, Anna?'

'Me and Ollie? Ooh nearly twenty years, this winter, in fact. What's the symbol for twenty years, do you know?'

'China,' he said. 'Porcelain or china.'

'I'll buy him a bed pot then.' I laughed at my bizarre joke, hoping to distract Fred from whatever course he was now set upon. 'Or a lavish cake plate, he likes cake as much as you do.'

He grunted, one of his twinkles, and he began working his pipe.

'Want me to help you plant your pots later?'

Another attempt to move us on, but who was I kidding? He *knew*.

'However.' He paused. 'I did have an affair.'

Silence. He continued drawing on the bowl of his pipe, while I froze.

'I wasn't proud, Anna. But then again I don't regret it.' The pipe caught and he looked up, his eyes piercing mine. 'Eve was her name. Shall I tell you about her?'

I nodded, unable to swallow.

'A business trip. Cliché. I met her in a bar after the conference. Another cliché. She had silken hair, and her legs… well another cliché I guess.'

We both laughed a little too loudly.

'I loved my wife, Anna. More than life itself. And she never knew. But that night, well I admit we met several times not just the once, that night I found something… It reaffirmed me as a man. And I like to think that Grace benefitted. No that sounds crass and self-justifying, maybe she didn't at all. But it rejuvenated me. Us.'

I stared at Fred. He seemed to have finished, but I had not the foggiest how to respond. Eventually, he reached across and covered my hand with his.

'The key is not to hurt others.'

I nodded and covered his hand with my other one. For a moment we sat, hands stacked up, his wisdom flowing through into mine, and then the shutter fell.

'Best get on.' He stood and began to clear our debris onto the tray.

12

On the Tube in to Soho, I flicked blindly through the *Evening Standard* then held it clenched at my knees. Once again, I wore my favourite jeans, though I'd opted for a more youthful crimson top which I hoped distracted from my craggy neck. My body was already jellified, my intentions too.

My phone pinged, a text from Scar, *Back from Cannes, meet at weekend?* I froze at the words, a quick glance around as if she was actually on the Tube, knew what I was up to. *Sorry, we're off to France ourselves, back end August.* Not strictly true, my response, but I'd hold her off until then; if Scar were to see me face to face she would know immediately.

Now that I was familiar with the club, I was fearful of piercing its darkness for a second time, of faking confidence among all those youngsters. Above all, I was terrified of rejection. Even if that would make it easier. Even if I'd mitigated my deceit by resolving that I'd do it once and then I'd stop. One time would sort me out and then I'd walk off into the sunset... or sunrise.

Mustering up courage, I hovered with the theatre crowds turning out, the brittleness of London's West End disquieting, almost to the point where I fled home. Finally, with a deep ragged breath, I slipped down the steps and inside the club.

Gabryel was on stage. Centre stage. My heart set about its

thumping, my face seared with a flush. He stood playing his sax, frowning as his fingers worked the keys. Around him, in the shadows, a band played too, but it was he who commanded the room. He wore jeans and the same snug white collarless shirt. With my back to the wall, eyes on him, I slunk around to the bar, perched on a vacant stool at one end and watched him. I waited. Would he look up? Could he even see his audience against the spotlights, if he were to?

He was playing some blues song I didn't recognise. When it ended, to solid applause, Gabryel released his sax and looked up, out at the room. I caught my breath, fixing my eyes on his as they seemed to scan the club in search of something. Of me? A double take and then he spotted me, his glance already moving on then snagging on mine, his mouth opening. In surprise? In excitement? I smiled. He smiled back, held up a finger, a gesture which I took to mean one more song, so I nodded. Once again his mouth found the reed, his fingers the keys, and the mellifluous *My Funny Valentine* drifted from the sax. To the patent surprise of his band mates who raised their eyes at each other, with a nonetheless flawless recovery.

I was mesmerised. Just one time? Who was I kidding? Beside this man is where I wanted to be. In those senseless moments I would happily have abandoned my home and family for him. A man I'd kissed once, and about whom I knew nothing, but for whom I had construed a whole existence. The Kew fantasy I had played out over and over, embellishing the detail each time and in my imagination this stranger's history, his values, his lifestyle, all were perfection. As was his soul. How utterly ridiculous, and yet somehow inexorable.

When the song ended, he acknowledged the applause before unclipping the sax and settling it on its stand. A brief rub of his neck, a few nods of thanks to the band, and he jumped off the end of the low stage and made his way towards me, his eyes never leaving mine. How is he going to greet me? I thought, aware of the sweat beading at my cleavage. His body was slight, boyish even, his hair thin and his flesh, even in the darkness, was bleachy white, but those eyes seared.

When he reached my stool, I raised my chin with a smile, and received a kiss, sweet and gentle. His arms slid around me, pulling me in, while I held him by the shoulders and returned the kiss. To anyone in the room it may have looked as if we were boyfriend and girlfriend embracing naturally, but the chaos was running ragged. For both of us, I could tell.

He drew back. 'I knew that you would come.'

His smile was open, his face splayed with the vulnerability which had so moved me, and I smoothed my hands down the front of his shirt, thrillingly conscious of the flesh beneath it.

'Oh did you now?'

Our language was not that of a temporary liaison, of a couple about to fuck and then part. It was that of a kindling relationship. I knew then that this would not be a case of once – or even five times. And although it could end in disaster, and probably would, I cared not a toss.

At my shoulder a glass of beer appeared on the bar.

'Thank you, bro.' Gabryel nodded to the barman and I smiled to myself. Bro.

'And one for my girlfriend too?'

The barman turned to fish a bottle of rosé from the fridge and flipped over a large wine glass with the hint of a wink. He'd remembered me, and he knew that I was no girlfriend, but Gabryel's use of the term had roused me. Me, the married woman.

We clinked glasses. 'Up yours,' he said.

I didn't even stifle the giggle.

'What?' He smiled.

'We say bottoms up.'

'Ah, my British friends…'

I smiled, a coquettish tilt of the head. 'Up yours has another meaning entirely.'

'I see. Perhaps you will tell me another time. So… bottoms up?'

'Bottoms up.'

Now what? I thought, watching him watching me, the desire in his eyes mirrored in mine. That beast was back scurrying inside, its claws catching at every nerve. I wanted nothing more than to take him by the hand and lead him into some sumptuous hotel suite, which would be conveniently sited in the adjoining room, all billowing white duvet and feather pillows. Two realities were clear, however. Firstly he had to play at least one more set, and secondly, the adjoining room would be a squalid office or staff room, stinking of cigarettes, its floor sticky with spilt drinks.

'I don't know what to say now.' Gabryel smiled. 'But you look beautiful.'

'I'm not sure either.' I hesitated. 'Is there somewhere we can go? Where we can be alone?'

He glanced towards a door at the back of the bar, then at his watch. How long did he have? I thought, stirred by the prospect of the very moment about to arrive. I watched him catch the eye of the barman and nod towards the door.

'Come with me.' He took my hand, led me behind the bar.

Trailing after him, I did half wonder if I was marking a well-trodden path to that door, but I was so exhilarated by what was to happen on the other side of it that the thought was titillating. It opened onto steps down, to the cellar I realised, breathing the dank cold smell of beer as the door swung shut and we left the club's hubbub behind. Down we went. With each step I left my life behind, a teenager again, about to claim sexual gratification with no heed of the consequences. At the bottom of the stairs we doubled back on ourselves, and I followed him around twists and turns, past shelves lined with wine and spirit bottles, until finally we reached a row of steel beer kegs. On the low ceiling a weak bulb swayed to the beat from the room above.

Gabryel's eyes clouded with lust as he pressed me against the blackened wall, and my stomach tightened. Lust. I had thought that feeling lost to me, vanished along with my youth, but there it was, a physical mayhem I had long since forgotten. That he wanted *me*. I breathed his heady perspiration, his earthy aftershave, and returned the force of his kiss.

He stood back and I slipped off my jeans while he dropped his around his ankles, no time to remove our shirts. We each produced a condom, which made us both laugh but defused none of the tension. He chose his own – a gesture that the item had been procured for me, and me only? Then he hoisted me up onto a beer keg, its steel chilling my thighs, and we found ourselves plying a rhythm in time with the thud of bass above our heads.

'Mum? Granny's on Skype.'

I was upstairs packing toiletries and I groaned, our flight was in a few hours.

Beside me Ollie laughed. 'My favourite mother-in-law? Let me at her…'

In reality both he and my mother were delighted to be living thousands of miles apart.

'All yours.' I threw a weak smile in his general direction, still unable to meet his eyes since Friday night, and trudged down to the living room.

'Here's Mum, Granny.'

Sophie waved at the screen and slid the laptop niftily from her knees onto mine as I sat down. I rolled my eyes at her and she back at me. My daughter, who when young would spend hours on Skype with her Granny and now couldn't wait to escape her. For a brief moment three female generations sat together and our bond thrummed, the power we held, the one over the other, mother to daughter, daughter to mother. Then Sophie stood and left the room and I was left looking into the face of the mother who, when I was eighteen, had left me alone in England to start over in Australia. I smiled vaguely at the screen.

'Hi Mum. We're off on holiday today.'

'Again? So much cash washing around that house. Now me, I live frugally.'

I smiled at her Aussie twang, she'd worked hard to lose the Home Counties. 'I know you do, Mum and I'm happy for you. How are you?'

'I'm good Anna. Hot as love's flaming climate here, mind. Fires mid-winter and all, can you imagine?'

'Not where you are?'

My concern fluttered to the surface. She was my mum, I loved her, and she had at times struggled to be a good mother after Dad died.

'Nah, further north.'

'That's a relief. So how is love's flaming climate?'

'Wayne's tickety-boo. Thanks for asking.'

'And the business?'

'Well that's one reason I was calling you. I need to get a shipment to England, gorgeous little wooden dolls, Anna.'

'And you want to avoid the tax on them again?'

'I was hoping you might help me out? Daylight robbery, adds a huge margin, and there's no need for it, is there? All that waste going to the government?'

'You may believe that we are awash with cash, Mum.' And so could she have been if she hadn't given it all away. 'But we do live by the rules, and it was such a hassle last time. I'm sorry, afraid you'd better bite the bullet, ship them to their end destination.'

I fixed my eyes on hers, I admit with a certain sense of satisfaction. Which proved to be a mistake, as I should have known. My mother considered me for several moments with a stern frown and I watched her eyes focus, she was calculating how to call me, it had always been thus.

'You're looking peachier than last time we spoke,' she said finally. 'Something nice happened?'

'Mum I'm going on holiday, in about thirty minutes actually, and I'm in a bit of a flurry. You know how I am before I fly.'

'I *do* know you.' She cocked her head. 'When life gives you lemons...'

I blushed; surely not?

'Maybe I'll come visit, shall I? Christmas time?'

Relieved by the shift I actually nodded. 'Why not? Bring Wayne too.'

That would shake up the old house even more than Jack had done.

'Wayne would love to visit Scotland too.'

'Great. Book it. You could even teach me about running a business. I may be starting one myself. Have to go, Mum, take care.'

I blew her a kiss and ended the session, closing the laptop with a resolute shake of my head; she did know me and had probably sensed what I was up to. Making lemonade.

13

In the departure lounge at Heathrow I felt the distance between Gabryel and myself already stretching out. For weeks I had been anticipating France with pleasure, but my body was now on red alert and I wasn't sure how I'd survive the fortnight with Ollie, especially as that was the one place where sex had always thrived. How could I possibly even go on holiday with my husband if I was cheating on him?

I gazed out at the planes taxiing and recalled that Government Minister who had left his wife in the lounge and fled back to his younger mistress. So many years together, then dumped en route to a holiday abroad, how ignominious – but the idea was appealing. I eyed Ollie sitting one seat away, our hand luggage a snug buffer between us. Opposite, Sophie and Jack were wrestling over his phone, their laughter rich and uplifting, at least they would ease the days.

On arrival at our old farmhouse, I meandered through the rooms, slinging open windows and shutters. When I shook our bedroom curtains free a gecko scuttled across the stone lintel. Hearing Sophie and Jack already running to the pool, I leant out of the window to see their tanned and perfect bodies take a flying leap into the water. I pressed my cheek against the cool wall and saw Gabryel, shirt buttons undone, my mouth at his hairless chest.

Afterwards in that beer cellar I had taken his hand in mine and turned it in wonder, smoothing the young flesh, caressing a new body, in a way I had not done for so long.

'Why me?' I asked him.

An imperceptible shake of his head. 'Something in your eyes. The way you looked at me.'

I smiled. 'I felt it too. From you, I mean.'

He nodded. 'It is true.'

'I don't... I've never done this before.'

'I am also surprised, but...'

He removed his hand from mine and slipped it inside my shirt, sliding fingertips down into my bra, catching at my nipple. A dizziness took hold and I swooned like some actress from a Forties movie, every nerve sending out feelers towards him. I'd lifted my mouth to his – my condom this time.

From the stairs I heard Ollie's tread and turned for the en suite to douse my face before he would come huffing in with our cases.

That first evening we four sat by the pool, tucking into a seafood platter we'd picked up on the drive from the airport. Ensconced in a darkness pierced only by a fat candle and the turquoise pool light, we were regaled by crickets and the odd bark of some faraway dog. The heat was luxuriant, the wine too.

Ollie was entertaining the kids with anecdotes from family holidays past. All of them at my expense – and actually very funny. I sipped wine, surprised to find that I was relaxed and enjoying the evening. To mask my deceit, I'd planned to amplify my levels of bonhomie over that fortnight, but my laughter was genuine.

I'd always wondered how men did it, how they could have

affairs while faking it at home so convincingly, leaving the wife totally oblivious. I had believed it must be such a tricky feat to pull off, but apparently it was quite simple; he'd nailed it for nearly five months, and now here I was smashing it too, for Ollie clearly had no inkling about Gabryel. Presumably it could prove tricky in the long run, but I'd cross that bridge as and when. Such subterfuge. Any guilt, however, was eased – erased even – by the knowledge that he'd succeeded so triumphantly. Perhaps it would even be possible for me to continue seeing Gabryel while still living with Ollie, to find some accommodation on a new level. To compartmentalise.

'Here's another one.' Ollie dipped his head conspiratorially at Jack, who was still chuckling politely at the last one.

I smiled my benediction at the boy and Ollie began the tale of Mauritius. In the milieu of our holiday home, my husband was also feeling relaxed enough again to indulge in some gentle teasing of me, as he had done freely in the olden days. Proof enough that he was clueless.

'So, we arrive at the wildlife park and Anna asks the man on reception if we could take Sophie into the lion's den and feed the cubs.'

'This one's cool.' Sophie's eyes sparkled at me.

'In my defence,' I said, beaming, 'on the poster at the airport the cubs were newborns sitting on the laps of toddlers.'

Ollie beamed back at me. 'And the guy looks shocked. 'No,' he says, 'we don't allow *children* in with the lions.' And when we got to the cubs, well they were the size of bloody Labradors.' A hefty guffaw to savour his own joke.

'Guess the poster was a few months old?' said Jack, his own laughter warm, a genuine kindness.

'It was, Jack. Thank you.'

The ambience boded well, I could easily pull this off.

Compartmentalise, compartmentalise, compartmentalise.

A sudden breeze blew the candle out, leaving us with an amber glow from house and a turquoise glimmer from pool. I struck a match and Ollie charged our glasses. He kept a stock of the local red in the cellar, even though in that heat I preferred a rosé.

'How long have you had this place Mr B?' asked Jack.

'Years. We potty-trained Soph out here.'

'Dad!'

'Ollie! Ignore him, Jack.' The boy was delightedly nudging Sophie.

'No big deal. We'd hose the patio when you didn't make it in time.' Ollie winked at his daughter.

'In answer to your question, Jack, we bought it fifteen years ago. Planted all the trees – lemons, olives, figs. Do you like figs?'

I had not intended the allusion, but Jack caught my eye, a sudden note of caution in his own. Surely he didn't know about the sexual connotation of figs?

'I've never had one,' he said.

'Ample opportunity out here.' Sophie smiled brightly. No hint of guile, even though we'd both watched the recent Sky Arts programme about figs as a sensual euphemism.

'Who fancies a game of something?' I said, closing the matter.

'Trivs!' Sophie clapped her hands. 'Me and Dad stick you two.'

'Cool. Thing is, Jack, Sophie is mistaken in thinking her father the more knowledgeable of her parents. I, in fact, am the queen of Trivial Pursuit.'

'We'll get you on sport, Mum.'

They always did.

'Any good at sport, Jack?'

'I, in fact, am the king of sport.' He stuck his tongue out at Sophie, a gesture more seductive than childish.

It took us a good hour to lose, but lose we did.

'When I said I was good at sport, I was thinking more of *this* century.' Jack frowned. 'Nothing against Henry Cooper, whoever he was, but you'd think they'd include some questions about Chelsea.'

'Ha! It's tradition to play this version,' Sophie teased him, folding up the battered board.

'Right kids, what's on the agenda tomorrow?' Ollie yawned widely without covering his mouth, so relaxed was he now with Jack around.

'Pool?' said Sophie.

'Awesome,' said Jack, stretching his arms above his head.

I caught the thatch of hair, a whiff of pheromones. Gabryel, his face, his body, and I felt myself flush. So much for compartmentalising.

'Perfection. Goodnight all.' Ollie gathered up our glasses and, with a loaded smile at me, sauntered inside.

I knew what the smile meant but was hoping he would be well gone by the time I reached our bed. The evening had brought a change of mood and I suspected he might also be anticipating a change of heart. However, his snores were puttering as, having tidied the kitchen, I climbed in beside him and stretched myself out thinly along the edge of the mattress. The next morning Ollie went off for provisions. Allowing Sophie and Jack some privacy at the pool, I slipped on my bikini and lay in the hammock beneath the olive trees, doused in music. Each song came at me with tales of love: new love, young love, broken love, *illicit* love, and I was restless. I was also acutely conscious of my own body, the warm breeze on

116

my belly, the brush of hair on my shoulders, the rope knots stubbing me, and I was back in that Soho club.

I had climbed off the beer keg and we had dressed, not without a certain shyness, then returned upstairs to the bar. A fresh glass of wine, another bottle of Becks. While I sat once again on a stool, Gabryel stood, inveigling his body to mine, my open knees parentheses around his thighs, pressing them in secret connection. He still had ten minutes, he said, before his next set.

'Where are you from?' I asked him.

'Moldova?' Those grey eyes teased in question.

'Ah, I'm afraid I don't...'

'Nobody does, it's OK.' His palms brushed my arms, letting me off the hook.

'I mean, I've seen it on the Eurovision Song Contest.'

He smiled. 'Is a very small country, but very beautiful.'

My lips parted to speak. To say that I'd love to go there sometime? I closed them again, then, 'How come you're here in the UK?'

'My studies.'

Jesus, was he that young?

He must have caught my flush. 'I am mature student. *Very* mature student. At London School of Economics. In Moldova I work for my government and they sent me here on a scholarship provided by your government.'

'How long have you been here?'

'One year.'

I nodded, calculating how long said scholarship might last. 'And you have a couple of part-time jobs to keep you going?'

'Kew is job. Here is passion.'

'Ah.' A wicked grin. 'Yes it certainly was that.'

We were still laughing when he pulled me in and kissed me

117

again.

'I'm sweating like a pig.' Ollie swung himself through the gate, several bags of shopping hanging off his wrists.

Jack was up off his sunbed without needing to be asked. 'Here you go, Mr B.' He relieved Ollie of one wrist-full and took them into the kitchen.

Ollie emerged a few minutes later in his swim shorts waving a plastic fly swatter. 'Bought this for the wasps.'

We'd been plagued by them at breakfast, a prolific year it seemed.

'G&T time?' He plucked a lemon from the tree and strolled back inside.

I watched him go. How relaxed he was around me. Maybe he thought he'd allowed me enough time to soften, possibly even believed himself fully back in the fold, all vestiges of his affair dissipated. But was I now actually having an affair myself? Sex on a single occasion would surely not count, but how many times would make it an *affair*? Affair. Such a bizarre word, especially when you said it over.

Scar had once told me about her own several years back. 'It all ends up the same. That initial thrill, well it lasts a few weeks tops. After that it's a case of diminishing returns. Nothing as delicious as that first chilled glass of wine, is there? The second brings less joy, the third even less. And so it is with forbidden sex.'

That would not be so in my case, however, because, oh the sex. I knew that *our* first glass would be bottomless, leaving us heady but always wanting. I thought back to his final look from the stage as I'd left the Tom Tom Club. Our eyes had lingered before I'd torn mine away and dashed to catch the last Tube home. I had asked him not to contact me on holiday, it was too

118

risky, yet I monitored my phone zealously, hoping that he would call. Each hour that passed without a message shored up my longing for another sip at that glass.

Ollie was back outside, placing a tray of plastic tumblers on a low table. 'Who's up for volleyball?' A gulp of his drink and he made a running jump at the pool, clasping his knees to bomb it.

'Da-ad!' Having taken the full hit, Sophie launched herself from her sunbed and into the pool, swamping his face as he came up for air.

Torn from my languid day dreams, I tipped myself out of the hammock and took a leisurely sip of my own gin and tonic before sliding into the pool. Jack downed his glass then pulled off a nifty dive and swam over to Sophie, forcing Ollie to join me on the other side of the net he'd strung up across the water.

So we took the kids on. I watched intrigued as Jack exploited every opportunity to grab Sophie for a victory embrace, occasionally slipping an arm beneath the water to pull her close. He'd come a long way since those first weeks in our kitchen and no longer cared about our presence. Bizarrely, Ollie began to copy him, grasping me for an occasional hug when we too won a point. And it did feel odd, his palms cinching my waist, his chest shrouding my back, its pelt swathing me like seaweed.

The peculiar sensation lingered when I was drying off on a sunbed – could Ollie have sensed that my body had recently indulged itself? The proximity of family life brought me a flutter of unease at having cheated on him, and the words guile and guilt sprang to mind. Each separated by one single letter. More of the guile than the guilt, Anna.

Because it wasn't cheating, it was getting even.

119

14

One evening towards the end of our first week in France, Ollie and I drove into La Rochelle for dinner at one of the fabulous seafood restaurants in the old harbour. Sophie and Jack preferred to stay at home. They'd had little time alone together, had accompanied us to the beach, joined us for dinner on each of the previous nights, and so we acquiesced.

Sunshine holidays have a knack of rekindling happy memories of previous vacations, times of togetherness, days of fun, later forgotten in the humdrum of home. It was a phenomenon Ollie and I were both accustomed to, indeed one which had reassured us in years past, that in France the frayed edges of our frenetic lives could be smoothed and rewoven. Against this backdrop, and lulled by the presence of Jack, Ollie's company had become not only more tolerable but pleasant. None of our past holidays, however, had hosted the ghost of adultery – and certainly no version that was alive and thriving. Amiable together we were, but the future of our marriage still lay beneath the carpet where we'd both kicked it some months before

It was his attentive behaviour, sliding my seat in before sitting down himself, which made me wary. He gestured to the waiter and ordered a bottle of the Chateau Moulin-à-Vent.

I caught the man's arm. 'I'll have a glass of rosé please.'

'Absolutely.' Ollie flashed his client smile and we opened

our menus. 'So what do you fancy?'

'Mouclade for me.' The local dish of mussels, cream and saffron.

'Me too. Starter?'

'The crab.'

Was it there in my voice? The self-fortification against any attempt at profundity? The waiter left us, and Ollie's smile shone.

'I wonder if it's time for us to talk?'

'About what?'

'About us.'

'Oh.'

I gazed around the night time harbour. Magnificent yachts, folk on deck draped in white linen, champagne coupe in hand, preening themselves for those of us still at shore. When I narrowed my eyes to slits, the strings of lights twinkled, reminding me of more innocent times, of simpler times. If my husband had raised this, even a week before, I might well have welcomed the prospect, may have been almost ready to climb back inside our marriage for good. But now, any conversation about 'us' would be muddied, like the swirl of balsamic in olive oil in the dish between us. I tore off a hunk of bread and dunked it, dispersing brown globules off to the sides.

'I'm not sure enough time has passed,' I said.

'Three months now.'

To the very day, I realised.

Ollie looked beaten then, a momentary sag of his cheeks, before he rallied and contemplated me with a more genuine smile. The impact surprised me, a wave of compassion; clearly he still had the facility to reach me.

'I am truly sorry, Anna. I was a total dick, I know that. What we have together. All those years. Sophie.' He paused. 'Jack

121

now…'

I granted the joke a wan smile, which prompted him to take my hand, but my heart I galvanised.

'We've been getting along better these past few weeks, haven't we?' he said. 'We seem happy again, if you ask me.'

'Do you think those two might have sex tonight?'

An imperceptible flinch. He leaned forwards, took my hand between his fingers and gently pumped it, as if that might speed me up. Before his own affair he had never been used to having to work at our relationship, hadn't bothered for years, but then neither had I. That's what he'd meant when he'd told me I'd allowed him to stray; we'd both allowed it of each other. I had realized that now.

'I do wonder if I left them alone on purpose,' I added. 'If our absence is my benediction.'

I thought again of the storm on the previous evening, the way she had clutched Jack at each crash of thunder, just as she once used to cling to me, and he had drawn her to him, folding her up in his arms. Young love.

'Do you remember our first time?'

He was so obvious, but I played along. 'In the wilds of Wales.'

As opposed to the wilds of Soho, that memory brought heat to my cheeks.

'It was a balmy night,' he said, heartened by the deceitful blush. 'The bracken was soft, I laid you down.'

'You sound like a Bon Jovi song.'

'Love at first sight, Anna. You can't quibble with that now, can you?'

'We already worked together in the same department.'

'Ah but I truly *saw* you that night for the first time. Your soul, Anna.'

He was right, it had been a thunder bolt. The precise moment of our eye contact in that bush camp; a love which had sustained us for many years, right up until his affair. Well that's what I had thought. In fact, the blur of the past months was causing me again to question the validity of our love from the very outset. Or was that simply to justify my affair with Gabryel?

'I promise never to do it again, Anna. Never. I want to go back to how we used to be.'

I threw him a sardonic look.

'I want to screw my wife again.' He ignored the sharp glances from the couple at the neighbouring table. 'And *only* my wife.'

Thing is, I wasn't sure I wanted to screw my husband again, but was I seriously going to continue living under the same roof, and screw Gabryel but not him?

'I need more time.' Was how I finally put the conversation to bed.

That old chestnut.

On our return, the house was quiet. Dark and too silent, as if playing hide and seek with us. I listened at Sophie's door and then lingered outside the guest room, but neither was revealing secrets.

I'm not sure why I gave in to sex with Ollie. The flop of his hand on my back as I drifted off, the caress of his fingers, skin on skin. It may have been guilt that caused me to turn around. Married sex was as familiar as scratching an itch, but the body I'd known intimately for so long felt alien, the ribs too padded, the arms too fleshy. As I faked an orgasm to precipitate his own, my thoughts clarified. If I gave up Gabryel then this would be the future. But if I didn't give him up then what catastrophe might lie ahead? It was all too convoluted to unpick. For the foreseeable I would continue to have them both.

Of course, I had known what I was sanctioning by leaving Jack and Sophie alone in an exotic setting, their bodies relaxed and glowing. Primed. But when I found the condom packet in his bed the following day, still I shed a tear. Whether it was a happy or a sad one is still not entirely clear to me.

It was late morning. Ollie had driven them off to the water park for the day, and I had been lying in the shade, revisiting the memories of Gabryel and indulging in a whole new set of invented ones. I rambled about the garden picking flowers, plumbago and marigolds to refresh the vases, and wandered through the cool house. Was it a conscious move? To have moseyed into the guest bedroom? To have shaken out his duvet? A glint of silver foil at my feet.

Alone at the pool, my thoughts washed poignantly. Sophie as a baby, playing Peepo! behind a fluffy towel; through the toddler years with its finger painting and picture books; all too quickly onto primary school and into her teens. Slipping through my fingers, as the song goes.

When they arrived back that evening, I led her by the hand off behind the oleanders into the privacy of the garden, where I held her in a long embrace and rocked her.

'What's up, Mum?'

'Nothing, darling. Nothing at all. I'm happy for you.'

She hugged me back. 'Thanks, Mum.'

It was a few days later that disaster struck. And it was from then on that I remained troubled. Not necessarily by Jack's reaction, but by the fact that I would never have credited him with it. Credited is not the word, of course, more like attributed, I suppose.

We were at the beach. Fortuitously so, as it transpired, given the distance of our old farmhouse from the city. The pair of them were in the sea, diving into waves as they crested. Ollie lay supine on his sunbed, reading a Jo Nesbo novel, shielding his eyes with one hand. My guide to business start-ups lay dog-eared and face down on my own sunbed, while I sat upright, scanning the beach, aware of bodies as I had never been on previous holidays. Before, I might have compared my own, in a favourable way given my fastidious diet, but that day it was the male flesh I found arresting; the trickle of hair into swim shorts, the flank of a thigh, the nape of a neck. So alive was I to the shape of a man.

Drawn to the sea by the occasional squeal from Sophie, or yell from Jack, I'd watch a wave build, reeling like a horse until it rose far above them. At times, they would brace their backs against its crash, at others spinning to face it, a nifty dive into its chest before it broke upon them. They were so good together, so happy that day. I watched them wade out of the sea hand in hand, and smiled from one to the other.

'Chill time,' Sophie said arriving back at our spot. She dried off her hair and laid out the towel on her sunbed. And then she reached for the open can of Coke on the sand.

I should have covered it while it had stood unguarded, should have warned her to check. As a mother who had spent her daughter's lifetime attentive to her safety, I do blame myself. When she lurched forwards, in what I could only describe as an eruption, spat out a mouthful of Coke, and screamed, I knew immediately what had happened. A wasp. The sting to the back of her throat. The anaphylactic reaction was instant. She fell to her knees, clutching at her throat, already gasping for air. Unable to speak, her eyes on mine were doused with terror.

Ollie and I launched ourselves up and I dropped to her side. She grasped me, her mouth gaping, lips and tongue swelling. Ollie gathered her up into his arms and began to stumble up the sand towards the car park.

'What's the emergency number?' I cried, grabbing my bag and desperately scanning the beach. 'Where's the lifeguard?'

'112,' he shouted as I staggered after them, jabbing my phone.

'Ambulance!' I shrieked at it. 'A la plage. Ma fille. She can't breathe.' I turned in circles, imploring those who had witnessed our panic and stood to help. 'What's a wasp in French?' I cried, frantic from one face to the next.

'Une gueppe,' someone shouted.

'Une gueppe,' I screamed into the phone. 'Une gueppe. She's been stung. In her mouth, her bouche.' I realised that I was being asked for the name of the beach. Again, I looked about me desperately. 'What's this beach called?' We called it Balzac Beach after its restaurant.

A hand appeared and a man took my phone. He gave the name of the beach and, still running alongside me, explained fully what had happened. Ahead of us I saw a lifeguard reach Ollie and take Sophie off him. His own strides towards the car park were much longer than my husband's.

When we reached them both, the man had laid Sophie down flat on a low wall. She was taking snatched breaths, barely drawing air, her pale face now blotchy. I took her hand, my eyes locked on hers as they flitted open, and desperately conveyed my love, my promise that I would not let anything awful happen to her.

'Slowly, Soph. Slowly in, slowly out.' I drew a long steady breath to show her how. 'You're going to be OK, the ambulance will be here any minute.'

'Don't you carry an EpiPen?' Ollie pleaded with the lifeguard, who shook his head, with a look that said he knew that he should.

Sophie's lips were turning blue. I watched on bereft as she drifted out of consciousness, as the lifeguard checked her pulse then took hold of her chin and thrust it back. He put his mouth to hers.

'Jesus, Ollie, no.'

I seized his arm and he fixed his eyes on mine, with fear, with reassurance. With the intimate connection between two parents who desperately loved their child.

When finally we heard the siren I began to weep. My daughter now appeared lifeless beneath the intermittent pumping of the lifeguard's hands, beneath his mouth locked on hers, and the next moments happened in slow motion. It was the fire brigade's ambulance which careered into the car park. The crew jumped out and the lifeguard stood back, but I was still kneading Sophie's hand as if I could pump oxygen into her through her palm. The EpiPen injection was swift and its impact immediate, Sophie's breathing was again visible and gradually began to steady.

The medics then brought out a stretcher, covered her and slid her inside the ambulance. With legs of jelly I managed to climb in too and watched them hook her up to an IV drip. My hand shook as I stroked her cheek, smiling into her closed eyes.

One of the medics allowed me a grim smile. 'You come, yes?'

Gripping the ambulance door to steady myself, I looked out at Ollie. 'I'll go with her, you follow on, OK?'

He nodded, his face ashen, so I fumbled for his hand and squeezed it. Then I looked beyond him for Jack.

'Where's Jack?'

Ollie frowned and squinted down the beach. 'What the…?'

'What?' I leant out of the ambulance and followed his gaze.

There was all our gear, closer now to the water's edge; towels, bags, umbrellas, body boards, the four sunbeds. And on one of them sat Jack, hugging his knees and gazing out to sea.

'I'm so sorry,' he said to us later.

We had returned to the house late that night, leaving Sophie asleep in hospital for observation; they hadn't allowed me to stay with her.

'Don't know what happened there, I panicked.'

'No big deal, son,' said Ollie, as we packed him off to bed, keen to sit alone by the soothing turquoise pool with a numbing glass. 'Sometimes odd behaviour is understandable after a shock.'

At the hospital he had kissed Sophie, had stroked her brow, full of concern then, but for me the sight of Jack on that sunbed lingered.

Ollie and I made love again that night. The fear, the shock, the anguish, what might have been, they all emerged in an intimacy we'd not known for many years. A closeness I'd been convinced was lost to us. Afterwards we both wept, before falling into a fitful slumber, spooned as one.

By dawn we were back at her bedside to discharge her. It was while Ollie was driving us all home from the hospital that Gabryel called. When I saw Gabby flash up, as I had been hoping to all holiday, I hit cancel, tossed the phone into my bag, and began chattering to my family.

Twenty years of marriage, one precious daughter, a fragile life together. How could I possibly allow lust to come between that?

15

Over the next days I succumbed to the shakes and relentless bouts of crying, and was still preoccupied with what might have been when I stood at Fred's door nearly two weeks later.

'How is your daughter, Sally?' he said, opening it.

We'd also had Susie and Sasha since I'd arrived home, but at least he got the S right, and his sustained concern was touching.

'She's fine, Fred, thank you for asking.'

'And you, love?'

'I'm good. Thank you.' I planted a kiss on his cheek and went inside. 'It's her party tomorrow night. A welcome distraction for us all. She's got some girlfriends round as we speak. Decorating the house, God help it.'

As ever, Dougal jumped up at me and I stumbled backwards, shoving his paws off so roughly that the dog actually yelped. I did feel bad, enough to smooth his silken ears, but thankfully Fred made no comment.

'And her O' level results?'

'Next Thursday.' I smiled with no wish to correct the antiquity. 'You're on the ball, aren't you? You should meet her sometime. And Ollie?'

Fred grunted and busied himself with the lighting of his pipe, puff puff at its snout. I smiled to myself, would that be a step too far? Did he want me all to himself? Just as I did him, he'd been such a comfort to me that week.

'You *do* know we have a hospital appointment, don't you?' I smiled.

He removed the pipe and gazed at me. 'Do we?'

'Charing Cross in forty-five minutes. Not sure they'll be impressed with that thing, or the smell of it on you.'

He glanced down at his sweater of canary yellow, to which a visible fug of tobacco clung. I admit it was a scent I now anticipated with pleasure.

'Best get changed then,' he said.

'Five minutes, OK?'

'Aye aye captain.' Fred saluted and took to the stairs.

Forbidden as he was from following, Dougal watched his master go before turning to me in full wag, it seemed I'd been forgiven. He lolloped after me to the kitchen where I opened the back door.

'Go and be a good boy.' The command I'd heard from Fred many a time.

I shut the door, leant against the work surface and smiled at the ceramic frog above the sink, a ragged Brillo pad in its wide open mouth. Then my eyes strayed to Fred's pill tin. Tightly shut, but from my online research I now knew that it contained the drugs Lisinopril for blood pressure, Atorvastatin for high cholesterol and Lyrica for anxiety, plus aspirin, and that, as he had once told me himself, Fred must avoid acute stress, which could send his blood pressure soaring, and even cause a stroke. That day's hospital visit was troubling me, however, because it did not seem to be linked to these drugs in any way.

Beside the tin a folded sheet of thin blue paper caught my eye. A letter. It lay on top of its envelope, a sharp nudge of which revealed a French stamp postmarked a few days before.

Listening to Fred moving about above me, for several moments I gazed at the letter. And then, surprising myself, I picked it up and unfolded it.

I began to read. *Nearly 86... Should be sensible... I can't.... You are being selfish by expecting.... should be in a care home.*

The words stunned me. So much so that, by the time I heard Fred's tread, he was already at the bottom of the stairs. I dropped the letter back in place and opened the back door.

'Come on Dougal,' I called, even though the dog had already bounded inside.

'Stand by your beds.' Fred reached the kitchen and his eyes seemed to flick instinctively to the letter.

'Looking dapper, Fred.'

I smiled brightly with a nod at the yellow sweater; he hadn't changed but I wasn't going to nag. 'Let's go, shall we?'

'If we must.'

Fred slid his large frame into my car with relative ease. Should be in a home indeed.

'I've a fancy you said your daughter is having a party, love.' He turned to monitor the road with me as I reversed out of his drive.

'For her birthday, she'll turn sixteen on Sunday.'

'A tricky age, as I recall. Are you close?'

'Well funny you should ask me that. Yes we are these days.'

And after the shock of France I'd prefer to be joined at the hip forever.

'She's been through a difficult spell, but I think she's out of it now. She's got this boyfriend, Jack. Lovely boy, and she's much happier with him around.'

As we all are, I didn't add.

Fred nodded but said nothing, and I saw my chance. 'How do you get on with your daughter? Beth, isn't it?'

He busied himself watching the passing houses. I think he knew, and I kind of wanted to confess.

'Well, Anna, as a matter of fact, she's written me a letter. She thinks I should be in an old people's home.'

'No? But you're still so sprightly.'

'Soon be eighty-six.'

'Going on sixty-six! Look at you, there's no way you should be in a home. You aren't being at all selfish.'

Fred smiled at me. 'You've read it, haven't you, love?'

My cheeks fired. 'Sorry. Yes I have. Totally out of order, I know. Totally. Don't know what came over me.' I paused in shame. 'I'm just so fond of you.'

He patted my knee. 'I should have liked a daughter like you.'

I teared up at that and drove on slowly to the murmur of Radio 4, blinking myself under control. Behind us, the cars began to stack up and soon an aggressive driver was clinging to us, inches from my bumper.

'I wish this guy would get off my back.' I nodded angrily at my rear-view mirror, grateful to break our silence.

Fred swung around to look at the open top Mercedes. 'Turn your windscreen wipers on him.'

He leant across, prodded the lever, and arcs of screen wash gushed back over my car roof, landing on the man. Fred pumped away and the man scowled, braked and fell back.

'Is there no end to this man's innovation?' My shoulders were actually shaking with laughter, spurred on by Fred's rich chuckles.

'I thank you.' He gave a seated bow, an arm at his waist, eyes twinkling.

With a sudden burst of acceleration, the driver then overtook me, as we both knew he would. He and I gave each other the middle finger as he sped past, and I glanced back at

Fred to see that he had done likewise.

I let out a delighted mock gasp. 'Fred!'

'It's contagious, Anna. You're quite formidable behind the wheel.'

We were still laughing when we reached the hospital, where I found a meter in a side street and parked up.

'Well, I won't let it happen, Fred.' I said, with an assertive yank of the handbrake. 'She's not going to put you in a home.'

With a nod which seemed to say, you don't know my daughter, he unclipped his seatbelt. 'Let's see what the quacks want from me today.'

'Which department is it again?' I asked as we walked, even though I knew precisely where we were headed.

'*I* don't know!' He threw me a look of consternation and stopped in his tracks. 'Thought you were in charge.'

'It's your appointment. The papers were on the sideboard, weren't they?'

'Quite possibly. Maybe we should leave it?' He turned back towards the car.

'Come on.' I smiled, linking arms with him. 'I'm sure they'll have your details in their super-duper computer system.'

At the hospital entrance, I was suddenly back in that French emergency room and my smile abandoned me. I steeled myself through the revolving doors and led us to reception, where they did indeed locate Fred in their system.

He grinned at me as he gave his date of birth, 20th August 1932.

I grinned back. 'It's your birthday on *Monday*? The day after Sophie's?'

He had been born precisely seventy years before my daughter. My thoughts turned again to the day she was born, as they had been doing all week, and I imagined Fred at seventy –

he'd already been getting on a bit back then.

He flashed his eyes. 'I should like to invite you out for a meal, Anna.'

'Thank you, I should be delighted to accept.' I traipsed him over to the lift. 'You dark horse.'

We arrived at the Mental Health Department with three minutes to spare. Immediately a strange aura settled itself upon Fred. After signing in, he shuffled to one of the winged chairs and sank down into it, as if to immerse himself in a parallel dimension somewhere beneath the lino. Judging by the packed room, we were in for a long wait too.

A silent TV screen with subtitles was showing the weather forecast. While swathes of red heat still smothered the country, there did appear to be gale force winds in the north of Scotland. *Bridges and fairies will be affected*, read the subtitles, and I smiled at the typing error, fairies for ferries. Fred laughed too – still in the real world then.

'Poor wee fairies, with their tiny wings,' he said, 'they'll be blown away in those winds.'

His Scottish accent was spot on but my laughter was far too hearty.

We lapsed again into silence. He sank back into himself, and I wondered again why we were there. The summons letter spoke of a mental ability assessment, which seemed extreme to me. Naturally, Fred was forgetful, but surely that was just old age? I myself had begun to walk into rooms and forget why. He had told me his daughter had recently trundled him off to the GP on one of her rare visits home, so this might well be a follow-up appointment. Whatever awaited, I deemed it best not to engage him in conversation, rather let him prepare himself, so I passed him a copy of the *Daily Mail* from the low table beside me.

'Poison,' he grunted, but he took it anyway.

My phone pinged a text, Sophie asking where we kept the fairy lights. *In the loft.* I smiled to myself. *Dad'll get them out tonight for you.*

I was slipping the phone back into my jeans pocket when it rang. Gabryel, well, Gabby. I stared at the name and felt myself flush, but dropped it into my bag. The man had been relentless; at all hours of the day, if not the night. I would have to take the call at some point, or return it to explain what had happened, how I had no choice but to stop. I owed him that. It's not that I didn't experience that thrill each time his name lit up, it's not as if I didn't dream about the sex, about the way he'd made me feel, it's simply that I had nearly lost my daughter. She had almost died, and it would be sheer madness to proceed with such frivolity in the face of that.

My focus now was on finding my way back into the heart of my marriage. In those days since the beach, Ollie too had made a volte-face. He seemed to be returning to his old self, the man I hadn't known for years and, bizarrely, in a few short days I was beginning to trust him again.

The announcement of Fred's name jarred me from my reverie; a young Asian doctor hovered in the waiting room.

'Off you go,' I said gently.

'You coming too, love?' He looked hopeful.

'Err...' I watched the hope evaporate. 'Yes, of course I will.'

I stood up, hanging back while Fred crossed the floor to the man who smiled first at him and then at me.

'I'm glad you've brought your daughter along, always helpful to have someone with you,' he said.

I nodded, declining to put him straight, and followed them both into his consulting room.

'Now, Mr Wildsmith. Your GP has referred you to us for

further assessment following a recent memory test you took.'

'With one hundred per-cent accuracy.' Fred sat proud, chin up, back straight.

The doctor smiled my way and I wondered if he was judging me for dragging my supposed father into the abyss of mental ability tests. Did he assume I hoped for a diagnosis of dementia so that I could more readily park him in a care home?

'Yes, you did do *very* well.'

His tone bordered on patronising. Don't mess with Fred.

'So, you yourself are not aware of any symptoms that might indicate a loss of memory capacity?'

'None whatsoever,' said Fred. 'I feel young at heart.'

'Good. Well, I'd like to carry out more tests, if that would be acceptable to you, Sir?'

That's better.

Fred shrugged. 'I'll play along.'

'Thank you, Sir. Now, first some questions about your general health. I note that you suffered a TIA some months ago.'

'It seems I had minor stroke.' Fred's voice was gruff.

This I had not known, and I took care to hide my surprise as the man began filling out his form of many pages in illegible handwriting. On questions about diet and lifestyle Fred soon found his stride – even admitting to copious enjoyment of the pipe, about which I'd expected him to lie. Then the doctor asked him to remove his sweater.

'Oh, shall I wait outside?' I asked, already standing.

'No need, love.' Fred raised the sweater up over his head.

I averted my eyes, but curiosity soon drew them back to him. A chest so frail that the shock hit me with a gust of heat to my face. Chicken white, paper thin and feathered with grey wisps, he seemed concave, as if one puff from a child even, would blow him out, would extinguish the man. But then what had I expected from a human body soon to have been on this earth for eighty-six years?

A poster on the wall behind the doctor's head became a useful focal point while I battled to stem my emotion, while the man took Fred's blood pressure and listened to his heart and lungs. I studied a grey image of the brain, colourfully highlighted with damage, and beside it a surprising array of products for those suffering with dementia – over-sized clocks, simple jigsaws, even toy cats curled up on laps. Dementia was big business.

'You can put your sweater back on, Mr Wildsmith.'

With a silent sigh and a smile for both men, I settled myself again.

'I have to agree, Sir, that you are in fine working order for a gentleman of your age.'

Fred grunted his approval. 'You mustn't give in.'

'Blood pressure's somewhat raised, but we may attribute that to some anxiety at being here in this room.'

Fred said nothing, but I think we all knew the doctor was right.

'Now to the cognitive tests. First of all, I'm going to give you an address which I'd like you to memorise, and which I will ask you to recall for me in a few minutes time. OK?'

Fred nodded.

'So, the address is 64 Langdon Lane.'

Fred repeated the address back to him, and I began to memorise it myself. There was a programme on telly when Sophie was small, *64 Zoo Lane*, and silently I hummed the theme tune, hoping that he would also find some quirky way to remember it.

'Now then, a few general questions. Can you tell me the date

137

today?'

'17th August 2018.'

'Good. And where are you right now, Mr Wildsmith?'

Fred shot the man a look of disgust. 'On the moon.'

The doctor raised his eyebrows playfully.

'At Charing Cross Hospital. But I don't for the life of me know why.'

'Who is the Prime Minister?'

'The Maybot.'

I stifled a laugh. The doctor glanced at me, lips twitching, then back at Fred.

'Do you mean Theresa May?'

'You're on the same page then?'

'Perhaps.'

He made a few notes, then he snapped up a sheet of paper and laid it down before Fred.

'Would you draw the face of a clock for me, please? Complete with all numbers in their correct places and showing the time now, which is 11.50am.'

Fred reached inside his trouser pocket and pulled out his pipe. I watched him from the corner of my eye – what now? He slipped it between his lips, mouth popping; all credit to the doctor who realised he was not going to actually light the thing. He picked up the pen and, after a considerable number of frog-like sucks, the deed was complete. A fine copy of his own mantel clock, a perfect dome, Roman numerals and all – he'd even embellished the hands with loops and curls.

The doctor smiled. 'Very good, Sir, thank you. Now, can you tell me the address I gave you at the start of the test, please?'

Fred looked blankly at the man.

Heart racing, I sent him silent vibes. 64 64 64 Zoo Lane, I

sang in my head. Lillie Langtry, I urged. The CIA are based in Langley, you must know that from your past? 64 Langdon Lane. Still he said nothing, the muffled pops of his pipe the only sound in that hushed office, we must have waited two full minutes.

'No. No, it's gone,' he said finally.

It was some moments before the doctor's eyes fell to his notes. Moments during which he contemplated Fred and his pipe assiduously.

'I'm still not sure if he was playing the man,' I said to Ollie that night.

We were enjoying the last of the day's hazy heat in the back garden. Tea-lights glowed inside a series of glass balls hanging from branches, a romantic touch of Ollie's. Sophie, upstairs with face pack on, had asked him to leave them up for her party.

'He sounds an exceptional human being, old Fred.'

'He is. I mean, I only managed to recall it because of 64 Zoo Lane. Bet you remember that programme too, don't you?'

Ollie began to sing the theme tune.

I grinned at him 'Hardly dulcet, darling.'

Darling was a word we were reaching for often since that day on the beach.

He smiled back. 'Seems like yesterday, watching that, doesn't it?'

'I can remember when we first brought her home from hospital, and you drove at five miles an hour, petrified of any collision.'

'And you sat in the back with her for the first two years, at least.'

I nodded. 'Sixteen. Still can't quite believe it.'

'We've come a long way, my darling.' Ollie raised his glass.

The *my* was a new addition. And I wasn't truly sure how I felt about it; certainly couldn't see myself echoing it just yet.

'We have.' I chinked his glass with mine. 'Here's to our daughter.'

Ollie dipped his eyes seductively. 'And to us.'

'To us,' I said, dismissing the wolf eyes which chose that moment to appear.

16

Scar and I were sitting propped up on my bed watching a film on Netflix when we heard the distant crash from the kitchen.

'Oops.' She made a face at me.

'Oops indeed.' I shunted myself off the bed. 'Pause that, will you? I'll be back.'

I stepped over Horace who, like us, had been banished to the bedroom, and left the room, entering the thrum of bass guitar which became deafening as I reached the landing. I grimaced at Ollie standing at the bottom of the stairs. We were taking it in turns to play bouncer and he had set himself up in the study with a novel and a clear view of our front path. Having emerged at the thunderous crash, he too frowned.

Between us young people of both sexes were lounging on stairs, draped across the banister, or leaning against walls, and I pushed my way politely down through them.

'OK?' I shouted, the bass line now vibrating the floorboards.

'Never been better.'

He hated having to skulk on the fringe of this teenage mass.

I swung myself around the newel post, stepped over the extended legs of two lads, who looked much older than teenagers, and entered the kitchen.

A large vase lay smashed on the floor, one of my favourites.

The flowers Scar and her son, Nick, had presented to Sophie earlier, were now strewn among the shards of glass. A gaggle of girls had made way for the mess, and now also for me, as I whisked out a dustpan and bent to pick up the larger fragments.

'Anyone got bare feet?' I cried above the music, glancing up at the stilettos which formed a crescent around me, and cringing at the thought of their impact on my wooden floor. The waxed legs rose a long way before finally meeting the hems of dresses which barely concealed crotches.

'Sorry, Mum.' Sophie, coming in from the garden, pushed her way through and bent down with me, extracting delphiniums and lilies with dainty fingertips.

'Long as nobody's injured.' I righted myself and leant against the island, now a makeshift bar.

Cans of beer and cider were stuffed alongside a few wine bottles in the vast ice trough we'd hired. Ollie had agreed to provide enough for two drinks per person, leaving teenage pique to evenly disperse, and I was pleased to note that much of the booze remained untouched. All the girls held glasses of water. I did briefly wonder about that drug, Ecstasy, which makes you thirsty, but I knew my daughter better than that, didn't I?

She followed me around to the sink and took out another vase while I tipped the debris into the bin.

'Having a good time?' I shouted, a motherly hand to her back, which was beautifully tanned after our holiday and shown off in a backless dress of cornflower blue.

'So cool, Mum. Thanks.' Her face glowed, her pupils gleamed, as she filled the vase and placed the flowers inside. Her recovery after France seemed so much more complete than my own.

I looked out onto the throng jigging along to the music in

the back garden. Boys throwing heads back in laughter, girls flicking flirtatious eyes sideways, the heat of the day still wreathed around them all. The lawn too was a victim of stilettos. The heels sank so deeply that the girls looked ridiculous, yanking the spikes out, only for them to submerge again. Think of it as aerating, I told myself.

Dusk was falling, the tea lights flickering through their special moment, and the radiance of young faces captivated me, nudging Gabryel's to the fore yet again. It had been a lucky escape, nobody had been hurt (as Fred had counselled) and I had revelled in the kind of sex I had thought extinct. The memories alone would sustain me now.

At the bottom of the garden, I spotted Jack, glass in hand, holding forth amongst a group of other boys, and smiled at the memory of his arrival earlier, joining we three for champagne before her friends arrived. He'd bought Sophie a silver necklace and its tiny S sat in the hollow of her neck.

The doorbell rang and I raised my eyebrows at her. 'Surely not more people? Already seem to be more than sixty here.'

'Didn't put it on social media, Mum, honest.'

'Well I'd better go and relieve Dad.'

Few of those hanging about the hallway were drinking beer or cider, mostly they too had water on the go, and again drugs crossed my mind, but, as I'd read, perhaps the youth of today simply lived much cleaner lives.

In the study, Ollie seemed to be no further into his novel than when he'd taken over from me an hour earlier.

'Cheers,' I said, handing him a can of beer. 'We appear to have bought surplus.'

He cracked it open. 'It'll go, you'll see.'

'Everyone seems to be having fun.'

'Just had ten lads at the door. Told them no room at the

inn.'

'Good plan, it's chocka back there.' I sat down on the arm of his chair. 'So I'm here to relieve you. Can't wait to get my hands on that novel.'

He smiled. 'You sure?'

I nodded and kissed his forehead.

'Back down in half an hour.' He heaved himself up and swept a hand at the chair. 'All yours Milady. Enough wine up there still?'

'Yep. Tell Scar she can watch the rest of that film, I'll catch it another time.'

I settled myself down, poured myself a beer and opened the novel.

It must have been an hour later when Ollie still hadn't appeared and I was desperate for the toilet. Preferring the prospect of my own en suite to whatever state our downstairs loo might find itself in, I stood up and stretched. I popped my head through to the kitchen, delighted for Sophie to see the laughter and revelry, and then threaded my way upstairs.

'Joint's a jumping down there,' I said, entering our bedroom.

Ollie was sitting on the bed beside Scar, legs outstretched, drinking wine, as I had been. Between them sat Horace working through a lettuce leaf. The TV remained paused.

'Oh, thanks, you waited for me.' I smiled at my friend and made for our bathroom, returning to slide onto the bed beside Ollie with a nod at the frozen TV. 'What great delights are you guys chatting about then?'

'Nick again. Your husband is a mine of information on the ills of boarding school and its remedies.'

'He is indeed.' Unwilling to be drawn into such tedium, I took Ollie's wine glass from him.

'All yours darling,' he laughed as I drank it dry.

'Can we finish the film?' I said. 'I'm desperate for laughs.'

'Suppose I'd better go back down there. Quick shufty around the camp.' He shunted himself off the bed and raised his arm, imaginary sword in hand. 'Once more unto the breach, dear friends!'

When he'd gone I smiled at Scar. 'A little bit of Ollie in the night.'

'You seem good together these days.'

'Not bad at all. I'll tell you about it.' I un-paused the film.

'Whenever you've time, Anna.' She laughed. 'Been weeks since you've fitted me in for Monday coffee.'

'You've been in Cannes all summer.'

'Only three weeks of it.'

'Oh, I thought longer. Well we've been away too, and I've been so busy with Fred.'

Downright lie. More like I hadn't trusted myself not to mention Gabryel. Imperative that he remained taboo as if he'd never happened. Had I confided in Scar he would have become real, existent, as would my guilt. Anyway, he was history now.

'But I can make next Monday,' I added.

'I'll hold you to it.'

Ollie threw open the bedroom door. 'Houston, we have a problem.' He paused for effect. 'Vodka.'

'Vodka?!'

'Bottles of the stuff.'

'The little minx, I'll bloody kill her.'

I scrambled off the bed and out onto the landing, with Ollie and Scar following close behind. Snatching a glass from one of the lads in the hall, I sniffed the liquid I'd assumed was water and drank. 'Urgh.'

On I ran to the kitchen, where there was now an impressive

145

pile of vomit around the ice trough, despite which groups of lads hung around the room chatting. Beside the sink stood a full bottle of vodka, encrusted with soil, clumps of rich black earth, and I gazed at it before stomping outside. In the garden, the mass was dancing, two girls were having a fight, actually kicking and pulling hair, and Sophie was staggering to the shed with a clinking black bin bag.

I bellowed at her. 'Come here with that!'

She stopped dead and dropped it. Turning around, she swayed and reached for the shed to steady herself. The fighting ceased, all eyes on me.

'Inside! Now!'

She teetered after me to the kitchen sink and clutched it, peering down at the white porcelain which was clogged with soil.

'How many bottles did you bury?'

She shrugged, clearly terrified, and her eyes fell on her father who had been chucking empty cans into bin liners.

'Come on, Anna, let's deal with this another time.' Ollie nodded towards the kids outside. 'Party's over folks,' he cried, clapping his hands.

'Jesus, Sophie, we trusted you.' I turned to leave the kitchen as she began to sob.

I walked along the hallway to our front door and sank my brow against its cooling glass panes. Behind me I heard the buzz of teenagers preparing to leave, so I stepped inside our study; peace and darkness were needed to process this fiasco. Closing the door, I leant back against it, palms and shoulders seeking comfort in its solidity.

I heard the couple immediately, but they didn't seem to hear me, so engrossed were they. Soft moans, sharp gasps. In the darkness, I watched the shape of them embracing, she appeared to be seated on our desk while he stood. When my eyes adjusted, I watched the shadows shifting rhythmically about their bodies, as they moved, obliviously, beyond the point of no return. Their actions I recognised, even if in all of my forty-five years I had never actually been witness to them in the flesh. For several moments I stood fascinated, until the moon appeared from behind a cloud and briefly illuminated the room.

It was Jack.

17

I flicked the light switch, illuminating Jack's bottom, the girl's legs clenched around it.

'For fuck's sake!' he cried, spinning around with a scowl, which instantly dissolved into recognition, and then fear.

My eyes dropped to his penis, still bobbing at half-mast.

'Get out,' I whispered.

He bent to pull up his jeans, while the girl scrabbled off the desk, tugging down her dress. It was Bianca, Sophie's best friend.

I glared at her. 'Both of you.'

I turned and left the room, my hand shaking at the door handle as I pulled it firmly shut behind me. Streams of teenagers were flocking from our home, and hovering in the hallway was Sophie, her face streaked with mascara. Our eyes locked and I reached for her, a tender arm turning her back towards the kitchen.

'I'm sorry, Mum.' She nestled into my shoulder and I pulled her close.

'It's OK,' I said gently.

She drew back and eyed me. 'Really?' Her cheeks were the mottled pink I recalled from so many childhood mishaps.

'I guess you *are* sixteen, we should have realised.' Anything to protect my daughter at that moment, anything to keep her from the hallway. 'Come on, let's help Dad and Scar clean up.'

Both had made impressive inroads into the mess in the kitchen. Scar, I noticed gratefully, was wiping up the vomit.

'You and I can clear the garden, Soph.'

With a nifty glance over my shoulder to see Jack and Bianca slipping out of the front door, I steered my daughter outside onto the patio. She slumped at our garden table, while I began blindly shoving cans and glasses into bin liners. The shock had me in its icy grip, my mind frozen with the image of Jack.

'Bianca's bag.' Sophie held out a tiny purse on a chain. 'Is she still here?'

'Everyone's gone,' I said without looking up.

'Jack left early too. Didn't even say goodbye.'

I said nothing, and Sophie dropped the purse onto the table and staggered over to me. 'That was a crap party.'

She flopped to the ground, and I sighed and sank down with her onto the grass, draping an arm around her shoulders.

'Seemed like a pretty cool one to me, Soph. The best parties end with a crazy parent scaring the hell out of their kid's mates. I was a great big flapping, squawking goose!"

'Nobody messes with you, do they?'

'Nope.'

Squeezing her tightly to me, I cast an eye about the garden. The tea lights had long since burnt out but the moon was full, picking out a vodka bottle balanced in a nook of our apple tree. I glanced at my watch, it was past midnight.

'Do you realise it's your actual birthday now?' I kissed her forehead. 'Happy birthday, darling. It's going to be amazing, I promise. And this can wait till morning, come on, let's get you to bed.'

That night I lay stunned. Arms behind my head, staring at the ceiling, I reeled in the shock of what I'd witnessed. This boy. How could he have done that to Sophie? How could he have done that to *us*? The weeks of his presence at the heart of our family, they paraded before me like a slide show: in the kitchen, at tennis, laughing, eating, drinking wine in France – all that warmth. Life itself. Had he bamboozled me into believing that he cared about Sophie? Had he duped us all along?

After several sleepless hours the shock eventually became fury, which finally formed itself into a plan. I wouldn't tell Sophie, Jack had to do that, hopefully sparing her the detail while extricating himself. I closed my eyes, saw again his naked flesh, and a tear squeezed itself out. Never again would I allow him in my house. Had he stuck around only until he'd secured his prize? Sex with my daughter. Had it been some sort of game to him? I fumbled for my phone and lit the screensaver. The photo of we four at the house in France, smiles sparkling like the pool in the background, taken little more than a week ago, a lifetime away now. We looked like a happy family. Well, we had been.

Beside me Ollie rolled onto his back and I glanced at him with annoyance, I'd give him two minutes before he began to snore. His sandy hair fell about in tufts, his face was beatific, the makings of a Mona Lisa smile. As yet unaware. Would I tell him? Probably not, he'd no doubt tell Sophie, so I'd have to suffer this one out alone.

The snores began to putter, amplifying my solitude, awake in distress while he slept on. Soon they had reached growl level and I frowned at my husband. What was it with men? This one had not been able to keep his dick in his trousers either. I dealt him a sharp elbow and the snoring ceased instantly. A slight judder and he turned onto his side, the subconscious reaction to twenty years of a wife's prodding.

I sighed and flopped away from him. Out in the street, the foxes of Chiswick were copulating as if mocking me, even if their pained shrieks were no advert for the joy of sex. Then there was Bianca. Sophie's friend for the past year or so. She had plenty of others, but there'd be ructions there too while the girl dropped her, as she would surely feel obliged to do. They were all supposed to be heading off to Reading Festival after results day too. Another plaintive sigh and I closed my eyes.

After a sprinkling of sleep I rose early to put house and garden back together, and set the table for Sophie's birthday breakfast. The kitchen echoed, already I could feel the lack of Jack in our lives. I set the radio blaring through the ceiling speakers, but no level of noise could mask the spectre hanging over the room – and neither Ollie nor Sophie knew just how ghoulish it would be.

Horace had managed to climb over the threshold from the garden and was pootling across for his breakfast, so I laid down a pile of spinach and slumped onto the floor beside him.

'Shit, Horace, he's gone. What a bastard, he's cheated on Sophie, he fooled us all.' I fed him a leaf. 'Even you, didn't he?'

When Sophie sauntered in some time later she turned down the music. 'Do you mind, Mum? My head hurts.'

'Happy birthday, darling.' I hugged her to me. 'You won't be wanting bucks fizz then?'

'Never gonna drink again.' She sat down at the table and sank her head in her hands, oblivious to the cards and presents I'd stacked at her place.

'Where's Dad?' I asked.

'Shower.'

Couldn't he get his arse up before her to greet her on her birthday?

I busied myself over coffee, chattering brightly. 'So how does it feel to be sixteen?'

She split her hands, a glimpse from beneath her hair. 'Sorry about last night.'

'No need, Soph. All forgotten. I'm sure I got up to that stuff when I was sixteen.' I placed a mug of coffee down with a smile. 'Of course it's not your actual birthday until ten past five this evening.'

Ollie finally arrived in the kitchen with a jig-come-shuffle towards Sophie and a tuneless, '*Happy Birthday Sweet Sixteen.*'

His presence grated. This should have been the happiest day and it felt hollow, as if the soul had been stripped from our family. Still, why was I cross with *him*?

'Thanks Dad.'

Sophie waved a limp hand before returning it to her forehead, and Ollie hugged her and sat down, waiting to be served.

'Jack joining us for breakfast?'

'No,' I snapped. 'I mean, he's coming for lunch with us later, isn't he?'

Sophie reached for her phone and wrinkled her nose at it. 'Still hasn't called. Think he was pretty well out of it last night.'

No, he was pretty well into it.

'Just we three this morning,' I chirped, a sense of doom looming as I arranged her birthday cake onto a plate and lit the candles. 'That'll be nice, won't it? I'm sure you'll hear from him shortly.'

Emerging from her lair, Sophie's eyes lit up. 'Did you make that, Mum?'

We sang *Happy Birthday*, my eyes shining at hers, while inside I was being dragged down into the abyss. Slinking from the hand Ollie cast about my hips, I walked around the table and nudged the pile of gifts towards her.

'Come on then, set to your prezzies.'

Her phone buzzed a text and she smiled at it. 'Ah, Jack's ill.'

Is he now? Giving himself time to work through the panic and couldn't even wish her happy birthday. But I was grateful that she would spend her special day in ignorance.

'Been throwing up all night,' she added.

Ollie let out one of his fake guffaws and I frowned. Was he also bothered by the thought of we three lunching alone? Jack had become a key part of his life too.

'Lightweight,' he said.

If only you knew.

'Ah well, no point calling The Wolseley,' I said. 'Won't make any difference if we're three or four.'

It would, of course.

Determined to make the day dazzle, I was fumbling over the hooks of dangly earrings, cursing my hands which still refused to stop shaking, when the landline rang.

'Put the boy out of your mind, woman.' I smacked my lips in the mirror, smoothed my dress and reached for the phone.

'Anna?' It was Fred, his voice strange.

'Fred? What's up?' I glanced at my mobile on the bedside table, two missed calls.

'Somethin' wron',' he said, and I knew instantly. I'd heard the same slur many years before from my Grandmother.

'What's happened?'

'Don' know.'

'I'm on my way, Fred. Five minutes. Sit tight.'

I dashed down the stairs. Sophie was fingering her S necklace in the hall mirror, smiling this way and that at her reflection, and I grabbed my bag and car keys.

'Sorry darling, it's Fred, I think he's had a stroke.'

Her hand shot to her mouth, eyes widening, so I pulled her to me.

'I'm so sorry but I've got to go to him. I'll meet you at the restaurant, you two will have fun until I get there, won't you?'

'Shall I Google that list of things to check for a stroke?' She was already thumbing her phone. 'I'll text you.'

'What would I do without you?' With a kiss to the side of her head, I rushed from the house.

En route I called an ambulance before even reading Sophie's text. *FAST. Face dropping. Arm weakness. Speech difficulty. Time to call 999.*

'Done,' I muttered. 'Fast.'

At Fred's door, I realised I had no key, and phoned his mobile.

'Nummer twenny-four,' he said.

I roused the old lady next door for his spare key and let myself in to be greeted by a frenzied Dougal, who trotted me through into the living room. Fred sat slumped in his chair, forlorn as a little boy lost. He gazed up at me, as if searching for an answer, his face etched with worry as to what that might be, and the sight of him tweaked me deep inside. Both his left eye and cheek sagged, the corner of his mouth too, releasing a thread of drool.

I knelt down, dabbed his lips with a tissue and took his hands in mine. 'It's OK, Fred, I'm here, I'm going to look after you.'

He nodded blankly. 'Can' spea'.'

'You don't need to. I'll take care of everything. Can you raise your arms for me?' I let loose his hands and watched his efforts but they remained on his lap.

A weak smile of apology. 'Tryin'.'

154

'Don't worry, I've called an ambulance.'

'Na!' His head shook violently, his eyes blazed, and I reeled but took his hands again.

'Fred. I think you might have had a stroke. Just a small one. If we get you to hospital quickly they can arrest it. Time is of the essence.'

He shook his head, squeezing my hands. 'No' goin' in a hom'.'

His confusion spiked my tears. 'Not a home, Fred, a hospital. Nobody's going to put you in a home. When you're better you'll come back here to your own home, I promise.'

He glanced down at the mobile phone in his lap and I bristled, had his daughter called him from France? Been onto him about going into a care home? Caused his blood pressure to rocket which could have brought on the stroke?

'I promise you, Fred, no care home, only hospital.'

When the medics arrived, he became subservient, furling up into himself, while I soothed him. In the ambulance I held his hand, and we retraced the journey we'd made two days before, to Charing Cross Hospital, only this time to A&E. It was a quiet Sunday afternoon and he didn't have to wait too long before his scan, so I took that opportunity to text Sophie.

What are you having for lunch?

Prawn cocktail. Dad's having oysters.

Is he now?

Yum, will try and be there for dessert

No chance of that, I knew.

When Fred emerged from radiology I learnt that he'd experienced another TIA, or mini stroke, a temporary lack of blood flow to the brain, as they explained. They settled him into a corner window bed on a small bay with three other elderly men.

'All good, Fred,' I said, when he was tucked in tightly, the bed raised at perfect angles for his comfort. 'They've said you'll make a full recovery.'

They had added the word *probably*, but he didn't need to hear that.

'They'll only keep you in overnight, I'm sure.'

Another bluff.

I pulled his curtains closed around us and sat by his bed, smiling as he drifted off to sleep. Conscious that I should phone his daughter, I decided that could wait until morning; he hadn't asked me to, and I didn't know her number, even if I had seen his address book lying around, even if I did now have his door key – and in my handbag also his phone. I pulled it out and lit the screensaver. Shit! Dougal. The mop of caramel laughed out at me, I would have to sort him later.

Once Fred was in a deep sleep, I sank back exhausted. It was 5pm, Ollie and Sophie would be home again, and I felt terrible about missing her special birthday lunch. Yet was that not a fizz of elation? In truth, had I been relieved to have avoided it? Not only because of the running subterfuge I'd have to have maintained towards Sophie, pretending Jack would soon be back with us after his hangover, ha ha. But also because we had lost him? All three of us. I took out my phone to call Ollie, but found I was unable to, so I settled on a text to Sophie, announcing the time at 5.10pm with a happy *actual* birthday message.

I slumped, raking fingernails through my hair, back and forth. In a bid for comfort, I tugged at an earring, fumbling also for the other one, which wasn't there, such had been my haste to get to Fred. The tears came then, and I didn't fight them; they'd be used to weeping visitors here and I was encased within my curtained sanctuary. When spent, I took long and steady breaths, restoring myself, but the curtain twitched and a nurse in navy blue popped her head through and handed me a box of tissues with the gentlest of smiles; a kindness which prompted fresh tears.

I watched Fred sleep on. Please let him be back to normal tomorrow.

Tomorrow. My thoughts turned again to home. Matters would come to a head with Jack... Sophie would be distraught... and I would have to be strong for her. That's what mothers did. But who would comfort me? Ollie? Huh. I yearned to step off the world again.

18

A plan forming, I walked Dougal to the park in the early morning. When I'd fetched him from Fred's house the previous night, the dog had launched himself at me. After so many visits, I'd no longer felt fear, only a slight revulsion as I'd pushed him off me. He'd raced through to the kitchen and with feral barks had jumped like a fox pounding the earth for forage – of course, he'd been crazed with hunger. An instant surge of sympathy saw me squeezing a whole packet of food into his bowl – an empathy which dissolved on the car ride home, when he'd stuck his head through between the seats, nosing my bare arm with snot.

'Oh my God, Mum,' Sophie had squealed, ruffling his ears. 'You got me a dog for my birthday!'

'Ha ha,' I said dryly. 'Outside with him.'

In the garden he made straight for Ollie, sitting at the table.

'What the…? A dog in Anna Bond's house?'

'Meet Dougal. For one night only.'

I watched Sophie sit and entice his paws onto her knees, sinking her face into his fur, immediately smitten, and it dawned on me that this could prove fruitful. After cocking his leg at the apple tree, the dog had then noticed Horace, lolloping over to give his shell a good sniff.

'You leave my tortoise alone, dog,' I said.

I'd never seen Horace retract head and limbs with such haste.

Now, Monday morning, Sophie was still asleep, Ollie was at the shop, and I had an ulterior motive for leaving the house with Dougal. With deep fortifying breaths of Fuller's beer which infused the air, I walked the breadth of Chiswick to the park behind Fred's house, where I let the dog loose. A quick once-over told me I knew nobody else there, so I found a stray bench, sat down and pulled out my phone.

Chest thumping, I scrolled my contacts to Gabby and gazed at the name. The rum of it was that he'd finally stopped trying to contact me, his last attempt being three days ago. Three *weeks* now since we'd met in the Tom Tom Club, so it would be totally explicable if he'd moved on, but I was going back in there, that was inevitable. I dialled the number.

The ring tone was distant, intermittent, so I hung up and tried again. Same thing, it rang out, then fell dead. Had he given me a dud number? In a panic I pulled up my recent calls and saw that, yes, he had rung me from this very same number, so I tried again.

It rang for some time and then, 'Alo.' A woman's voice, remote yet brusque.

I cancelled the call and tossed the phone onto the bench with a scowl. Then I snatched it up and called again.

'Alo.' This time a man's voice, rich but still far-flung.

'Gabryel?' His name flopped out of me, but then he hung up.

I gazed at the screen and surmised immediately; he'd returned to Moldova, that must have been his wife, he had felled our tryst with the click of his thumb. Dougal rambled over to me with a stick and dropped it at my feet.

'You can fuck off too.' I picked it up and hurled it into the branches of a nearby tree.

All my elaborate imaginings, none of them had included a relationship for Gabryel, he had been designed only for me, no complicated others hanging on. How utterly foolish I'd been. I sank my head in my hands, if only I'd returned his calls, if only I'd done this sooner. I was now completely alone.

The phone rang again, a long unknown number, and my heart leapt; he'd found a way.

'Is this Anna Bond?' A female voice, haughty.

'Who's this?'

A laughing Dougal had returned with a new stick which he dropped onto my skirt, saliva and all.

'Urgh!'

'Sorry?'

I frowned. 'Who is this please?'

'Elizabeth Wildsmith. Fred's daughter. You left a message for me last night.'

'Yes I did. I'm afraid that your father's in Charing Cross Hospital.'

She sighed. 'But I only spoke to him yesterday morning.'

'He's had a stroke.'

'Oh dear, not another one.'

'Just a minor stroke.' I paused for my repetition to impact. 'They've said he's most likely going to recover.'

'Well that's good news. Thank you for letting me know Anna, were you with him at the time?'

'No, he called me and I went to him. I'll be going in to visit him this afternoon, if there's any message you'd like me to pass on?'

'Please do send him my greetings.'

Greetings?

'Unfortunately, this has not come at the best time for me.'

'Guess Fred would say the same about himself.'

'Of course.' Her turn to pause and I allowed it to linger. 'And I'll try my utmost to fly over this week sometime.'

'Well if you manage to do so, he's on Nine South Ward.'

'Unbelievable,' I said to Dougal when I'd hung up.

I still held his stick, poised for launch, while he was jumping from paw to paw, ears pricked, mouth agape. *'I'll try my utmost,'* I mocked, and hurled the stick across the park.

We repeated the game a dozen times, each fling of the stick releasing a notch of anger at the woman, until I was calm again. Then I resumed my state of misery over Gabryel. It was my own fault, I should have returned his calls, and in any case his wife would be much younger and more attractive, so the whole affair had been a farce. I would have to galvanise myself and ride this anguish alone. I clipped on the dog's lead and began to walk the short distance to Fred's house, where I intended to gather some personal effects.

Again the phone rang and my heart leapt, but it was Scar.

'You *swore* you'd make it today,' she cried.

Shit, it was Monday.

'Sorry Scar, bit of a crisis.'

'Your life is one constant crisis these days.' She hung up.

I stopped in my tracks. 'Et tu Scar.'

I texted, *Sorry, Fred's had a stroke,* and watched the screen for her response, breath bated at the pulsing dots, until eventually *xxx* appeared. But three kisses would not do the trick – a universal over-and-out, and these were undeniably passive aggressive. Every friendship requires nurturing, I got that, but surely as my closest she could cut me some slack?

We turned the corner and Dougal strained on the leash at the sight of his home, so I jogged with him to the front door.

161

'Let's find some of your toys too, shall we?' I said, letting us in.

The house resounded with an eerie vacant ring, amplified by the hollow ticking of the mantel clock. The dog trotted through rooms in search of his master, returning to me with a quizzical cock of the head.

Moved by this, I knelt down to fondle his ears. 'He's not here, Dougal, but you can come home with me again until he's back. You're gonna help me take care of Sophie, aren't you?'

He wagged his tail and set off again to double check, with an anticipation which brought a pesky tear to me.

Upstairs in Fred's bedroom, an interloper's guilt took hold and I froze, as if the room was criss-crossed by laser rays which would trigger an alarm when breached by my criminal move. The double divan with its faded pink duvet cover made me smile, had he never invested in new bed linen after the death of his wife? On the wall hung the wedding bouquet he'd told me about, dried pink peonies pressed and mounted in a golden heart-shaped frame. I took a step towards his chest of drawers and hovered over a hair brush clogged with his fine steel-grey strands. Beside it sat a packet of his tobacco which I brought to my face. Closing my eyes, I took a deep draught of its sweet aroma, an instant comfort. Please let him be alright. My mentor, my rock.

In search of clean pyjamas I opened a drawer and found a pair ironed and neatly folded. Smoothing the fabric with my palms, I mulled over his daily life, whether he would be capable of such household tasks on his return. I laid them on the bed and began to open another drawer, slamming it shut again at the sudden ring of my phone. Caught red-handed, discovered snooping, well that's how I felt. It was a lengthy unknown foreign number – Elizabeth effing Wildsmith again?

'Hello,' I barked.

'Hello Anna.' It was Gabryel.

I closed my eyes, tears already spiking. 'Where are you?'

'In Moldova. I'm sorry I could not speak to you.'

'Your wife?'

'Yes.'

'Are you coming back?'

'Of course. On Thursday. Can we meet?'

The relief engulfed me. 'Where?'

'At the airport? I will send you details of the flight.'

I saw a hotel room. A perimeter fence. Anonymity.

'Sure.'

I hung up to find Dougal's snout on my lap, a hopeful look, a feeble wag of his tail, and I sank my face into his. 'You're not allowed to be up here,' I said, my voice thick with joy.

At home, I dropped the bag of Fred's clothes and toiletries in the hallway and let Dougal loose. Hanging up his lead, I was aware that there had been something more satisfying about walking with a dog, purposeful and uplifting.

'You up, Soph?' I called at the stairs.

'In the kitchen,' she sang back.

Then I saw the bike propped against the wall.

In the kitchen, at our island, mug of coffee in his hand, sat Jack. A growling Dougal already stood at his feet.

'What the...?' I frowned at Sophie, feeling the colour drain from my face.

'What's up, Mum?'

I contemplated Jack, who was unable to meet my eyes. His hand at the mug was shaking. You'd better be shaking, I thought, you'd better be in my house for one purpose only.

'Nothing,' I said, and glared at the boy, waiting until his eyes finally met mine. 'Didn't sleep well last night, that's all. I'll leave you two to it.'

I stomped along the hallway to the study and slammed the door behind me; if ever he needed propelling towards the decent thing. I sat down at the desk, with its recent tang of lemon cleaning fluid, switched on the Mac computer and brought up *Angry Birds*.

'Deceitful little shit,' I muttered, slinging a bird at a cartoon pig.

It was only a matter of minutes until I heard footsteps along the hallway and the front door opening.

'Bye.'

I froze at Sophie's tone, far too friendly. And was that the sound of a kiss? The door closed and I watched Jack wheel his bike down the path, turning with a furtive glance at the study window as he shut the gate behind him. Our eyes met and I flooded mine with hate, bringing a flush to his cheeks before he hurriedly mounted and cycled off.

'You OK?' Sophie stood at the doorway. '*Angry Birds*? Some secret addiction?'

I swung around, mind tangled in confusion. 'What did Jack want?'

'What do you mean, what did he want? He arrived back in the land of the living and couldn't wait to wish me happy birthday. He's taking me out for dinner tonight.'

'Dinner?'

'Yes, you know that meal you have together at night. He's booked La Trompette.'

'La Trompette?' Surely he wasn't going to tell her there? 'How can he afford that?'

'You *know* he works for his Dad sometimes. What is *wrong* with you today?'

I shook my head. 'Nothing, sorry. I'm just upset about Fred. It's visiting time soon, guess I'll feel better when I know what's happening. Can you believe it's *his* birthday today too?'

Her eyes widened and she shook her head, swivelling on her heels. 'And they say charity begins at home...'

What was that supposed to mean? I'd hardly strayed from her side since our return from France. Slinging birds at the screen, I refused to think it through; I was juggling too much emotion already and, while my subconscious was aware that her moodiness was a result of so much more than me having missed her birthday lunch, that is what I settled upon.

Fred was sitting up in bed when I arrived with my carrier bags. The drip dangling at his arm had worked its magic, returning colour to his cheeks, plumpness to his flesh.

'Happy Birthday,' I chirped, dropping a copy of *The Guardian* onto his bed.

He nodded at the punnet of grapes I placed on the overbed table. 'Won' be staying in long enough to ea' those.'

I smiled, his wit was restored if not his crisp vowels, and the left side of his face definitely drooped less.

'How about this then?' I removed a small shop-bought cake on which I'd iced his name and the number eighty-six.

His eyes lit up. 'I love ca'.'

'I know you do. Eighty-six today, Fred.' I kissed his forehead, pleased that it smelt recently washed, and pulled up a chair. 'How are you feeling?'

'Moun'ain ou' of a molehill. Thas wha' this is.'

I wondered if he could hear himself slur.

'You look so much better. Nearly back to full health I'd say. Bet you're flirting with the pretty nurses, aren't you? Do they know it's your birthday? Must be in your notes?'

165

All those questions.

'They are lookin' af' me, Anna. So kin'.'

The man in the bed opposite called over to us. 'Your birthday today is it, Fred?'

'Eigh'y-six, I am,' said Fred.

'This your daughter?'

'Anna is a frien'.'

'You old rascal. A lady friend, no less?'

'She's a frien' and a lady. Now, if you don' min'?'

The man flapped out his *Daily Mail* with a chortle, while I smiled at the twinkle in Fred's eyes.

'*He's* los' his marbles,' he whispered, far too loudly. 'He's goin' home toda' an' they've said I can soon.'

'Brilliant Fred. But they're obviously looking after you, so why don't you let them pamper you for a while longer?'

'I've go' Dou'al to thin' abou'.'

'He's fine, Fred, he's staying with me.'

'Than' you, Anna.' He smiled warmly.

'And I called Elizabeth.'

An exasperated sigh. 'Wha' did she wan'?'

'No, it was me who called her. She sends her love, she's very concerned.'

He blew out a disdainful lungful. 'Don' need her here, bossin' me aroun'.'

'Don't worry, I'll take care of you, and we can get somebody in to help around the house.'

I'd checked it all out online, had already spoken to the discharge team about social services, after all, how many days would they entertain him until he was bed blocking?

Still disgruntled, Fred fumbled for his newspaper. 'Thans fo' this, Anna.'

'I've brought your glasses too.' I placed them by his side and began to empty the contents of the carrier bags into his cupboard. 'Here's some pyjamas, and clothes for when you're ready to get dressed.'

He gestured to the glasses. 'Can you help me with thos' pleas'?'

I slipped them up onto his nose and watched him continue to grapple with the newspaper, reluctant to step on his pride.

'Anyone else you'd like me to tell that you're here, Fred? Next door neighbour? Your Thursday club?'

He shook his head and I smiled, what now?

'Shall we do the crossword?' Gently, I took the newspaper from him and found the right page. 'OK. One across. Felt hat. Six letters.'

Fred gazed blankly at me.

'Tricky one,' I said. Though he had once told me he used to own a Fedora. 'Wasn't there a particular type of hat they wore in old detective films?'

He nodded but said nothing. The moments lingered until his gaze soon dropped to his bedspread, and eventually out onto the darkening courtyard outside.

19

Thursday morning. Results Day. Reading Festival. Fred was leaving hospital. Gabryel was flying in. Compartmentalising had made a comeback, but unless I was especially cunning that day my lives would converge. At 6am, I sat in the kitchen with a mug of coffee, perusing the mental spreadsheet I'd concocted; precision timing for when each event would have to happen in order for me to be a part of it.

I needn't have bothered on the first item, as I should have realised after the previous evening's outburst. Incredibly, Jack appeared still not to have said anything. Tuesday had come and gone, and by Wednesday I was fuming with the notion that he was mocking my daughter – and me. So I'd taken Sophie into the garden, Dougal lolloping at our side, and had broken the news. Naturally, I'd rehearsed my spiel, at the mirror even, but emotion was running high.

'Soph. Look, I need to tell you something.'

'More wise words for Reading?'

She was fondling Dougal's ears, treating them like the handles of a motorbike, twisting and squeezing to her voiced soundtrack of changing gears. The dog was loving it. Whenever she stopped he'd nudge her hands with each side of his head in turn. I confess, I wanted a go, it would have calmed the sandstorm within.

'I saw Jack kissing another girl at your party.' The words blurted out irrespective of me, and I waited, eyes locked onto the side of her face like an Exocet missile.

It was Dougal who suffered first, an extra hard squeeze of the ears, a yelp, and then my daughter's dark face was upon mine.

'No, you didn't.' Her eyes glittered.

'Yes, I did.' A calm voice. After all, I was the adult, wasn't I?

'What the fuck do you know?'

'Because I came across him. After that fuss with the vodka. In our study.'

Such resort to detail, already I was losing control.

'Did you, fuck?!'

I held her eyes with mine. 'Sophie, why would I make this up?'

'Jack wouldn't do that.'

'I'm so sorry, but he did.' I reached for her hand but she swatted me off.

'He loves me. Do you know how much he spent for my birthday dinner?'

A gentle shake of the head. 'I'm telling you the truth, darling. For your own sake, before you go off to the festival.'

'Why do you always have to ruin things for me? Just because Dad has an affair behind your back. I'm not surprised, I would have done if I were him, because you're horrible!'

She'd run inside leaving me reeling. She had known about the affair? At my feet, Dougal, then lying prone, chin flat with the gravity of the situation, had attempted a smile and a lame flop of his tail.

The outcome of this little mother and daughter conflab had

169

been that Ollie was the sole parent invited into school that morning to open her GCSE results with her.

He was first down, soon after 7am. Whistling, of all things. Had he reverted to a fresh game of *play the parent*? I contemplated his jaunty back as he busied himself boiling eggs, and suddenly the notion of chucky eggs and soldiers for breakfast seemed unmanly. Feckless. A few more hours and I would be with Gabryel.

When Sophie arrived in the kitchen, she refused me eye contact and sat at the island, back square on.

Ollie threw her a smile. 'Hello lovely. Boiled egg?'

'Please Dad.'

'Nervous?'

Her back shrugged.

I butted in. 'No need for nerves, you'll have done brilliantly.'

Another shrug, a gesture I took as placatory. We'd never before found ourselves at this level of conflict, and the thought that she might be smarting as keenly as I was distressed me. Her endurance of the past two years was about to culminate in the moment she would open that envelope and we should have been sitting close, cheek to cheek, devoted mother to loving child that morning.

'Will you text me as soon as you open them?' I faltered.

Ollie kicked in then. 'Absolutely! Won't we, Soph?'

I could take no more and rose from the table, stacked my mug in the dishwasher. 'I'll take Dougal out then.'

Another task to be slotted into this day of many colours.

It was just after 9am when they called me. Ollie's phone, Sophie's voice.

'I got all As!'

The top mark was A*.

'Fantastic!' I cried. 'Well done you!'

Guess she heard the quiver of disappointment.

'Ten As.'

'Fabulous Sophie, absolutely fabulous.'

'It is, isn't it?' Such hope, such belief in my words.

I closed my eyes. The ropes that bound us, currently so slackly coiled, were stirring, beginning to tauten, tugging us closer, but I had wounded her. She must have known that there was truth in my words, that I would not have lied about something so earth-shattering, but right then she felt betrayed more by her own mother than by some wayward boyfriend. A kid I now despised.

I took a deep breath. 'Coffee and humungous slice of chocolate cake to celebrate? Dougal and I are in the park near school.'

'Can't, the coach is here.'

'Coach?'

'The school laid it on to take us to Reading, remember?'

Some distant recollection of having paid for that, but my mental spread sheet had not incorporated it into the day, and nothing had been mentioned at breakfast. I braced myself against the threatening tears.

'Got your bag with you?'

'Yeah.'

'Text me when you're there?'

Silence.

'And be careful.'

'You've got us a pod with a loo in it, Mum. Luxury compared to everyone else.'

The *Mum* felt good. And I had indeed, forked out for a means to cocoon my daughter at her first scary rock festival, along with some of the other mums, including Bianca's – how would that pan out?

'Well you have fun, you deserve it, Soph. Fabulous results. I'm so proud of you.'

Did they even matter to her? Eclipsed by the miserable prospect that the first boy she'd fallen in love with was a cheat. I scrunched my eyes with the pain I was unable to protect her from.

'Bye then, everyone's getting on.'

'Text me?'

Ollie came on the phone, laughing, just as I was letting a tear fall.

'Our daughter, Anna. Doesn't get better than that.'

Well it did actually, my tiger goal for her had been ten A*s, a mania now pathetic in the face of her distress. I hung up.

Fred was already dressed, bolt upright in his chair, eyes locked on the door, when I arrived. Eyes which widened with excitement when he saw me.

'Here I am,' I sang, relieved to see his overnight bag packed. First hurdle crossed.

'Good morning, love, I'm all ready for you.' His speech appeared much crisper and the facial drooping had all but disappeared.

The clock on the wall said 11.30am. Sophie would be setting up camp in her pod. She'd text me soon, no doubt, and I had determined to put her from my mind until then. As for Gabryel, his flight was due in at 2.05pm, so plenty of time there.

I kissed Fred's cheek, scooped up the bag and held out an arm, bent at the elbow. 'Shall we dance?'

He got to his feet, steadied himself with a walking stick, and we set off, his arm looped through mine. He managed to lift the stick at his ward companions.

'Well gentlemen, my chariot awaits.'

'Bye Fred. See you later.' The men waved their newspapers in that particular manner of farewell in films from the war years.

'Not if I see you first.' He chuckled and set the stick down to set off around the bed.

A male nurse appeared in the bay. 'Not so fast Frederick. Need you to sign this discharge notice for me. And we're still waiting on your drugs from the pharmacy.'

'Strike a light!' He flopped back down into his chair, and the guy laid a clipboard of notes on his lap.

I dropped the overnight bag onto his bed. 'I could fetch his drugs for him?'

'No need, they're on their way.' The man gestured to the door. 'While you're signing your autograph, Fred, I'm going to pinch your daughter.'

'I'm not his daughter,' I said, following him to the nurses' station out in the corridor, where he pulled up Fred's details on a screen. 'I volunteer for a charity, that's all.'

The man smiled his amusement. Yep you got me, Fred's so much more to me than that.

'Well you're the best we have,' he said. 'No next of kin, are there?'

'A real live daughter, actually. Can't believe she hasn't been in touch.'

A brief flash of his own disbelief, eyes on the screen. 'Was it you who requested social services to visit on discharge?'

'It was. He's going to need help, you can see his mobility's been affected. I'm hoping he can still get upstairs.'

'Do you perceive a change in his mental capacity also?'

'Not really,' I lied, with an imperceptible shrug.

He typed a few notes. 'I've passed his case on to social and somebody will go round later today. Oh, and here comes the

173

prescription.' He took the paper bag from a porter and checked its bounty.

'And we're off,' I said, returning to Fred and stuffing the drugs into his bag.

At Fred's house, the dodgy paving stone had been repaired, but if he noticed this he didn't comment. Dougal awaited us, along with a full fridge and fresh flowers from Fred's garden. Having discovered vases galore beneath the sink, I'd assumed he was wont to cut his pride and joys, and had only clipped roses from the back of the bush; rosette heads stuffed with pink petals, a pastel blush the colour pink should be.

'Goo-ood boy.' Fred ruffled Dougal while the dog's paws scrabbled for purchase on his thighs, knocking him back against the closed front door.

The mantel clock struck an ominous quarter to one. Still no text from Sophie. The heatwave had broken that morning, in time for August bank holiday weekend, and it was tipping down; she would probably be standing in a muddy field in front of a stage knocking back some form of alcohol. I'd tried to access her Facebook page but she'd blocked me, and that stung. How would she deal with Jack?

As for Gabryel, well it was getting tight but my duty lay to Fred. I settled him in his armchair, handed him the pipe he'd been deprived of for several days, and made us a cup of tea, knocking up a sandwich of his favourite breaded ham as I went. Laying the plate onto his lap, I smiled at his pleasure to be home, his mouth working the pipe against a multitude of thoughts. This man, my father figure. We would make this work between us, but what needed to be done now? Home from hospital. New drugs. A different person, in as much as he was shaky on his feet and physically diminished, even if his speech was almost as clear as before. Would he make the stairs? Would it be alright to leave him alone? I hoped social services would arrive soon.

The clock struck one. I had thirty minutes tops.

'Good to be home?' I asked.

He nodded. 'Thanks, Anna. For all you've done.'

'My pleasure. You'd do the same for me, I know.'

He bent to sniff the roses beside him. 'Wild Eve. Beautiful scent they have.'

'Ah.' The name of his lover.

'Used to grow this rose myself.'

'Yes, Fred, they're from your garden.'

'Really?'

'I thought, why not bring your beautiful lush garden inside for you to enjoy?'

'I had them at the old house, I know…'

Old house?

I gestured to his sandwich. 'It's ham, Fred, your favourite.'

'Thanks.' He reached for it. 'Good to be home.'

'No place like home.'

And at this rate I was going to have to click my heels to reach Heathrow on time.

'Where's *your* sandwich?' About to take a bite, he held his mid-air.

'Well, I…' That hurt expression. 'If you don't mind me using some of your ham I'd love one please.' I jumped up.

Old house? I thought, as I buttered the bread.

Back in the living room guilt kicked me in the gut. Fred had waited for me, had returned his own sandwich to its plate, as if we were going to spend a pleasant and leisurely afternoon together, which is what we should have been doing. I forced myself to eat at his snail pace, casting from my mind all that

175

awaited me in a hotel room near Heathrow airport. Gabryel would surely wait for me if I texted him.

When we'd finished eating, I picked up the bag of drugs. 'Shall I sort these for you, Fred?'

'No thank you, I need to keep operational, you mustn't give in.' He began to rummage through it. 'Have you got somewhere to be Anna?'

I met his eyes sheepishly. 'Actually Fred, I'm meeting a friend, at the airport.'

'That's nice. Where's she flying in from?'

'Moldova.'

He raised his eyes to mine. 'Moldova? I went there once, Chisinau, isn't it?'

I shrugged. Gabryel said he was flying via Bucharest.

'After the fall of communism. We set up a university course in economics. Nice place. Nice people.'

'My friend is very nice.' I realised that I was playing motorbikes with Dougal's ears. 'And she's a he.'

'Then you must go and meet him. Dougal and I will be fine.'

'If you're sure? I'll pop back later, and they're sending someone round soon.'

He gestured to one of the blister packs of drugs. 'Would you pour me a glass of water before you go, love?'

'Sure.' I almost skipped to his taps, my flight with impunity now imminent.

He began to pop his drugs dutifully. 'Pretty dress,' he said, mid-pill with an unmistakeable twinkle.

'Thank you.'

I winked at him – this secret needed some outlet – and he returned it, an exaggerated pirate wink.

'I'll be back around seven, I'll walk Dougal too,' I added, not wishing him to consider my return a well-being check.

'Don't you worry about me. Now off you trot.'

I kissed his cheek goodbye.

'Turn the telly on, would you, love?'

Fred had always said daytime TV was a slippery slope, but I did as he asked and left the house, unlocking my car with a shadow of unease. Clearly there were no long-term memory problems if he remembered Moldova from years ago, but *old* house? I'd certainly be back later.

Then I set off on a winged horse – nay a unicorn – to Heathrow airport.

I fell off Gabryel and flopped onto my back. We lay panting together, contemplating the white stippled ceiling. As ceilings go, this one must have seen its fair share of illicit love. Beyond the double glazing, a silent Lufthansa was soaring into the cloudless blue sky.

'Again?' I said.

He laughed, took my hand and squeezed it. 'May I have a few minutes?'

'You can have all the time in the world.'

I rolled onto my side and kissed him, overwhelmed by the haze of joy, by the intensity of my feelings for this man – to be wanted again, to feel adored, it had been so many years. His body was taut as a drum, the skin on his chest almost squeaked when rubbed, not an ounce of surplus fat. Was I falling in love? Was some kind of future with him tenable? Right then it seemed as if no obstacle was insurmountable – not even Sophie.

I got up off the bed and breathed in, aware of his eyes on my body as I forced a stroll rather than a sprint to the bathroom. The round magnifying mirror lured me to its scrutiny and I screwed up my face at the wrinkles, exacerbating

177

them horribly.

'Urgh,' I whispered, then peered at the normal mirror above the basin. 'Much kinder, thank you.'

But why had I recently had my hair cut into that business-like style? All flat and feathery. '*Too short*!' Mum had exclaimed during our last Skype session – and my mother's estimation still carried excessive weight; anyone else and the words would not have stung so painfully or throbbed for so long. *Gamine*, Scar had called it – much kinder. Still, I didn't want to be boyish for Gabryel, I wanted to flick the shoulder length waves I'd now lost.

At least my body was tanned, and lithe, if nearly ten years older than his, and I'd even clipped my pubes the previous evening (a wax was out of the question, and if Gabryel was used to his women shaved then he hadn't let on). Ollie had almost caught me at it, an *M&S* bag at my crotch for the tumbling hairs which I'd hurriedly scrunched into a drawer before he saw it.

Back in the room, I took a running jump onto the bed, blurring, I hoped, all imperfections.

'I watched you from the café. At Heathrow,' he said, once I was stretched out luxuriantly beside him again.

'While I was waiting for you to come through at arrivals?'

He nodded.

'You mean you were there already?' I frowned. 'Why would you do that? I thought I'd missed you.'

And had been frantically prowling up and down, as he'd no doubt observed – but the sense of vulnerability was not unpleasant.

He pursed his lips. 'I was wondering…'

'Wondering what?'

'Why you did not respond to my calls.'

'Ah.'

'Ah,' he began to laugh. 'Now you will invent some false story for me?'

'It's complicated.' I pressed a finger to his chest.

'The lady says it is complicated…'

'That was your wife I spoke to on the phone earlier this week?'

'Yes.'

'Well then… and you've also met my husband. Like I say, it's complicated.'

I turned the finger and scraped a nail, tracing his flesh.

'Anyway, I'm back, aren't I?'

Ignoring his winces, I scored an indent between his nipples, applying pressure as I dragged my nail down.

'Ouch,' he said finally and grabbed my wrist. 'We both can play like this. If this is what you enjoy?'

Both my wrists in his grip, he flipped me over onto my back and thrust my hands behind my head, clamping them to the pillow with a force that made me gasp in pain. The longing in those wolf eyes sent an almighty thrill skittering through me. I tensed my body and flashed my eyes at him.

'Come on then.'

The shadows of the planes lengthened against the runway, but I had lost all sense of time in that hotel room. While Gabryel was in the bathroom, I checked for news of Sophie. Still nothing. After a few seconds wondering whether she would already have had it out with Jack, I decided that it was in her hands and tossed the phone onto the bedside table. Sod Sophie, if she couldn't be bothered to text me. That afternoon was about me, and no concern for my daughter would cloud it, I'd been through tough times and deserved my moment of hedonism.

The phone pinged – joy of joys, a text from Fred's daughter, Elizabeth. She'd flown in from France that afternoon and was at his house, so I wouldn't have to call by again today. I stretched out and scissor-kicked my legs, no need for me to abandon my opium den.

And so we lay naked on top of a white, much-laundered duvet (hollow-fibre not goose) while my every sinew wanted to reach for him again. So much for that glass of wine and its diminishing returns, each time left me heady for another bottle, a whole cellar would not cut it. The sky was darkening, lights flooding the airport when I finally tore myself away and dressed.

'I will pay the room,' he said, still naked on the bed as I stood at the door.

The languid sight of him drew me back for a final kiss, my lips trailing to plant one just below his navel.

'My turn next time.'

'Tomorrow then?'

A certainty rather than a question.

20

The phone call came in the early hours of Saturday. Bianca's mother. She'd tracked our landline from the school reps for Sophie's year, having received frantic calls from her own daughter.

We were both in a deep slumber. I since around ten, Ollie since I didn't know when as I hadn't heard him come in; that week he was lording it up as patron of a local art exhibition and was out with his Chiswick crowd. It must have taken several rings, intrusions into my dream, hijacking it, before I came to and fumbled for the phone. The news punched me awake and I pummelled Ollie's arm until he was too.

'It's Sophie. She's in A&E.'

I was up and off as if at a starter's pistol, pouring my jellified limbs into jeans and T-shirt. Surreal steps through the house and out to the car, with Ollie traipsing behind me, muttering questions, exuding fumes of alcohol. He joined me at the driver's side.

'You'll still be over the limit,' I said, pushing him away, and sliding behind the wheel, while he obediently lumbered round to the passenger door.

'What's happened? Tell me.'

I felt his eyes locked on the side of my face as I dug a scrap of paper from my jeans pocket and put the car into gear, wiping the tears which would blur my progress.

'Put Royal Berkshire Hospital into the Satnav. And call Bianca's phone, number's on there.'

'What's *happened* to her?'

'She's had her stomach pumped.'

'Sophie?'

'No, the Queen!' I shrieked. 'That was Bianca's mother calling. She didn't say whether it was booze. Or drugs.'

'No.' Ollie began to weep effusively, hands cradling his face.

'Give me the phone, I'll call her.'

Jaw clenched, I snatched it from his lap and drove one-handed out towards the M4 (for the second time that day...) while the girl's voice came over the car's speaker.

'Bianca? It's Sophie's mum. Is she OK?'

'She's sleeping now.' Her voice quavered.

'We're on our way.'

'My mum's here.'

'We'll be half an hour max.' I refused to soften my voice for this girl, who had probably been caught with Jack, the bastard, and catalysed the binge of whatever had brought Sophie to this point.

I hung up, tossed the phone at Ollie, wincing at his continued sniffles, and floored the accelerator. It was all my fault of course, I had not been shielding her with motherly thoughts, had been greedily shagging Gabryel again that afternoon; if only I'd been mentally safeguarding her, sending her protective vibes. What kind of a despicable mother was I to allow my daughter to wind up in hospital twice within one month? Such negligence.

When we reached Reading, I followed the Satnav Ollie had finally managed to negotiate, parked up and sprinted through the front entrance to reception, my voice faltering as I gave Sophie's name.

Ollie and I were led along corridors, gliding as if in a dream. Bizarrely, I was alert enough to take in the slick refurbishment, none of your old-fashioned radiators with their glutinous layers of apple green paint, and my subconscious was keen to affiliate this investment with a parallel high level of care. On into a ward, another corridor, a nurses' station, then through a door into a single room. To Sophie. At the sight of my daughter I crumpled to the floor, crawled to her bed and clambered at the side rails to hoist myself up.

She lay peacefully asleep on her back. Her blonde hair with its platinum fringes was fanned around her tanned face as if a stylist had arranged her. Instantly, I was back in her nursery, watching her sleep, imagining her dreams, pouring love into her – it seemed a matter of weeks ago. How could my daughter be lying here after yet another brush with death? I could still count her time on this earth in months – and had done so on her sixteenth birthday. There had been just one hundred and ninety-two of them, each single month suddenly distinct for me as a tumble of vivid montages. I bent to kiss her, brushed a strand of hair, stroked her cheek.

'Bianca called the ambulance the moment she found her.'

I looked around to see a woman sitting against the back wall. Beside her, Bianca, her eyes as red as an albino rabbit's.

'Was it drugs?' I asked the girl.

An imperceptible nod.

'Which ones?'

'Don't know. They looked like sweets.' She shrugged at her mum, who took her hand and squeezed it. 'Pink teddy bears.'

I eyed the comforting hand and Bianca bit her lip.

'She said they weren't kicking in, so she took a load more.'

'Why would she take them at all? Sophie's dead against drugs.'

'Bianca said they were everywhere, that you couldn't avoid them. Everyone was taking them.' The mother sparred with me.

'Tell me why *she* took them.'

Bianca flushed. 'She saw Jack with someone.'

'*Someone?*'

'Anna!' Ollie whipped out my name but I was not for turning.

'Was it *you?*' I cried. 'You little slut.'

'How dare you?' Her mother launched herself up and stabbed her finger at me. 'It was because of *my* daughter's quick action that yours is lying here and not dead in some field!'

'Yes,' I hissed, 'it probably is because of *your* daughter that mine is lying here now. I found her having sex with Sophie's boyfriend at her party last weekend, did you happen to know about that?'

I turned on Bianca who was weeping softly. 'Did you tell your mum that? Eh? Did you?'

I was silenced by an intake of breath from the bed, followed by a sigh, and Sophie rolled her head as if seeking a more comfortable position on the pillow. We all stood statue-still and waited.

'Enough, Anna,' whispered Ollie.

I grasped the bed rails for support and nodded; after all, this girl had probably just saved my daughter's life.

'She did see Jack kissing someone else,' Bianca's small voice, 'but it wasn't me.'

I cocked my head at her resignedly.

'Let's get you home, darling.' The woman glowered as she led her daughter towards the door.

184

'Thank you,' I said then, 'for calling the ambulance.'

'S'OK. I hope she'll be alright now.' Bianca lingered.

I managed a wan smile and turned back to gaze upon my daughter.

After they'd left, Ollie brought a chair and gently pressed me down into it. I placed a soothing palm on Sophie's forehead, provoking a murmur as she slept, a sound which pierced me.

A nurse entered the room. 'She'll be sleeping for a good while yet.'

'Can you tell us what happened exactly?' asked Ollie.

'Lucky her friend was so vigilant, got her to us in time to pump the stomach. Any longer and the drugs would have been absorbed into the digestive system. And then we'd have been looking at a totally different scenario.'

I felt Ollie's hand on my shoulder and covered it with my own. After fussing with the chart at the end of the bed, the nurse left us, and we sat on, watching our daughter breathe.

'Come on,' said Ollie eventually. 'Let's get a cup of tea, she won't wake up for hours yet.'

I nodded and, with a final brush of my fingers, I stood, allowing him to take my hand.

In the foyer Ollie fed the drinks machine, but the lights were painfully bright so we slipped outside and found a bench. The night was muggy after the heavy rainfall, fanning my bare arms with comfort. Darkness enveloped us, but a glance at my watch told me dawn was not so far off.

'Thanks.' I took the lidded cup of tea from him and we sat in silence.

She's OK, I thought. She's sleeping now, she's going to be alright. But the swirling sands of my mind would bring me no relief.

Ollie took my tea from me. 'Don't let it go cold,' he said,

removing the lid and folding my hands again around the cup.

I sipped. 'She's going to be OK, isn't she?'

'She is. Bit of a sore throat, that's all.'

'When I think what could have…'

'Don't Anna.'

'No.'

We watched a group of nurses arriving for their shift, sensible shoes, walking in step, sharing a joke, but what was there to laugh about?

'What was all that with Bianca?'

I shook my head. 'Nothing.'

'You saw her having sex, with *Jack,* at Sophie's party?'

I nodded.

'Why didn't you tell me? I'll kill him, cheating little piece of shit.'

'I hate him too.'

We lapsed once more into silence, cocooned by the velvet dark of night, lost within our own shock.

'Do you think it was an overdose?' I said finally. 'Or that she chucked more down her neck because they weren't kicking in?'

'The latter. The lad never meant so much to her that she'd try and top herself.'

I winced at his words and fumbled for his hand.

'Not Sophie. She's strong, oozing with self-esteem. You saw to that, Anna, you've been a wonderful mother, you know that, don't you?'

I heard an odd squeak emerge from me and closed my eyes, only to see once again the images that had been haunting me since our arrival at the hospital. One of those animal posts on Facebook, the kind you expect to make you smile, set you up for the day. A tiny fawn slips into a river. Probably in Africa, because it's followed into the water by a crocodile which has been watching from the bank. The water ripples with the reptile's unseen progress which is much faster than the fawn's – and where is the baby animal swimming to anyway? Then its mother, clocking the situation, jumps into the river and swims her heart out to intersect the two animals, head up, moving boldly towards her fate. When she reaches the spot, she treads water, waiting, and the crocodile jaws take her, drag her down to her death. The ultimate sacrifice. Now that was a proper mother.

We sat on. Eventually, birdsong struck up in the hospital grounds, sweet wisps which bathed us as the sky paled and our shelter of darkness lifted.

'We should get back to her,' I said.

We were both there when Sophie awoke. Each with a tender smile.

'Oh my God,' were her waking words, that glib mantra of youth, and she covered her eyes.

'Shush,' I said.

'It's OK,' said Ollie.

We tripped over each other's words, both parents saying the right thing at the same time. 'We love you, Soph. That's all that matters. You're going to be alright. Let's get you home.'

It was some time before the doctor released her, with stern words and an avuncular hand to her back. She'd showered and dressed, and a clean T-shirt had appeared.

At home, we sat on the sofa with our daughter between us, each of us pressed close to her, and she took my hand, resting it on her thigh. We watched a family film, *Moulin Rouge* with Nicole Kidman and Ewan McGregor. Wrangling with sleep, I fell into a daze, soothed by the presence of Sophie's flesh and bones beside mine, by the swirling haze of Paris rooftops, by the blood red silk of a ball gown. And those songs, all about the greatest thing in life. Which is to love, and be loved.

Afterwards, we took to our beds for the remainder of that afternoon. I slid into slumber as if anaesthetised, succoured by the knowledge that my daughter was safely asleep mere yards from me.

It was the next day before we spoke about it. Ollie cooked a momentous fry-up and we sat around our kitchen table with jazz music flowing. Louis Armstrong was just the ticket for a sunny Sunday morning, for a family breakfast.

Then Ollie set about the dishwasher and I asked Sophie to join me in the living room. She didn't ask why, trailed me in, sank onto the sofa, tucked her feet beneath her, and hugged a cushion. I sat down beside her and carefully marshalled my thoughts.

'Will you tell me about it, Soph?'

I'm sorry, Mum.' She began to weep silently.

I handed her a tissue and waited, but she was stifled by gulped tears.

'Why did he do that to me?' she managed finally.

The age-old question. Was it ever thus? What the male did to the female? How was I to respond? Because he only thinks about himself? Because he's a rogue and can't keep his dick in his pants? Because he's young and has just discovered sex?

Because he's a bastard, is what I really thought.

'I don't know, darling,' I said, gentle smile in place.

Her wide eyes flooded, piercing my heart. I saw her again as a baby, enormous eyes looming in a miniature face – blue-eyed girl, Ollie and I used to sing.

'Because all men are bastards,' I joked softly.

'But I told him I loved him.'

Ah. So he'd run a mile from that.

I looped an arm about her shoulders and she melted into me. 'I think it's horrible what he's done, darling. I don't understand it either.'

'Do you think he'll come back to me?'

'Do you want him to?'

She sniffed. 'Don't know. Not sure I can live without him.'

I kissed her hair, breathing in her shampoo. 'You can do better, Soph. I know it must hurt right now. God knows, I've been there, when I was your age.'

'Really?'

'Oh yes. Matt McGarvey when *I* was sixteen. He dumped me.' And I'd begged. 'The key is never to beg, Soph.'

'What do you mean, *beg*?'

'Never demean yourself. Never let him see that he's hurt you.'

'Think he might know that.'

'Well next time you see him, give him the ice queen treatment.'

She began to cry again. 'I love him.'

'I know you do, darling.'

What did she know about love at her age? Well, possibly everything. Who's to say that finding love at a later age was more authentic? More valid? Ollie and I were no showcase.

'But you'll love again, I promise. You might even fall in love several times before you find the one, you'll see. Trust me on that?'

She stuffed a wet tissue beneath her thigh, cuddled in further, and we sat closer than close, our bodies rising and falling.

'Soph?' I said eventually.

'Hmm?'

'You weren't trying to…?'

I felt her stiffen. 'No,' she whispered. 'Just wanted to feel numb.'

'Yeah. I get that.'

'It wouldn't happen. So I took more.'

I sighed. 'OK.'

'Stupid, Mum, I know. But I saw him kissing another girl, and he told me we weren't exclusive so he could do whatever he wanted.'

Exclusive? What the hell did that mean?

'Well he's a shit for cheating on you, but you're home now, and we both love you very much, Dad and I.'

I had no wish for us to move from the sofa, and seemingly neither did she.

'So, what shall we do today?' I asked lightly.

'Bianca wants to come over. She's got my stuff from Reading.'

'Sounds like a plan.' Presumably also to confess. Or at least to take care of Sophie and work herself up to it. Whatever, the girl had guts after my treatment of her. 'I'll be pottering.'

'Pottering? Not a word I associate with you, Mum?' She dug me in the ribs.

'Oh yes, potter here, potter there, that's me. Little known fact in this household, clearly.' I drew back with a smile. 'Think I've been neglecting our home of late, haven't I?'

My daughter did something then which she'd never done before, she pulled the crown of my head down to her lips and kissed it.

I was euphoric. 'So I'll be home all day if you need me.'

21

I had intended to visit Fred that bank holiday weekend, having left a diplomatic gap for him and his visiting daughter to bond, but of course I didn't make it round.

When I arrived at his house on the Monday morning, in some trepidation at meeting the woman, a key safe had been fitted to the wall beside his front door. That was quick. I knocked. No response, but he did answer his mobile.

'I'm in the garden. Do you have a key?'

I did, and I found him clipping his roses with a pair of pliers, a sight which tweaked my heart. I hugged him, both with affection and relief that his daughter was not home, and a delighted Fred held his pliers aloft, allowing my arms the full scope of his torso like hoops around a barrel. I pressed my face into his shirt savouring the scent of tobacco, happy to see him pottering about his garden as ever, despite the pliers.

I did yearn to tell him about Sophie, to offload my heart as I was by then wont to do, but this visit was about his welfare, so I took a seat and watched him tugging and twisting the stems, eventually resorting to snapping them with his fingers.

'Ouch,' he said. 'Damn thorns.'

At the risk of upsetting him I decided, on balance, to fetch his secateurs from the shed. 'Here, try these,' I said nonchalantly, swapping the tools over.

He frowned at the secateurs, then at the pliers, and turned back to his roses with a shrug. 'Now that's much better, thanks Anna.'

I sat back down. 'Where's Dougal?'

He looked around him, surprised not to see his dog on the lawn, and contemplated the question. 'I've a fancy he's out with Beth.'

'Ah. Coffee?'

'Love one, I'm parched.'

I was waiting for the kettle to boil when his daughter arrived home. Dog first, she strode into the kitchen, where I stood in a mild panic at the thought of being judged red-handed. Seeing me, she stopped short, while Dougal bounded on, jumping up and pushing me back against the work surface.

'What's happened to Dougal?' I cried.

The dog had been shorn.

'He needed a good clip.'

'But he looks like a normal dog now.'

'Precisely.'

In fact, he resembled a fox with an oversized rugby ball for a head.

'He's supposed to be long-haired, it's his breed.'

'It was unhealthy, all matted. If Father can't remember to groom him.'

That was rubbish, the dog had received more grooming at our house over the last week than a prize racehorse. Eager to console, I fondled his ears, while Fred's daughter and I took each other in.

A thin woman, she was as tall as me. Her hair was a shimmering mass, not left to grey but highlighted with various shades of silver, her nails were perfectly manicured (crimson naturally) and she wore a silk scarf patterned with horse paraphernalia, its Hermès logo carefully on show. I'd put her in her fifties, though she looked younger. French younger.

Aware that my gaze must have been semi hostile, I forced a smile; this woman held some power over Fred and it was crucial to keep her sweet.

'I'm Anna,' I said, holding out a hand.

'Elizabeth.' She took it.

Was that grip gauged to hurt? Did she mean to grind her rings against my fingers?

'I'm making Fred a coffee, would you like one?'

'Splendid idea, thank you.' She bent to remove Dougal's lead. 'Smelly dog. Go on, out to the garden with you.'

A soft kick with an out-turned calf and Dougal lolloped off, bald as a springtime sheep, leaving us alone in the kitchen. The woman washed her hands at the sink, dried them on a tea towel and slotted it neatly over the small radiator on the wall. Meticulous like Fred then. The kettle began to whistle so I busied myself with the drinks, sensing her weighing me up as I found the mugs.

'I can't thank you enough, Anna,' she began. 'My silly old father. What would he have done without you there?'

The *silly* rankled and I heard myself inhaling, like some cartoon bull about to charge. 'Your father is a very special man,' I said primly.

She scratched her neck, head tilted, considering me as if I was struggling to understand the facts.

'He is, isn't he?' she decided on finally. 'Shall we go and find him?'

Tray in hands, I followed her out to the garden, where Fred was taking a break, sitting with his sunglasses turned up to the sun. Dougal sat at his feet, and I wondered how he'd reacted to the shearing of his beloved pet. On the table sat pliers and secateurs, so I set the tray down and surreptitiously removed both tools to the shed, while Elizabeth dragged her chair and mug into the shade.

'You're enjoying that sunshine, Fred,' I said fondly, sitting down beside him.

'That I am.'

'It'll give you cancer,' said Elizabeth.

'Got to go somehow.' Fred still hadn't acknowledged his daughter's presence.

'Yes, well you very nearly did last week, didn't you, Father?'

'I'm still here. As are you, it seems.'

I hid my smirk behind a sip of coffee, elated to hear his brain still so sharp.

A young woman in a white medical coat appeared in the garden.

'Morning, Mr Wildsmith.'

Fred tipped his head from the sun to face her. 'Who are you?'

'I'm Sharon, one of your carers, duck, we've met a few times already.'

'Don't need anything, thank you, I can manage.'

She smiled warmly at him. 'I can see you're dressed, so no help needed there.'

'And I brushed my teeth too, nurse, all by myself.'

'I'll sort your medication, duck, and I'll leave you be.' Completely unfazed by Fred's infantile voice, the woman wandered back inside.

'That was rude, Father. You know these visits are necessary now.'

Fred was already soaking up the sun again. 'Don't need a nurse maid, thank you. Specially one who lets herself in. How *did* she get in?'

'For God's sake, they are here to help you.'

Fred raised his sunglasses and rested his eyes on his daughter. 'What happened to you, Beth? Where did this nasty streak come from? I never noticed it before your mother died, but was it always there?'

Silence. My heart began to thump. I would have welcomed Dougal as a prop, but Fred's need was greater, his fingers twisting what remained of the dog's fur.

'You never noticed me at all, Father.'

I took a furtive glance at the woman, her eyes glittering amidst a face which was now ashen, and I scalded my mouth in my haste to escape.

'I'll be off, Fred.' I placed my mug resolutely onto the tray. 'How about lunch in the park later in the week? We haven't celebrated your birthday yet.'

'Good luck if you can get him out.' Elizabeth was already on her feet, as if to shoo me off. 'Sadly I have to return home tomorrow.'

Both Fred and I seemed to sigh with relief at this news.

I bent to kiss his cheek. 'I'll call you.'

Righting myself, I caught a sneer on Elizabeth's face. 'How charming,' she said, and swung around to lead me inside the house.

On the way in we passed the carer, glass of water and plastic cup of drugs in her hand.

'I'm Anna,' I said to her retreating back. 'I'm a regular visitor…'

'Sharon,' she said, turning with a grateful smile.

At the front door, Elizabeth rested her forehead against the wooden panels, as if gathering her thoughts. Then she turned on me.

'Look, my father is going to have to go into a care home,

195

that much is clear.'

'Is it? I think he copes admirably on his own. For saying he has no family nearby.'

'This morning, he asked me five times what day of the week it was.'

'Well, he's a little disorientated after his stay in hospital.'

'Yesterday, I came back to find his lunch in the oven, burnt to a cinder. He'd completely forgotten about it.'

I shrugged. 'His memory's not as sharp as it was.'

'And he's constantly feeding the dog.'

'Maybe he does need some support around the house, I mean he is eighty-six now. That carer seems to have got the measure of him.'

She shook her head. 'The situation is not sustainable, his attitude towards her is abhorrent.'

'Understandable, I'd say, strangers letting themselves into your home, taking over.'

'He's had a stroke! And this is his second one.'

That I knew, of course, but still I fought her.

'He's had a TIA, a minor stroke. It's very common apparently, and there's unlikely to be lasting damage.'

'As you say, he *is* now eighty-six, and he must be sensible, do the right thing.'

I raised my chin. 'By whom?'

A step too far, and she glared at me then. 'Who are you anyway? What's my father to you?'

'He's become a dear friend, if you must know. I live around the corner, and I can take care of him.'

'What? Wash his bottom?'

'He can do that himself, you know full well, but I'll pop in every day.'

What was I saying? Ludicrously unfeasible, but I kept going.

'Your father does the crossword every day without fail, did you know that?'

She rolled her eyes. 'My father has now been diagnosed with vascular dementia.'

'And you've been trying to secure that diagnosis for a long time, haven't you?'

'The decision will be mine.' She looked me up and down. 'Not some busybody's.'

'If you put him in a home he'll go rapidly downhill, you know that.'

'I've visited several homes this weekend, all perfectly suitable.'

'*This* is his home!' I swept a hand at Fred's coat rack, the barometer, the clothes brush, and as if for effect the mantel clock began to strike eleven.

'The house is in my name. His decision, after Mother died. And, naturally, with the diagnosis I now have Power of Attorney.' She opened the front door and stood back with a Walter Raleigh flourish.

'Where's your heart, woman?' I stomped past her and left the house.

My hands were shaking on the wheel. I pulled out of Fred's drive and parked up a few houses down, aware that I needed to calm myself before driving on. Thankfully I hadn't actually sworn at the woman; Fred might well have suffered the fallout from such anger. I would have to play it carefully.

Once I was less agitated, I drove to Earl's Court, admittedly with a couple of near misses, and parked up outside the address Gabryel had given me. The Heathrow hotel was untenable, unless I were to play Lady Bountiful, we both knew that, so he had suggested we meet at his place. I'd been longing to see him again after Sophie's... Well, Sophie's what? Mishap? Accident? I thought again of my guilt at having been in bed with him oblivious to her knocking back the drugs, I saw that fawn, the crocodile, and I got out of the car and fed the meter. This man was a drug.

Finding myself at the grubby front door of a Victorian terrace, I scanned the name plate and realised I didn't know his surname. There was a G. Lupu, no other G, so I rang the bell, smiling at the sound of his voice as he answered. He buzzed me in and I took to the thinly carpeted stairs, slipping on what felt more like underlay until I reached the very top of the building.

At his doorway Gabryel awaited me, that burning look in his eyes. I hauled him to me, pouring my need into the frantic embrace, into my parallel universe where nothing of my real life would intrude, and he pulled me inside his studio apartment.

'Welcome to my den.'

Apt word for it, I thought, clocking the single bed set against one wall and covered with a dingy brown candlewick bedspread.

'Drink?'

'You must be joking.' I threw the door shut behind me, kicked off my shoes and whipped the summery cotton dress up and over my head.

I did have to smile at his own rush to get naked, such comedy about the way he yanked off his shoes, hopping on one foot, the way he fumbled at his jeans, while I took a running leap onto the bed and landed on a loose spring which speared my ribs.

'Ouch,' I said, laughing as Gabryel slid more carefully down beside me.

Nothing careful about what followed, however, as the bed

acknowledged with its brisk squeaks of protest.

'Do you know the person who lives below?' I asked as we lay on our backs afterwards, looking up through the skylight, the flat's only window, I realised.

'I believe that now it is he who knows me.'

Gabryel's body was half hanging off the side of the bed, so I rucked myself up onto an elbow and pushed myself back against the wall. He edged towards me, and for a fleeting moment I felt trapped against that wall, on his territory now, no longer mutual ground. With a glance at the candlewick bedspread I was transported back to my childhood bedroom, my own had been purple not brown, but how I'd loved to pluck at the tufts.

I smiled at him and took in the sparsely furnished room. 'So this is your den.'

The same thin grey underlay, no rug, a table with two wooden chairs, and a water heater suspended above a tiny sink. On top of a small fridge sat an empty wine bottle, a candle stuck in its neck, and hanging from the ceiling was that ubiquitous white spherical paper lampshade I'd had in my digs at uni. There was just one door, which I assumed led to his bathroom, and on the back of it Gabryel had sellotaped a film poster, *The Wolf of Wall Street*. Memories of my own teenage posters floated to the fore – and with them the tiniest sliver of disdain for such a childish act.

'That is my goal,' he said, nodding at Leonardo di Caprio's glowing face. 'To earn lot of money.'

I nodded with a kind smile, should I let on that the man had ended up in prison? Best not. I kissed him again.

'Drink now?' he said.

'Please.'

He padded over to the fridge, the carpet buckling beneath

his bare feet, and retrieved a bottle. An overly tart Chilean Sauvignon Blanc, I saw from its label.

'Driving, so a small one for me,' I said, watching him fill two tumblers.

'Up yours,' I said as we clinked glasses.

'Up yours.' He smiled.

After a tiny sip I kneeled my way towards the foot of the bed and placed the glass on the floor. I turned to see him watching me, that desire in his eyes again, and the familiar thrill skittered. He fell to his knees on the carpet and held his hands out to me, grasping my haunches as I too knelt down, back to him, face buried in the bedspread. I turned my cheek from its fusty scent.

'Like animals,' I said, bracing my body.

'I am an animal,' he whispered in my ear. 'My name is Lupu, which in my language means wolf. And I am hungry for you.'

A hungry wolf? Did I find this cheesy? Well, given the height of my arousal, not in the slightest. And as Gabryel let out a mini howl and his teeth gnashed at my neck I was all for being eaten. By the *Wolf of Wall Street*, as I joked afterwards.

That evening, Ollie and I met up with Scar and Alex at High Road Brasserie. Exhausted by the events of the past few days, I had considered backing out, but Scar and I needed to patch things up, and I was relieved to have no depth of focus but the evening ahead. More of an inability to process thoughts than a compartmentalisation.

'Keys in,' said Alex, referring to our loyalty keyrings which conferred a hefty discount on Mondays.

This gave him the chance to slink an arm about me, to wiggle us around a bit. So I dropped my keyring onto the table and allowed myself to be wiggled, while Scar and Ollie rolled their eyes and pecked cheeks as they always did.

'Sorry about last Monday, Scar,' I said, settling myself onto the velvet bench beside her.

'No worries,' she said coolly. No mention of Fred's stroke and that smarted.

I distracted myself by texting Sophie, basking in the single heart emoji which bounced back, she had another friend round: pizza, coke, Netflix and the run of the house.

A prosecco glass appeared, a waiter pouring the most welcome bubbles, and I relaxed.

'So what's new?' Alex leant towards me, his scent of metrosexual origin drifting.

'Not much,' said Ollie, and we shared a diagonal glance, having agreed not to discuss *Reading* as we were calling it.

When I reached for my glass, however, the comedy of his words hit home, because a more eventful week had not transpired in the whole of my life. I let out a snigger and with it a fine spray of fizz, coughing to give myself time.

'We had a dog living with us,' is what I came up with.

Ollie took his cue. 'Should have seen it guys, Anna the dog whisperer.'

'Whose dog?' said Scar.

'Fred's,' I said tightly.

'Oh, *Fred's*? The old codger.'

I threw her a quizzical frown. 'Yeah, he's had a stroke, remember? So we were looking after his pet.'

She nodded, reached to prick an olive with a cocktail stick.

'What kind of dog?' said Alex, drawing my eyes back to his.

'A Lhasa Apso.' I sank my prosecco and reached for the bottle in the ice bucket. 'Called Dougal.'

He laughed. 'Like the dog from the *Magic Roundabout*?'

'Yep. Looks just like him too. Well he did, he's recently been shorn, bald as a coot right now.'

I held forth about Dougal's haircut, masking the sour mood, while I continued topping us all up. Eventually I raised the empty bottle at the waiter for a second one.

'But it'll grow back,' I finished with a reassuring shrug.

'Glad to hear it.' Alex glanced up from his menu with a sardonic roll of his eyes. 'Any other riveting news?'

'What about you guys?' Ollie jumped in. 'What bands have you seen lately?'

'The Killers,' said Scar, eyes on her menu.

'Let's order,' said Alex, tossing down his own with a scowl for his wife.

At home later, Ollie suggested a final glass outside.

While he found a bottle from his cellar I sat at our garden table and closed my eyes, allowing the day to wash over me. Lately my mind had been chattering not only with thoughts and worries but endless dazzling images, and that day it had banked a veritable feast.

'Sophie OK?' I asked, as he stepped outside.

'In her element.'

'Have you also had a chance to chat with her now?'

'About *Reading*?' He nodded. 'Didn't let on that I knew about Jack.'

'Good.'

'Deceitful little shit.'

'Wish he'd never walked through our front door.'

Ollie pulled out the cork and sniffed it. 'But then. So was I,' he said.

'What?'

'Look. I know that we're back on an even keel, Anna, but I feel the need for closure.'

I squirmed beneath his words, that intense look. 'It's fine. Really. Doesn't matter anymore.'

'Absolutely,' he said, pouring the wine. 'I can see you're happy again, you seem to have found your vocation with Fred. I reckon voluntary work could be the way forward, don't you?'

Such audacity, and he knew I'd been working on starting my own business.

'But I just wanted to get the affair off my chest and behind us for good.'

I shook my head. 'Water under the bridge, Ol, let's let sleeping dogs lie.'

What other metaphors could I mix in my panic to shut him up?

'It's done and dusted.'

Well there was another one.

'As long as you didn't sleep with her in our bed, or anything awful like that,' I laughed.

'Well, no, but,' he paused and glanced away. 'I did take her to France.'

'To our *house*?'

'But we used the guest room.' His palms fluttered to lessen his guilt.

'To *our* holiday home? In *France*?'

The bastard, that hurt.

Ollie began swirling his wine and we both watched the streaks appearing inside the glass, the legs as he called them. When had he been in France? Must have been that buying tour over Valentine's Day, and he'd left me a card too, sent flowers even. My own deceit paled in comparison.

I sipped my own wine, tipped my head back and looked up at the moon, full now but still pale in the darkening sky, and I processed the impact of his news.

'OK,' I said finally. 'Let's put it behind us, shall we?'
He stopped twirling the glass and smiled hopefully.
'Absolutely. And thank you. For being so understanding.'
I smiled back at him. 'Let's move on.'

22

The last week of the summer holidays slipped away smoothly enough. Sophie seemed to have bounced back well after *Reading* and was happily hanging out with various friends. The resilience of youth, it could not have been more striking, whereas I was still plagued by cataclysmic dreams of me saving her. Usually from falling – slipping off a cliff, tripping from a skyscraper, tumbling from a plane.

I packed the fridge with her favourite fresh foods, and spent mother-daughter time, including a trip to IKEA where I treated her to a raft of bits for her bedroom. Anything for my daughter. In a spectacular feat of compartmentalising, I also bought a lilac sheepskin rug for Gabryel's flat, fibbing to her that it would look nice in the guest room, a place where she rarely ventured.

I longed to tell Fred about all that had happened to Sophie, but his life had slowed, in every dimension, and he no longer showed the slightest curiosity about her – or me. I missed the balm of his concern. That week, I found time for him most days, mowing his lawn, brushing Dougal to stimulate fur growth and busying myself with jobs in his house. While I too had caught Fred over-feeding Dougal, forgetting his own meals in the oven, and one day had even found his pipe in the fridge, I was determined to keep him buoyant. Having silently secreted the pipe to its home on the sideboard, I pretended to us all, including his carer, Sharon, that everything was under control.

However, the poster on the wall of that Asian doctor's office had never left me. I had been delving online into products for those living with dementia (the *living with* rather than *suffering from* was an important distinction, I'd learnt) and with each foray I was experiencing a peculiar mix of emotions. Excitement. Respect. Compassion. From the vast range of ideas on offer, for Fred's birthday I had chosen a jigsaw, a simple 1950s dance scene, with just sixty three pieces. I returned to the websites, astonished both by the array of challenges that might await my dear friend down the line, and the innovative products that could help him cope. A business idea was forming.

That week I also took myself off regularly to Gabryel's lair, as I was now calling it, feigning attendance at a workshop I'd sourced online: *Motivational Skills for Women*. I'd even printed off the programme, hole-punched it for a lever arch file, which I touted at home and added to daily. A flamboyant alibi. In the face of Ollie's revelation my deceit was blossoming. Guilt about the affair per se had still barely featured. I was stepping not through the wardrobe but through the stars, for another galaxy. The state of Gabryel's flat alone was so alien to my own home, or that of my milieu, and it carried me back to a time when I too had been a poor student, not only in its sparseness, but also in the feelings it engendered: carefree, fancy free. Just, well, *free*.

One day, I arrived with the lilac sheepskin rug.

'So the lady wants to transform our lair into our home.' Gabryel slid his arms around me as I laid it down beside his bed.

'No, I simply want to save our knees from rubbing raw on your bloody carpet!'

Sadly, he didn't share in my laughter. My fantasy of building a new life with him still glowed magically, but it would not comprise living in that dump; I had my dad's shares, half the house, savings from a lucrative, albeit short banking career.

The fusty candlewick bedspread I also tackled, taking it home to wash. And that was a colossal mistake. The presence of this brown eyesore in my washing machine, creating a sudden overlap between the Venn spheres of my lives, caused me all manner of grief. That these two worlds might even collide. Once clean, I'd bundled it at the bottom of our linen cupboard before then smuggling it out of the house, chest thumping. It had taken me an age to clear the fluff from the barrel too. Never again.

With this gesture I believe I had also hurt him. Perhaps he felt reproached for lacking domestic hygiene and sought to regroup, because he invited me out for dinner, and then on to the Tom Tom Club where his prowess would be restored. But surely this relationship was beyond power plays? Ours was a stripped-down beast of lust and hunger. Nonetheless, I too was keen to revisit a display of his talent, to witness the reverence of an adoring crowd, to return to where it had all begun.

On the Friday evening, having arranged to meet him in Soho, I came downstairs in a new dress of cobalt blue.

'You're wearing *that?*' Sophie gaped at me as I entered the living room where she was watching TV with Ollie.

I glanced down at the shift dress which stopped well above the knee, and beamed. 'And why not? It's been a fabulous few days at this motivational workshop and I'm feeling all motivated and ready to shine for my new sisters at the final motivational dinner.'

'It's too young for you.' That po face. 'And your make-up, Gothic went out with the Stone Age.'

I gazed at my daughter, unable to mask the hurt in my eyes

207

– after all we'd just been through together.

Ollie, however, smiled with an appreciative once-over. 'Out all week and now dressed to kill, any other husband might think you're having an affair.'

Clearly, my suggestion that we *move on* had brightened his life.

I tapped the side of my nose at him. 'Women dress for other women, you know that.' Unable to sustain the eye contact, I cocked my head at Sophie. 'And you, madam, will soon discover that too, if you haven't already.'

Before leaving, I did nip into the downstairs loo and dab at, what I had considered to be, my smoky eyes. The shift dress, however, was staying put, even if on the Tube it ruched itself up my thighs, provoking the odd glance or two. Was I mutton dressed as lamb? I hoped Gabryel wouldn't think so.

We met inside a small tourist bistro. He was waiting at a table in the far back corner, and his eyes shone, a reassuring whistle at the dress as he stood and kissed my cheek with a covert brush of my breast. I blushed, thrilled by his hunger, and half wished we'd met at his flat instead.

I sat down, nodding at the saxophone on the chair beside him. 'You've brought your friend, then?'

'We will both enjoy entertaining you later.' He patted the case. 'Glass of wine? It is a good one.'

A bottle of Retsina sat open on the table. My heart sank as he poured for me but I clinked glasses with a warm smile.

'Up yours,' he said.

'Up yours.' I took a sip.

Yep, just as I remembered it.

I reached for the menu. '*Bistro Blue*, what a lovely name.'

'You belong perfectly here.'

I laughed, I did blend in with the walls of Greek blue.

'You know the meaning of Bistro?' he asked.

'Nope.'

'It is a Russian word, meaning fast.'

'Russian?'

He nodded. 'Speedy, quick.'

'You speak Russian?'

'Da.' He smiled. 'My mother's family is of Slav origin. Moldova once belonged to the Soviet Union.'

I visualised monolithic grey blocks, tanks and vast public squares of marching soldiers. Why was he highlighting his foreignness?

In a bid to lighten him, I mustered a sexy smile. 'So you're Russian?'

'Ethnically half Russian, yes. Most Moldovans look more like Romanians, dark hair not blond.'

Well, mousy. The thought was out, chastising me, but this date was not how I had imagined it. Did he want me to get to know him? Is that what I also wanted? Sex is what I wanted. Another sip of the Retsina and I longed to be beamed up to his den or the Heathrow hotel. Where could we go to gorge ourselves on sex? Without having it cut short by his work, or by my family? Well, I knew just the place, didn't I?

We ordered his favourite dishes, sharing plates of calamari, hummus, vine leaves, haloumi, and the waiter left us alone.

'So,' I said, keen to reveal my sudden plan before I might have time to reconsider, 'how would you like to spend a few days in France with me?'

I arrived home after midnight, showered, and slid into bed beside a snoring Ollie. Unable to sleep, my ears still smarting from the bass and my core still smarting from Gabryel after our brief descent to the beer cellar, I began to plan France. I'd told him about our farmhouse, the pool, the way the light spilled pink at sunset. He said he'd never been before, that it might be difficult for him to obtain a visa.

That, I had not even considered. I'd Googled it while he performed at the Tom Tom, and discovered that Moldovan citizens no longer required a visa for France.

'Zip-A-Dee-Doo-Dah!' I cried when he jumped off the stage after his first set.

'Zipadee…?' he laughed. 'This is new English word for me.'

'It means we're going to France.'

Lying in bed, hands splayed behind my head, I actually chuckled to myself in anticipation. A brief glance at Ollie, his messy hair, and again I felt cross at having been conned by him so royally. Let's move on, I'd said. Well I could dupe too. There must surely be some term, possibly in a foreign language, for the joy in secretly cheating back on a cheat without them ever knowing about it. A sly smile and I rolled over and found sleep.

Late the following morning, I sat with a coffee at the island. Beside me, splayed prominently, a sheaf of glossy documents extracted from my bogus file awaited Ollie's entrance. Sheets peppered with photos of shiny happy women with headings such as, *Who is the Real You?*

After booking flights for France with the new email address I'd concocted, I began yet again trawling the internet for dementia products. Exhilarated to discover a simple gadget which would remind Fred when Dougal had been fed, I then found yet another to locate his lost keys. To launch a business selling such compassionate products, to make a difference to the lives of people like Fred, well it would nourish my soul, but there were already so many companies out there, so many devices, that it must surely be a saturated market. No room for new invention even if I had been at all creative.

Mulling it over, I jabbed away the irritating pop-up screens, but then my eyes snagged on one of the adverts – for music therapy. I clicked through to the site, where a cornucopia of activities reeled itself out on screen, not only music, but art and animal therapy, singalongs, re-enactments. A whole world of pursuits to stimulate people living with dementia.

Ollie ambled into the kitchen, mobile phone at his ear. His deputy manned the shop whenever Man Utd were playing a London team and I caught half a conversation about a delivery of Montrachet. I reached theatrically for the sheet headed, *Communicate your Passion to the World*, frowning in fake concentration, while Ollie picked up, *Who is the Real You?* A cursory glance and he gave it a nod of appreciation.

'Right.' He hung up and tossed the sheet down. 'I'm off then.'

Sophie appeared in the kitchen. 'Me too.'

Turning to her, both Ollie and I did a double take; a skirt which skimmed her bottom, tights with ladders you could climb up, and a top that must surely have been a bra.

'You are not going anywhere dressed like that!' I cried.

Mock astonishment, followed by a downwards sweep of those wide blue eyes which hardened as they rose again to mine. 'Like what?'

'Like a tart. Go and change.'

'Oh, so it's OK for you to go out looking like a tart…'

My gasp prompted Ollie to wade in, clearly wishing he'd left a minute earlier. 'Come on, Soph.'

'All my mates are wearing this gear.'

'Where are you going?' I said.

She dipped her eyes, a defiant shrug. 'Up town.'

'Where exactly?'

'*Up* town! Just back off, will you? I'm sixteen now!'

'Yes you are, just sixteen and –'

'And I can do what I like.'

'Not while you're still under my roof.'

Really? My mother's words verbatim. I can't have been much more than sixteen myself.

'Soph, just change your top, yes?' Ollie turned his palms up at me and I shrugged, but Sophie was already taking defiant steps away, then she ran and the front door slammed.

Ollie looked at me aghast. 'What the…?'

'Fuck,' I finished, feeling the blood drain from my face – and I had thought we were close again.

My hands shook as I gathered the sheets of paper, tapped them together and slotted them into their folder. But then had I really needed to speak to her just as my own mother would have done? Mum had once called *me* a tart too, and the memory still stung; the heft of a mother's criticism.

'Might be latish.' Ollie kissed the side of my forehead, and with palpable relief he too left the house.

In the ensuing silence, I gazed around the kitchen. Hollow since Jack. He had infused our house, the charm, the jokes, the buzz with Sophie, and now that he'd gone we'd fallen into an even greater abyss than before. I longed for all of that life back. And yet I despised him. Exclusive? I now knew what that meant, and in my day there was no such nonsense, if you were boyfriend and girlfriend there were no declarations, you simply did not screw around.

I picked up Horace, set him down on the island for company, and we eyed each other intensely. 'You wouldn't do that, would you, Horace?'

Jack the lad. When I look back now, of course, I realise that it was easier to nurture such hatred towards a sixteen year old

212

boy than it would have been to take a good hard look at our family, but I attributed all our woes to him.

My phone rang. A Facetime call.

'Mum?' I said, answering it; speak of the devil. 'You've got yourself an I-phone?'

'Aw hello, Anna.' She was frowning down her nose. 'Wayne bought it for me.'

'I was just thinking about you.'

'Just as well because I've booked our flights for Christmas.'

'Already?'

'Heck, they were pricey.'

'When for?'

'Monday third of December. Cheapest deal going.'

'Great!' My heart sank; weeks before the day itself. And she sensed the lie.

'"Course, we'll be travelling about a bit first, Wayne wants to see Scotland.'

'You'll spend a good length of time with us, though?'

Would *us* still be *us* come December?

'Aw, yes.'

We smiled at each other, a few moments too long.

'Everything rosy, Anna?'

I nodded, then sighed. 'Mum? Was I a problem teenager?'

She laughed. 'Hope so. Only way a child can detach from its mother, full on rebellion.'

This was news to me. My recollection was of a mother I'd never been close enough with to detach myself from.

'Why? You having problems with young Sophie?'

I allowed her an imperceptible nod and her face softened.

'It's a tough time for you both, hon. My advice would be to turn a blind eye. That's what I did.'

The *hon* felt good. 'Blind eye? You don't have the foggiest

213

what I got up to…'

'Aw, like the time you had sex with Matt McGarvey on the living room floor?'

'You knew about *that*?'

'And a hell of a lot more.'

We both laughed.

'We might just have to get to the bottom of this,' I said.

'It's high time I came over.'

'I'll stock up on the port. Bye Mum.' I blew her a kiss, and she disappeared.

The kitchen fell silent once more. Staring at Horace, I sat straining for memories of times with my mother. Since Sophie's drive for independence, I'd been dredging my mind, but had found no more to add to the paltry pile I'd consigned for preservation years ago. And that troubled me, because increasingly I was aware that Mum must have invested so much of herself in me, just as I had done in Sophie – but I could remember none of it. What if Sophie grew up oblivious to my love and care, to her own mother's devotion? What if all she would recall was our conflict?

I felt suddenly alone, abandoned by my family. A couple of empty hours loomed before I was due at Fred's that afternoon, so I texted Gabryel, *Are you in the lair?* Within half an hour I was in his bed, needy, and needed.

'OK, Fred, three down. Used to make stockings, five letters, beginning with N.'

Silence. Legs crossed, he was sitting in his favourite garden chair, popping at his pipe. At his feet Dougal was asleep on his back, legs akimbo. *Nylon*, I urged silently.

'Think of your wife when you were courting. I bet she wore stockings?'

An hour in and we were struggling, even with my prompts, but having read that a simple crossword was good for brain muscle, I persevered. I now knew, however, that cryptic crosswords would only confuse and frustrate a person with dementia because of the lateral thinking involved, so those beauties belonged to our past.

'Aha!' He raised an index finger, flicked it in triumph. 'Nylon.'

'Yes! Brilliant.' I laid down the newspaper for a few moments of respite and smiled at him. 'You look totally chilled, Fred.'

He smiled back. 'While you're here, would you help me with my bank statement, Anna?'

'Of course.'

'Only there are a couple of items niggling me.'

Amidst the fug, he seemed to have remained lucid about his personal admin and I found the statement easily in the sideboard where he kept all his papers.

'See here,' he said pointing, 'and here. I've a fancy I must have withdrawn cash to buy something, but I can't for the life of me recall what it was.'

I scanned the statement. Two withdrawals of £500 each during the month of August, made exactly two days apart. I broke out in a chilling sweat, Elizabeth had Power of Attorney.

'Do you think you might have withdrawn bits and pieces and stashed them around the house?'

Bemused, he gazed at my bright smile and produced deep furrows at his brow in a display of extra hard concentration, helping me out. The sight plucked my heart and I squeezed his hand to spur him on.

'Don't think so,' he said finally.

'Well, if you like, we can go to your bank on Monday and

check it out.'

'Thank you, if you have time, Anna. I'm sure there's some explanation, but my memory's gone out the door.'

He smiled at me, knowingly, as if in a rare moment of clarity he'd realised what was happening to his mind.

'I've always got time for you, Fred. I'll make an appointment now.'

Early that evening, I returned home to find the house still empty. Ollie would have lingered in the pub with his mates after the match and, as for Sophie, she had not checked in all day, which was fair enough given our spat. It would still be light for a couple of hours and, as she'd said, she was sixteen now, could legally marry. Yet the sensation of wanting her home and safe began to prickle.

I sank into the sofa with a large glass of white wine and flicked through Netflix, until I found *Just Alice*, a film about dementia. On Monday morning, I would distract Fred somehow and ask the bank manager to explain just how this Power of Attorney malarkey worked. I'd found the official document in his sideboard and would prepare myself in advance; was his daughter really able to withdraw cash from his bank account? With one eye on the time, I settled back to watch the film.

A good hour in, I heard a key in the front door. It slammed, Sophie ran up the stairs and I sighed; she was still angry, whereas I myself was not at all. Pausing the film, I emerged to refill my glass and listened at the foot of the stairs; she was in her room, door shut, but I'd give her space.

When the film had finished, I was overcome by the unfailing love of the woman's daughter who cares for her when she is lost to the disease of dementia. I hauled myself up from the sofa, downed my glass and took to the stairs. After all I was the adult here.

A tentative knock on her bedroom door. 'Hi.'

I heard her thump from bed to floor and the door opened. 'Yeah?' Her eyes shone.

'Jesus Christ!' I clamped a palm to my mouth.

'What?' she said, thrusting out her chin.

And with it her nose, one side of which had been pierced with a silver hoop, large enough to hold a set of keys.

23

I couldn't stop staring at her violated nose. Normally small and snub, it was now mutant, encrusted with apparatus.

Ollie was particularly pissed off. 'You look like a bull being led off to market,' he cried the next morning. 'To the meat market!'

Harsh, I thought, as she screamed at him and flounced off to her bedroom. Impossible to turn a blind eye as my mother had advised, however, because the hoop hanging off her snared the eye.

'Sorry about Dad,' I tried later, with a soft knock at her door, mug of herbal tea in hand. The gap widened and I snuck in, sat down on her bed. 'Think it's just the shock. He'll come round, I already have.'

She sat down beside me and took the tea, weighing my words for sincerity.

'Everyone's got them.'

'I know, I've been looking online. Could have been worse, could have been through your septum. Those girls do look like bulls with nose rings.'

I was rewarded with a soft smile.

'I'll have to put a stud in for school.'

'I'll buy you a tiny green peridot for Christmas.'

'My birthstone?'

'Or a diamond even, make it really sparkle.'

'Thanks, Mum.' Her finger sought out the hoop and twizzled it.

I relaxed, deemed it safe to step further in.

'So how are you doing now? After Jack?'

An instant scowl. 'What's that got to do with you?'

I balked, hands up in surrender. 'Sorry, just thought you might want to talk about it.'

'Well I don't.' She stood up, slammed her mug down onto her desk, and yanked on her headphones.

My cue to leave then. It was Sunday, too tricky to slip off to the lair, but how I wished I could have escaped my family that day.

At the bank, Fred and I joined the queue, unbuttoning our coats against the stuffy air. Catching a drift of stale sweat, I took a covert sniff of my armpit, was I *so* nervous about this meeting? A furtive breath at Fred and I realised that it was he who stank.

'Anything wrong?' He must have clocked my astonishment.

'No Fred. All good.'

I was beside myself; the man was no longer looking after himself and didn't even realise it. In that moment it dawned on me that a care home would soon be a reality, even if I would continue to refute the prospect.

'Why are we here again?' he asked.

'Just for a chat.'

Was I right to patronise him? However protective my motive.

'What day is it?' The third time he'd asked that morning.

'Monday. Pension day, we've just been to collect it. Remember?' I winced; the one question you should never ask of a person with dementia.

The clerk who invited us into one of the private booths was bearded but still burdened by acne. I passed him the statement, attempting to speak in code about the two withdrawals.

'Fred doesn't recall taking this money out.' I flashed my eyes wildly.

Frowning at my odd histrionics, he brought up the account on his screen. 'A further withdrawal of £500 was executed last week. Have you been abroad on holiday, Mr Wildsmith?'

Fred looked at me in surprise. 'Have I?'

'Mm, not sure.'

The man contemplated Fred, while I decided finally on a coughing fit.

'Sorry, may I have a glass of water.' I stood and beckoned him outside the booth, lowering my voice to a hiss. 'The money has been stolen by his daughter. He has no idea. He's already had two strokes and this stress could bring on another one.'

'I see.' He threw a concerned glance at Fred's tapping foot which extruded from the booth. 'His daughter has Power of Attorney?'

'Yes.' I pulled out the document. 'She's allowed to withdraw money for his benefit, but she's taken this lot out for herself. Which is illegal, isn't it? Would you cancel her debit card? Please?'

'And who are you?'

'I volunteer for a charity, Old Friends.' I showed him my badge, which he scanned with a shrug of the mouth.

'How do I know that you yourself are not coercing Mr Wildsmith? He's clearly lacking in mental capacity.'

'Just ask him if his daughter has withdrawn all this money for his benefit, he'll tell you himself.'

Back in the booth the man beamed at Fred, who regarded

us both with suspicion.

'So, Mr Wildsmith, you don't recall making these withdrawals?'

'Withdrawals?'

'Two in the UK, which are marked on your statement, and last week a further £500 from an ATM abroad.'

Fred's face darkened; there was no avoiding it.

'Elizabeth has Power of Attorney, doesn't she?' I said gently.

He looked at me blankly. 'Does she?'

'And she has a debit card for your account.' I reached for his hand. 'I think she might have drawn the money out.'

'Strike a light.'

'You can have the card stopped, Fred.'

'Stop it. Yes, stop it,' he cried, and my heart crunched. 'This account is in my name not hers.'

The man looked from him to me, weighing us up, and then consulted his computer.

'Well, Sir, I can see that the account does remain in your name, which means that I may indeed take your instructions.' A few clicks of the mouse and his hands flew across his keyboard. 'There we go, that particular debit card is cancelled.'

'Thank you. Wonderful. Let's go home, Fred.'

The man stood up. 'You should discuss the POA with your daughter, Sir, if you wish to reduce her powers, however.'

He reached out to shake Fred's hand, his eyes softening to a sympathetic smile, and said, 'My gran has dementia.'

Spoken in all kindness, but Fred turned to me, his face crumpling.

'Dementia?'

On our silent drive back to his house, Fred sat wringing his hands. Once home, he slumped into his armchair, beckoned Dougal onto his lap and wrapped his arms around the dog. I left him with the succour of wet tongue in face, and made us both a coffee, pouring a generous tot of whiskey into his, then I knelt down before him and rummaged for words.

It was Fred who spoke first. 'Have I got dementia?'

'We don't know that, Fred. Nobody has said anything,' I lied. 'Just that your memory's not so good, right now, is it?'

'No.' He gazed worriedly up at the ceiling, as if searching for an elusive answer to an unknown question.

'Am I going in a home? Beth said I'd have to go in a home if I got dementia.'

'No.' I squeezed his hand.

I was fumbling for more reassurance when Sharon let herself in and Dougal rushed barking to the front door.

Fred raised his hand in a stop sign. 'Don't need anything, thank you.'

'Morning, Fred.' She nodded at me. 'Shall we get you showered, duck?'

'I've showered myself already. Every single day, without fail. You mustn't give in.'

I made a sorrowful face at Sharon, who nodded, equally sad.

'Can I borrow Anna for a sec? Could do with a hand to make your bed, Fred.'

He grunted, took a hefty sip of his Irish coffee and sank back, closing his eyes on the morning.

Upstairs, Sharon opened the bedroom window against the rich smell.

'He won't let me near him,' she said. 'He's festering. It's not only a matter of personal hygiene, you know, it's potentially dangerous for him. If he's cut and it becomes infected then we're heading for trouble.'

I slumped onto the bed. 'It's possible that he really is showering himself occasionally?'

She rolled her eyes at me in response.

'But he's always been so meticulous. This thing only happened two weeks ago. How can it have had such a massive impact on him? He's a changed man.'

She sat down beside me with a sigh. 'Vascular dementia, Anna. With a stroke, blood is lost to the brain and the damage can be instant. My guess is he's had a series of these mini strokes, sometimes it's not obvious, and what with him living alone.'

I nodded. How many websites had I trawled over the past fortnight?

'It'll kill him if he goes into a home.'

'Sometimes they perk up with the company.'

'What about the dog? Dougal's his lifeline.'

'Doubtful they'll take a dog. He could visit, though.'

'But can't we give it a go? You and I? He's stubborn, I know, but between us can we try and keep him here in his own home? There are so many gadgets out there to help him.'

'And he seems to have acquired most of them.' She smiled. 'It's you who's been on that spending spree is it? Shame he hasn't got you for a daughter, rather than that Cruella de Vil.'

'Yeah, bet she made a coat out of Dougal's fur.'

We both laughed.

'She'll be back. We might have until then.' Sharon stood, walked around the bed and took hold of the duvet. 'Here grab this, will you?'

I took my end and shook.

'Because it'll be her who makes the decision, duck, not me.' We locked eyes as the duvet floated back onto the bed. 'And certainly not you.'

The jungle drums beat across the Channel within a matter of days. Must have been when she next came to use the debit card and found it defunct.

I was lying post-coital in Gabryel's single bed when she rang. Ollie was having a busy September, as always, supplying wine for the Chiswick Book Festival, judging at the Chiswick House Dog Show, all those pillar of the community roles he relished, and that month I had found greater freedom than ever to visit the lair.

I did consider ignoring Elizabeth's call, but feared she might harangue Fred if I refused to absorb her sting myself, so I reached for my phone.

'Elizabeth. What a lovely surprise.'

This panache was partly for Gabryel's benefit.

'Anna.' She paused.

'Elizabeth,' I repeated, I would never call the woman Beth.

'You have no right to mell.'

Mell? Surely she meant *meddle*? I realised she was slurring and glanced at the clock. Only 10am, albeit an hour later in France.

'Meddle?' I echoed, with perfect diction.

'Yes, meddle.'

I smiled but remained silent. As did she. I heard the scrape of a chair on tiles as she sat down, the dull thud of a glass on wood, and I visualised her in some vast farmhouse, honeyed in summer, frigid in winter.

Gabryel rolled off the bed and padded into the bathroom, closing the door behind him. I contemplated his *Wolf of Wall Street* poster, the empty wine bottle with its candle, and again it occurred to me that Scar would make some sarcastic remark about both. I had done well to keep this affair to myself and would never divulge it to her. After her snappy text in the park that morning, and her coldness at our recent dinner, I had made a supreme effort to meet up with her again on a couple of Mondays, but she was unpredictable these days in a way I couldn't pin down. Aloof somehow.

Finally, Elizabeth spoke. 'I'd rather you kept out of our private affairs. My father agreed for me to have Power of Attorney several years ago, and naturally it was activated after the dementia diagnosis.'

I heard the shower running, a sign for me to join Gabryel there after the call, so I hurried it along.

'You are a thief, Elizabeth. Your father did not intend for you to filch from his bank account.'

She sighed. 'Do you know anything about my childhood?'

'Oh, spare me! Your father had a brilliant career at the United Nations. He has gravitas, clearly none of which has rubbed off on you.'

'Yes, he was at the UN. And I was packed off to boarding school.'

'My heart bleeds…'

'When I was six.'

That did pull me up a beat. 'And where was your mother?'

'With him. Living it up, life of Reilly, both of them. He even owned a smoking jacket, can you picture that?'

I could actually, Fred in a smoking jacket, and I allowed myself an indulgent smile.

She seemed to feel it. 'Oh, you like that image, do you?'

'Why are you telling me this? I don't give a toss about you, I only care about Fred.'

Gabryel threw the bathroom door open and stood naked amidst a rush of steam, arms out, legs apart, his body dripping. I threw him a wicked grin, a hushing finger at my lips.

'Listen,' I said to the woman. 'Fred is coping exceedingly

well at home and that's where he wants to be. Sharon is a marvel. If you try and dump him in a care home, you'll have me to contend with. I'll make damn sure that social services are crystal clear on your motive.'

Gabryel frowned at me in fascination and dropped his arms to his side. A wink brought him over to the bed, where he dropped to his knees and nuzzled my stomach; I'd long since stopped sucking it in.

'Pretty speech, Anna. It's a matter of time, that's all.'

'I'll fight you,' I said tightly, Gabryel's lips now trailing downwards.

'How tedious.' And she hung up on me.

24

I watched Gabryel padding around the kitchen of our French farmhouse. Butt naked.

'A backside like marble,' I said, as he opened the fridge in the corner.

He turned to me with questioning frown. 'A backside?'

'Your arse, it's like marble. They used to say that about some footballer, it's a compliment.'

He removed a lettuce from the fridge, wandered over to the battered oak table and bent to kiss me.

'My backside, as you call it, is not hard like marble, but my cock will soon be.'

True to his word, there it was. Day three of our holiday and, if I'm honest, there had been so much sex I was beginning to tire of it.

'I'm hungry, let's eat,' I said.

While Gabryel was perfectly at ease with his nakedness, I wore a sarong over my bikini as we ate our prawn cocktail, a ragged concoction he'd thrown together of leaves, avocado and prawns the size of my thumb. It boded well, but then he'd gone and doused the lot in tomato ketchup.

'It's good?' he asked.

'Delish.'

He sucked the tail shell off a prawn, leaving a smear of

ketchup at his lips.

'My Grandmother taught me cooking. She raised me, you see. It is quite common in Moldova, the parents find work in the city and leave their children in the countryside.'

I nodded, without the faintest curiosity to hear more, and was struck then by a sudden realization, hitherto buried deep beneath the tiers of sexual yearning – that our bodies were in communion, but our minds were far from aligned. Our values too. How had I'd become so embroiled with this man?

He absorbed my nod with one of his own, deciding not to offer more, and we lapsed into yet another silence.

Often these pauses lasted so long they were beginning to echo. As this one lingered, the sudden sense of panic at having invited him to France saw me probing my careful preparations yet again. The housekeeper I'd called from London to ensure she wouldn't pop up to water the garden; the pool man I'd dealt with on arrival, secreting Gabryel in the house while he topped up the chemicals; we were not overlooked, and came and went with a jaunty confidence, as if he were a family friend.

'We could have dinner in the harbour tonight,' I said finally, pushing my bowl away.

And eat some decent food.

'I would like that.' He smiled and wiped his mouth with the back of his hand, even though I'd laid out paper napkins and modelled their usage.

He stood and reached for my hand; the guest bedroom beckoned yet again.

Later that afternoon, we lay side by side on sunbeds by the pool, headphones on, but I was unable to relax. With his determination to remain naked, Gabryel's white body was now striped red with random sunburn, and he had finally donned a pair of swim shorts he'd found in the guest room. Jack must have left them behind, and I'd watched with gritted teeth as my lover had slipped them on. An even more shocking discovery, however, had been the bumper box of condoms. Gabryel had held this aloft, trophy-like, counting out the remaining foil packets.

'Six extra times!'

They must also have been Jack's. For use on my daughter. And I'd flinched at the sight, could focus only on the eighteen bloody condoms that were no longer in the box. I'd moved us then out of the guest room and into the marital bed; Ollie would never know.

At the pool, however, I was still fighting to kill the image of Jack. He had popped up, grinning like a Punch and Judy puppet, and I was taking mental thwacks at him with a wooden club. Eighteen condoms. After which he had hurt and humiliated my daughter.

I yanked off the headphones and reached for my guide to business start-ups. Having now researched fully the market for dementia products and services, the seeds for something special were shooting, and I was engrossed in the chapter on social enterprises when Gabryel sat up.

'Will you do me the honour?' He held out the sun cream.

'Sure.'

Miffed at the interruption, I smothered his shoulders just as I had Ollie's, year upon year, by the side of that pool. Gabryel's back was skin stretched on bone, each vertebrae distinct, while my husband's was fleshy, flabby even, but I was becoming aware that spending so much time in close contact with this man was tedious in a way it never had been alongside Ollie out there.

'And my neck,' he said.

A roll of my eyes at his back and I squeezed out more cream.

'You study economics, don't you?' I said.

Might as well make use of the moments.

'Yes.'

'What do you know about social enterprises?'

'There is no profit with social enterprises.'

'Yes, I know.'

He spun around to face me, incredulous. 'But the only goal of business is to make profit. Why would a person want not to make profit?'

'What about to put something back?'

'Only in the West can you afford to *put something back*, as you call it.'

I frowned. 'I thought communism was all about the people? Solidarity? I want to set up a business that helps some of the weakest in our society. Isn't that what life was like in Moldova?'

He let out a disdainful snort. 'You have no idea what it was like to live under communism. Your life has been easy, but my life...' he smacked his chest, 'my life has been hard. I want to make money. A lot of money, Anna. Money is all that is important.'

He shocked me into silence with that, but the fire in his eyes blazed on, until it seemed to dawn that this behaviour was out of character and he shook it off, his smile sliding back.

But I was not ready to smile. I lay back down and pulled on my headphones, mind whirling. Money is all that's important? What about his music? What about his family? I pumped up the volume. What about me? A rogue thought winkled itself in – what if he was a gold digger? As if this man was ever going to make big money off his own bat. But surely Gabryel was too attentive to be so deceitful; I had only ever witnessed kindness in him – that and a certain naivety.

I struggled to impose relaxation on myself through mindfulness, loosening my toes, my feet, my legs, all the way up to my shoulders. Allow yourself to be in the moment, I told myself silently, pretend he's not there; the pool glistening turquoise, the dragon fly diving to pluck water, the gnarled olive trees lined up like old men on parade. I closed my eyes, saw the colour blue, and eventually began to drift off. Then a shadow fell, darkening the blue, and his wet lips were upon mine.

'Oh!' I recoiled, eyes shooting open.

Gabryel was laughing down at me. 'Were you sleeping?'

'Yes.'

Couldn't he leave me alone for a few moments?

'Drink?'

'Sure.' That would be the only way to relax. 'But then we should stay in tonight, can't drink and drive.'

Which meant more crappy food.

'That is good for me. Dinner in bed?' He was already walking towards the house, plucking a lemon off the tree as he went.

Spell broken, I sank back irritably, mind and body railing at that prospect. Sex was becoming a chore. There, it was out. This affair revolved around one thing only and I was having too much of it. I now wanted some *decent* interaction, grown-up conversation. I closed my eyes and gave in to the chattering mind.

Was it really worth cheating on my husband with this man? But then was my marriage worth saving anyway? Surely yes, if only for the sake of Sophie. She, I was also deceiving, of course, had even lied to her on the family WhatsApp – how much I was enjoying *the retreat in the Cotswolds*. Appalling, but would she care if I left? After my prying about Jack she'd withdrawn again. We were on lowest common denominator terms, barely interacting to avoid all possibility of conflict, and I even wondered if she might be back with the boy. Truth was that I didn't much like my daughter right then, even if I loved her as fiercely as the day she was born. Imagine leaving her with Ollie and moving into that grotty pad with Gabryel? I shuddered, would it be wiser to end it before Ollie found out?

A clink of glass on the low table at my side and I opened my eyes to see Gabryel, so I sat up, forcing my shoulders to slacken.

'Up yours.' He chinked his gin and tonic to mine.

'Up yours.' I took a hefty sip.

'Pool?'

'Why not?'

He turned and took a running jump at the inflatable unicorn, landed and rolled onto his back and under the water, still gripping the white beast so that it ended up on top of him. I had to smile. Sure, the diminishing returns had set in, our cellar was all but drunk dry, but why not eke it out until empty? I hauled myself up and water bombed him, as Sophie had done to Jack so many times that summer.

It was the morning of our last day when I saw it. Gabryel was still walking around naked, still preparing my meals. Relieved to be on the homewards stretch, I was feeling benign; a break from him might be all it would take for that almighty thrill to skitter through me again.

I don't even know why I was looking up at the ceiling, perhaps I was mildly searching for cobwebs. In any case, there it was, fixed at the corner of our French dresser. The camera.

I froze. Jam-laden knife above my croissant. A rush of prickles swept my body and my face was an instant furnace.

Without moving a muscle, I flicked my eyes at Gabryel. He

was making coffee, his backside of marble in full technicolour view of the lens.

'Gabryel,' I hissed, through ventriloquist lips. 'Get out of the kitchen.'

'What?' His willy bounced as he turned around.

'Quick.' I jerked my head at the dresser. 'There's a camera.'

He looked up and stood motionless. 'Oh shit.'

Lowering his eyes, he slunk from the kitchen, while I slid sideways out of my chair and followed him.

'Fucking hell!' I cried when we were out on the patio, where I scanned the side of the house, the guttering, the roof for more cameras.

'Your husband?' His face was ashen.

'Yes, my fucking husband. The bastard!'

'You think he knows about us and set the camera?'

I shook my head. 'No, it'll be for burglars, but he could have fucking well told me he'd had it installed. I bet it hooks up to his PC. What are we going to do?'

'Keep out of the kitchen?'

His attempt at humour set me off laughing manically. I slumped onto the steps of the house and sank my head between my hands as the laughter became sobs.

'Three days we've been here, he'll have had a field day. It'll be grounds for divorce if he wants. What about my daughter? What am I going to do?'

Gabryel sat himself down beside me, draping an arm around my shoulder. It hung there, heavy, invasive, and I longed to throw it off.

'Leave him,' he said. 'I will also divorce my wife, I want to be with you, Anna.'

I screwed up my face at him, wiping snot and tears with the back of my hands. 'Are you crazy? It's not as simple as that.

233

Maybe it is for you, but for me there's too much at stake. My daughter…'

He fell silent then. After a few moments he removed his arm from my shoulders and allowed me to cry myself out. When I had no more tears to shed I sat staring at the dusty ground, my mind a top spinning with consequences. Gabryel lifted my chin with one finger and turned it to him, and I watched him watching me, figuring out my thoughts, which I no longer wished to conceal. In my eyes, where once he would have seen laughter, desire, esteem even at the outset, there was now only regret. And his own gaze, weighted with understanding, held a sadness I had never seen before.

'Let's go,' he said.

We left the kitchen as it was. Half-eaten breakfast, dirty pots at the sink, flip flops by the window. Just in case Ollie had not yet seen us. Just in case we might escape scot-free.

25

After a nerve-wracking journey, much of it spent furiously Googling security surveillance devices – how did they work? how did you monitor them? – I returned home early on the Thursday evening to find Ollie and Sophie eating dinner together at the island. Heart thumping, I'd dallied at the hall table, perusing post, fanning my cheeks, and the familial scene brought a flurry of panic. Father and daughter in communion – without need of a mother? What if Ollie knew? What if he filed for divorce, kicking me out, or taking Sophie with him?

'Hi family,' I said brightly.

Sophie glanced up. 'Hi, how was the course?'

'Brilliant, thanks.'

A surge of guilt; those lies I'd spun her on WhatsApp. I wandered over to kiss her, with a glance at Ollie who appeared to be struggling with a string of spaghetti, his focus on sucking it up. I rested a hand on his shoulder in greeting and turned to make for the kettle. He let out a soft grunt.

'I think I've decided on my business,' I added daringly. 'How's the week been here?'

'School. Dad's got himself a huge new client.'

'Oh?' I chanced a return to the island. 'Who's that?'

Ollie's eyes met mine. Inside I balked, hoping the boiling kettle was masking the clunk of my swallows, that my demeanour did not betray the panic. He smiled mildly, giving nothing away. Perhaps I was safe, but my shoulders were still clenched.

'Wedding caterer,' he said, 'Home Counties. Could be lucrative. So what's the business idea?'

'Oh, still needs mulling over, some due diligence too, but I'll reveal all soon.'

His eyes held mine, his tongue rolling inside his cheeks. 'Intriguing.' He returned to his meal with a smack of the lips.

I aimed for nonchalance. 'Well I'm knackered. Think I'll take my tea up to the bath. Anyone want a cup while I'm making?'

'No thanks.' Spoken in unison, if not necessarily in collusion.

I ignored the glass of red wine at Sophie's place, the open bottle almost empty. I should probably have nagged, for authenticity, but I was aching to escape and wash off the holiday, its smells, its shame.

It was just after 8pm and I was pottering around the bedroom in jim jams when my phone rang. Gabryel had made several attempts that evening already, so I reached to cancel the call, but it was Fred. That week I'd spoken to him daily, well-being calls from afar.

'Hi Fred. Everything OK?'

'Anna. I'm on the floor.'

'On the *floor*?'

'One minute I was standing on the bed, changing a light bulb, next thing I was down here.'

Standing on the bed at his age?

'Are you hurt?'

'Can't seem to get myself up. I wouldn't have bothered you,

but I know you're just next door, aren't you?'

'Yes,' I lied. 'I'll be there as soon as I can.'

I pulled on clean jeans and T-shirt and rushed downstairs, keenly aware that I would not be able to lift him up off the floor alone. Bracing myself, I sought out Ollie, now watching the news in the living room.

'Ollie.' My heart quickened to be in the same room. 'Fred's had a fall. He's on the floor. Would you mind helping me?'

He glanced up and smiled, the eye contact painful. 'Absolutely.'

'Thanks, only I don't think I can lift him myself.'

He stood up. 'Let's go.'

'Hope he's not hurt himself.'

My mind was chattering. Had Ollie seen us in the kitchen? Sharing food? Kissing? Gabryel naked? I gabbled on.

'He was trying to change the light bulb above his bed.'

'Ah,' was all that Ollie offered.

'So silly. I just hope this isn't the beginning of the end.' I saw the camera up on the dresser and added quickly, 'I mean of Fred living at home.'

We drove the few minutes without speaking. His proximity smarted – I'd almost succeeded in slinking off to bed without any further interaction that night. Above us hung a full harvest moon, blood red rather than juicy orange, and he began to hum cheerily, plumping for Sinatra's *Fly Me to the Moon*. With a tight grip on the wheel, I analysed the lyrics glumly for some coded clue.

At Fred's house I let us in, greeted Dougal effusively and flicked the hall switch to no avail.

'Urgh, stinks in here,' said Ollie.

The fusty air of self-neglect.

We switched on our phone torches and headed upstairs

with ghoulish swoops of the walls. I sensed Ollie behind me with trepidation; what if he were to confront me in that darkened house?

In Fred's bedroom, the bleeding moon spilled light enough and I cut my torch. Fred lay on his back in the bay window, his head having missed the sill by inches. In his stripy pyjamas he was fragile as a small boy. I knelt down beside him.

'Fred. Have you hurt yourself?'

'Can't seem to get myself up.'

'This is Ollie, my husband.'

'Hello Fred,' said Ollie kindly. 'Anything broken?'

'Bit stiff in the old ribs. Don't want to be a nuisance.'

'Shall we help you up?'

Ollie knelt down in the confined space beside me, our thighs rubbing, and together we took hold of Fred. I was relieved that I had bathed, that I wouldn't smell of sex, even if possibly I exuded the stench of betrayal.

'Deep breath,' said Ollie. 'Gently does it.'

Fred managed to roll over onto his front, then struggle up onto hands and knees and reach for the windowsill.

'Does he have a Zimmer frame?'

'No, I do not.' A sideways glare at Ollie.

In the gloom he and I shared a smile, eye contact which brought again the shock of that camera and a desperate hope that he'd seen nothing.

Eventually, one of us on each flank, we managed to haul Fred up to his feet and lowered him gently back onto a chair.

I placed a comforting hand on his shoulder. 'Shall I fetch you a whiskey?'

'Please, love.'

I left the bedroom, encouraged by the way Ollie and I had worked calmly as a team; each passing moment a step towards safety. Surely if he'd known, he would have disclosed some sign by now? Some barb?

When I returned with the glass of whiskey, he was standing on the bed, torch in one hand, light bulb in the other. He gestured to the screw bulb and then to the ceiling fitting, which was a bayonet; Fred had been trying to force one into the other.

'Think you might have blown your lights, Fred,' he said. 'Do you know where your fuse box is?'

'Fuse box?'

'Don't worry we'll find it,' I said. 'Back in a tick.'

After rummaging beneath the stairs, we finally found the box, fortunately a modern one, in a kitchen cupboard, and Ollie flicked the fallen switch.

'Then there was light.' I braved eye contact. 'Thank you, Ol.'

There had been such genuine kindness to his manner with Fred, a gentle patience I'd been witness to on many occasion with his own father, and the memory of distant happier family times had moved me.

His eyes lingered on mine. 'Look at this place.'

I took in the heap of unwashed crockery, spilt dog food, a grubby T-towel trailing on the hob.

'Nothing broken,' I said brightly, heading back to the stairs. 'I'll help him into bed and call the doctor out tomorrow.'

I was steadying the whiskey glass at Fred's lips when Ollie re-appeared in the bedroom doorway. 'Shall I help you to the bathroom, Fred?'

'Thank you,' I said on the drive home. 'Wasn't sure how I was going to tackle that.'

'He can't keep going like this,' he said as I parked up. 'You're deluding yourself, you know that?'

I hesitated, something pertinent about his tenor, but said blithely, 'I'll go round early to check on him.'

Once inside the house I took to the stairs and bed.

Ollie was still soundly asleep when I returned to Fred's shortly after dawn. Already the air was pervaded with Fuller's brewery, and I savoured the yeasty aroma with deep restorative breaths while walking Dougal. Then I took breakfast up to Fred and cleaned his house while he remained in bed, until the doctor arrived to deliver his edict.

'It may be time to consider a residential care home, Mr Wildsmith,' he said.

Fred's beseeching face would remain with me forever. I was impotent, not a thing I could do, but still I called Sharon and asked if she could increase her hours.

'Doubt the agency will sanction that,' she said, 'but I can ask.'

Back home, Ollie had left for the shop, Sophie was at school, and I spent much of the day with a chattering mind, mulling over the previous evening, analysing our interaction. Self-soothing. Something about the steady quiet with which we'd worked around Fred was affirming. A possible foundation on which to re-build our marriage? Assuming I was home and dry.

The memory of Ollie with his aged father had generated others from happier times. Our bike rides in Richmond Park when we'd first bought the house, our honeymoon in the Maldives, and the wine tour to Italy when his mother had looked after young Sophie for a whole week. And, of course, when he'd first purchased the wine shop; a leap of faith from his banking career, but it had brought him such pleasure – and me too to see him living out his passion. From more difficult times too there were memories to cherish. Well over ten years now since I had nursed Ollie with a broken leg from his five-aside football, and not so long after when he had cared for me during a bout of painful shingles. We had known such gentle nurture.

After school, I drove Sophie out to Kew Retail Park, on the pretext of exchanging some underwear I'd recently bought her which didn't fit. I'd suggested we return the items and request a bra fitting at M&S, tea and cake to follow, and was ready to lavish my attention on her.

On the High Road we came upon Jack cycling, no helmet, tennis gear in a precarious backpack, and my hackles rose as we passed him.

'What's *he* doing in Chiswick?'

'Goes to school here, remember?' said Sophie in a tired voice, gazing out the window with that teenage disdain.

'Fulham not big enough for him?'

She gave a hollow laugh. 'Cougar!'

'What?'

'You fancied him, didn't you?'

'I did not!'

She clicked her tongue.

'Of course, I didn't fancy him. He's a boy, he's sixteen!'

'Well you've been all weird since I dumped him.'

'Have I?'

'And he's seventeen now.'

Smirking, she reached to change the radio station. A blast of Capital, but I didn't react; as it currently stood she held the power and I would suffer all manner of behaviour.

'And now you hate him, don't you?'

'What I hate is disloyalty.'

Listen to yourself, Anna.

'Well I'm over him. *Totally* over him.'

'Good for you darling.' My heart crunched; I knew she was

lying but I raised a palm sideways on. 'High five to that.'

She allowed me a pat. 'Keep your eyes on the road, Mum.'

Result – the first *Mum* since I'd arrived home from France.

While Sophie was being fitted in the changing rooms, I wandered through the menswear section; would boxer shorts for Ollie be akin to flowers, guilt wise? I chucked a pack into my basket. My phone rang, Gabby, and I tossed it back into my bag. While I'd convinced myself that the surveillance system must have been switched off, and was beginning to relax, I'd totally had my fill of him. Possibly even forever. Imagine, that I'd once dreamed of running off with that man.

Sophie emerged with a raft of new underwear, most of it black and lacy.

'We'd like to exchange these for these,' I said to the young man at the cash desk, who took the plastic carrier bag from me and tipped out its contents.

We all three watched on, as not only bras and knickers fell onto the counter, but also a mass of pubic hairs.

I gasped. 'Where did you find that bag, Sophie?'

'Your bedroom.'

I'd clipped them before meeting Gabryel at the Heathrow hotel.

The man looked at me in disgust. 'These items are soiled Madam, I'm unable to exchange them.'

'No, no of course, I'm sorry.'

Sophie was already walking away, deserting me, as I began to brush the underwear back into the bag, pubes and all, scraping stubborn hairs off the counter. After I'd paid for the new items, with an embarrassed smile at the queue, I set off around the store, finally tracking her down outside on a bench. She glowered at me.

'You are *so* embarrassing!'

'I meant to throw them away.'

'*So* gross.'

'It's just hair. They were clean.'

'Why can't you wax?' She jumped to her feet.

Crazily then, I attempted the old parenting mantra: acknowledge, value and hold to account. 'I agree that it's embarrassing, and I can understand that you're angry, but you will not speak to me like that, Sophie.'

But she was already half way to the car.

'OK, that's enough.' I shouted, trailing her. 'Let's go.'

Thus our shopping trip was ruined.

'Has to be the most excruciating thing that's ever happened to me, Scar.'

Having missed Monday morning coffee that week (she too thought I'd been on a course in the Cotswolds) we were catching up with a cocktail in The Old Fire Station. It was my idea, to avoid contact with Ollie; some superstition that my luck would hold out if I could just last the full twenty four hours without challenge.

'You must have wanted the ground to swallow you up.' Scar's mascara had smeared with her laughter.

'Mortifying. Queue full of people, and the *look* on the guy's face, but I can't stop giggling about it now. Sophie was livid.'

'Guess she doesn't have pubes. Get rid of them, girls today, don't they?'

That smarted, such a personal comment about my daughter.

'Maybe Nick does too?' I said.

Scar flashed her eyes at that, but she backed off with a sip of Margarita, licking the salt carefully from her lips, and I followed suit with a sigh; I'd so wanted to keep the evening light too.

'How is she doing now? After the drugs?'

I started, slopped my cocktail. 'Who told you about that?'

'You did.' A shrug, another sip, another measured lick of the lips.

'*Did* I? When?'

'Last time we had breakfast. You remember, you ordered poached eggs with smoked salmon, and I had them with avocado.'

'Really?'

Mopping up the spilt drink with a napkin, I lingered over that detail. So much in my head these days, thoughts and secrets tumbling like clothes in a dryer, hence it was completely feasible, but *Reading* was a chink in my armour I'd intended not to share with Scar. Surely Ollie wouldn't have told her? If he'd wanted to confide, there were others he would have chosen above a woman who was primarily my mate.

She pulled out her phone and began scrolling. The mood between us had curdled yet again but a glance at my own phone told me it was still too early for me to go home.

'So…' I said, placing it face down as a prompt for her to do likewise. 'Think I've finally come up with my business idea.'

'Ooh tell all.' She dropped hers too and leaned forward. 'I was going to ask how the retreat went.'

'Well, it'll be something to help people living with dementia.'

'Go on.'

'A combination of products and services. An online shop for products, you know, like clocks which show days of the week, gadgets to locate objects mislaid around the home, that sort of thing. Combined with activities. Dogs as therapy, art, music, dance, even fashion. All sorts really.'

I'd hardly paused for breath. It was the first time I'd voiced my plan and a long draught of Margarita was required to prepare myself for her reaction.

She nodded, weighing it up. 'That's impressive, Anna. Sounds a huge undertaking.'

'It'll be a social enterprise, not for profit. My plan is to cross-subsidise. So I'll use profit from the lucrative products to co-fund the services, making them cheaper, and therefore more widely accessible.'

'And you're thinking Fred will be your first customer, so to speak?'

I nodded, grateful for her interest in Fred. 'I've been trying a few bits out on him already. Nostalgic jigsaws, large pieces, you know.'

She squeezed my hand. 'I'm loving it, Anna. You're onto a winner.'

At home, Ollie was in his usual habitat, at the island, glass of wine at its master's side. With a swift glance I gauged his mood – laid back – and I relaxed. Surely if he was going to, he would have erupted by now?

'I'll join you,' I said, opening the fridge to pour myself a large glass of Montrachet. 'Sophie around?'

'At a party.'

'*Party*? Where?'

'Not sure, said you'd agreed it.'

'Well I didn't.'

'She'll be fine, let her hair down a bit, why not?'

'Guess so. I'll track her whereabouts though.' I pulled out my phone.

He waited until I was seated opposite him, until we had clinked glasses.

'Any lemons left on the tree?'

26

The strike was nuclear. The shockwave punched me in the gut, almost causing me to vomit, and thumped through my organs, my limbs, out to each extremity. Then the ball of heat, a furnace in my core, flushing chest and face.

My eyes locked onto Ollie's, but at first I said nothing, furiously analysing the question. Could it possibly have other meaning? He sat silent and still, giving nothing away. When I'd computed all the options, I returned to the only possible connotation. He'd had me at lemons. My husband had bided his time until Sophie was out of the house, that's all. Like a stalking leopard awaiting the dusk.

'Yes,' I said quietly. And a sudden calm settled.

Somehow it had been better to say yes than no, and I was glad for those last few lemons that remained on our tree. I sensed embers of defiance kindling, if I held my silence I would also hold the power.

It was a good minute before Ollie spoke. 'A backside like marble, eh?'

So the camera had recorded sound as well as movement. What else had he heard us saying? Seen us *doing*? It was so grotesque I wanted to laugh.

'Guess it's a case of touché, is it?' he said.

He'd blinked first, and the embers burst into flame.

'You rather sold the idea of taking a lover to France, yes.'

He shrugged his agreement. 'How long has it been going on?'

'You don't need to know that.'

Let him stew.

'I need to know if you're going to leave.'

I glared at him, a bid to mask the rising panic, but said nothing.

'How could you do this when we were back on an even keel?'

'Oh, so *you* have an affair and I'm supposed to accept it, little wife like, but when I go for it, that's different?' I watched his jaw clench and I hurried on. 'For all I know you might be having another one!'

A bizarre accusation, but defence by attack had its merits.

'Why would I want to do that?'

'Because it's in your nature.'

'Bollocks. I went nineteen years without straying, Anna. Not once. It was only when you changed, that –'

'Yep it was all my fault, I know, long leash.'

'Well we'd been happy, hadn't we? Until you started wanting more.'

'Until you shagged another woman, you mean.'

'I'm sorry?' He shook himself dramatically, arms flailing. 'How have we arrived here when we were talking about *your* affair?'

'Because I suspect you're hiding something too.'

'You've gone stark raving mad, woman!'

The front door slammed – I hadn't heard it open – and Sophie walked through to the kitchen, the palpable silence bringing her to a halt. Saved by my daughter.

'Am I interrupting something?'

'Not at all.' I slipped off my bar stool. 'Did you have a good time?'

'Yeah.'

'Want anything?'

'No thanks.' She glanced from me to Ollie, gliding backwards as I approached her. 'Night then.'

I caught a whiff of cigarettes as she left the kitchen.

Churlishly ignoring Ollie's empty glass, I poured myself more wine and leant back against the fridge, soothed by its cool solidity. With a surreptitious flick of the eyes, I caught my husband staring into his glass, twirling the stem, and was astonished to find that the sight moved me.

'Are you going to end it?' he asked, softly then.

I shrugged.

'I'll leave you, Anna.' He looked up. 'And I'd bet you any money that Sophie would choose me. What kind of a mother lies to her daughter on the family WhatsApp?'

What kind of mother indeed? We gazed at each other, looks loaded with sadness despite our wrath. That it had come to this. I pushed myself up off the fridge, the terror of losing Sophie slithering through me.

'I've already ended it,' I lied, and left the room.

Upstairs, I gathered my night things and headed for the guest room, tiptoeing past Sophie's door.

Saturday morning found me alone in the kitchen at an early hour. I sat silently nursing a coffee and staring out at the garden. Last weekend in September, and although bathed in glorious sunshine the foliage was beginning to turn. Autumn always found me melancholic, but as summer's lush drained I was engulfed by the sense of an ending. Yet whatever it was that was coming to an end eluded me.

Marriage was supposed to be challenging. We'd weathered nearly twenty years, and perhaps muddling through is what is left to all couples once life's demarcations of baby, child, teenager, have blurred and melted. The two of you popping out the other end. Alone.

It had been a December wedding. Shotgun, as we'd blissfully joked – because who gets married in the depths of winter? But then we'd lost the baby some weeks in, and several others thereafter. Sophie was an only child simply because I couldn't bear the risk of more harrowing miscarriages. Last year we had celebrated our nineteenth anniversary at La Trompette while his affair was raging. This year? Would there be a this year?

Were we bound now only by a mutual fear of losing our daughter to the other? I thought again of the look we'd shared, loaded with the grist of those long years by each other's side. And I thought of Ollie's kindness towards Fred. We had united, each of us instinctive to the other's move, an intuition exclusive to couples bound together for so long. Surely there was some way back? If that is what I wanted.

My own mother had once told me that real love is what's left once lust has subsided, that she and Dad had been among the lucky ones who had sustained that love. Ollie and I were not in their league, but then they hadn't been in it for the long haul, just a few short years together.

Footsteps on the stairs, and Ollie, clad in his Man Utd garb, made a brief appearance in the kitchen for his keys. They were away that day at West Ham.

'I'll be home late.' The clipped tone of angry humiliation, after all he was now a cuckold.

'Okey-doke.' I said softly. 'Hope you win.'

And that was that. The beginning of reparations?

After he'd gone, I toyed with the idea of calling Scar, of spilling my heart about the affair and Ollie's reaction. But she, my closest friend, I had also deceived about my whereabouts that week, and somehow I doubted she would be understanding. Instead I reached for my laptop and immersed myself in management structures and working capital, the only way to take my mind off the misery of my predicament.

My phone rang, Gabryel, and I stabbed cancel, letting him know instantly that I was declining his call. Surely he'd realised that we were going to have to end it? I fired off a text, *Can we meet at yours in next few days?* My formality did trigger a pang of regret, no mention of the lair, but the words had flown, no chance of recall. No response either.

Just before noon, Sophie arrived in the kitchen. Her party trickery of the previous evening outweighed our shopping fiasco in terms of outrage, which meant that I currently held the cards, but I wanted to play them wisely, so I closed the laptop to give her my full attention.

'Good party?'

'Yeah.' She busied herself over coffee. 'Want one?'

'Please. There's croissants in the fridge.'

When she sat down opposite me with her mug and plate, I pushed my papers aside to make room, delighted that she'd joined me.

'What's Dad hiding?'

'Sorry?' I felt the heat at my cheeks.

'Last night when I got in, you were screaming at him, *you're hiding something too.*'

'Nothing.'

Far too quick.

She pressed a finger onto flakes of croissant and dabbed it at her tongue.

'Why did you sleep in the guest room, then?'

'I just wanted to be alone.'

Again, such haste.

'You're not going to get divorced, are you?'

Those clear blue eyes, which despite our conflict had never ceased to stir me, now held a flicker of fear. Suddenly my child was tiny again, the bravado, the sullenness, all of it vanished, and I crumpled. I'd feared she had outgrown me, but she still needed me. What a weasel of a mother. To focus on my own selfish satisfaction, altruistically caring for an old man or hedonistically shagging a much younger one. Altruism or hedonism, they both funnelled into the same jar – it was all about me. With a steady shake of my head, I slipped from my stool, walked around the island and hugged her, drawing deeply on the scent of her hair. She was still slipping through my fingers but it was not over yet. Not yet.

'No. I promise you, that will never happen.'

Was I reassuring myself too?

'But you *were* arguing again, weren't you?'

'We were, yes. But we will clear the air once Dad comes home tonight.'

I held her for a long time, taking pause for reflection, and I vowed to be a better mother, a better wife; I would make everything alright for her. Eventually, I sensed her relax, and with one last squeeze I released her and wandered back to my place.

"It'll be OK, Soph," I said, with a gentle smile.

She sighed, smacked her hands free of crumbs and picked up one of the product brochures.

'Is this your business idea?'

I nodded.

She flicked through it. 'All stuff for old people with

251

dementia?'

'Sometimes younger ones too.'

She stopped at a page. 'Magic painting? Like we used to do when I was a kid? You brush water on it and the colour appears? Then vanishes when it dries, so you can do it all over again?'

I was heartened by her reference to herself as a child; that she remembered those days too.

'And you're going to sell these things?'

'Through a social enterprise. Not for profit, you know. I'm looking at activities too. Anything that might help stimulate them, or take them back to a time when they were happy. The plan is to use the profit from products sold to discount the cost of activities so that more people with dementia can benefit from them.'

'Cool. You should go on *Dragon's Den*.'

I laughed. 'Maybe I should.'

'Need any help with your website?'

'You could design it for me, if you like?'

I beamed at my daughter. Relenting on my previous tiger insistence of a purely academic path, I'd allowed her to take an A level in Business Studies.

'Just say when.' She rapped a drumroll on the granite surface. 'Better get down to some homework now, though.'

A poignant joy fizzed. Mother and daughter, the power we possessed over each other without being aware of it. I feared her the more powerful, whereas she believed the same of me, and thus we danced around each other, thus we nurtured conflict. Guile-free and candid moments such as those were rare.

But, naturally, I couldn't let the cigarettes go unmentioned.

'You weren't smoking last night, were you?' I kept it casual.

An imperceptible shake of the head as she bent over the dishwasher. Was she as surprised as I was to be taking her on after such a golden interlude? Or had she been distracting me all along to get away with it?

'Must have been off Jack, he was smoking. Dropped me in his Uber.'

I stiffened. 'Jack was at the party?'

She said nothing.

'I thought you were done with him?'

'I am.' She righted herself and locked eyes with me. 'Are *you*?'

'I'm pleased to hear you're not smoking, that's all, I would have been disappointed in you.'

''K, Mum.' Her nod bore a brisk trace of the military, and she left the kitchen.

With a plaintive sigh I gazed down at my papers. Would I ever learn?

I made more coffee and drifted out into the garden, where Horace was nosing a rubber ball left behind by Dougal. Settling into a chair, I watched him nudge the toy then scuttle in pursuit as it rolled off. Well who would have known that a tortoise had it in him?

And, really, would I ever learn?

Ollie was right, of course. Sophie would probably much rather live with him if we were to split up, their relationship was benign and he would run a loose ship, but the thought of losing her was a knife to my ribs. It had been a good move to tell him I'd ended the affair, and it was only a white lie. Angered as he was, I suspected he was going to let me off – not least because we were evens now. But the deed was still to be executed.

In the early afternoon, I took a stroll over to Fred's. Even before his fall that week I had visited several care homes, armed with the invention of an elderly mother, leaving no contact details. The quality of these places varied astonishingly, some were dingy and stank of urine, others were fresh and south-facing. One of the best sported an actual pub, with horse and hounds wallpaper and bottles lined up behind the bar. All, however, were marred by one common blemish, the inhabitants sat in winged chairs facing each other around a large TV room. I couldn't imagine Fred wasting away in soft furnishings.

Turning the corner into his road, I saw the commotion, a bundle of people in his front garden. As I drew closer, I heard the smoke alarm too, and ran the last few yards, pushing my way up the path to his door. I let myself in, no Dougal to greet me.

'Fred?' I cried, and sped through to the screeching kitchen.

No Fred there either, but a T-towel was on fire on the hob. While impressive enough to provoke a scream from his elderly neighbour, the flames caused me only mild panic and I turned off the gas, filled the washing-up bowl and hurled water onto the remains of the towel. Steam shot from the sizzling flames, smothering my face as I re-filled the bowl. When the fire was out, a blackened pan sat forlornly sporting the remnants of two boiled eggs, the stench of burnt metal steeping the air.

The howl of a siren, and within seconds two mighty firemen were upon me. I stumbled to the hallway and watched them clattering around his kitchen.

'What's that fire engine doing outside?' Fred was on the front step. 'Strike a light.'

He walked into the hallway, staggered back against the wall and I rushed to steady him.

'It's all out, Fred, don't worry, no damage done.'

I led him gently back outside and sat him down on his front garden wall. While the other neighbours had dispersed to a distance, the old lady from next door had remained to restrain Dougal on his lead. Fred's breathing was racing, his chest heaving in snatches, so I sat down beside him with an arm around his shoulders and held him tightly against me.

'It's OK, it's all over.'

'I went to the shop,' he managed between pants. 'Wanted a loaf to go with my eggs.'

He gestured to the carrier bag on the front step, its shape betraying a couple of cans, no loaf, and I exchanged sad glances with his neighbour. Suddenly then, Fred's bulk slackened beneath my arm. His head slumped onto me and there he lolled, his face vacant, all expression drained.

'No Fred, no!' I cried, struggling with the weight of him.

Dougal began to whimper, straining to get to his master as if he too recognised what was happening.

'Would you get the firemen, please?' I think I managed to say. 'Ask them to call an ambulance?'

27

This time Fred appeared to have suffered a more serious stroke. The weakness in his left arm, the droop to his face, and slur to his speech, all lingered and his hospital stay was an extended one. I duly informed Elizabeth, who once again duly flew over, but I avoided all contact, leaving Sharon to keep me informed of the nefarious daughter's plans. It seemed she'd already had the house valued.

Dougal had moved in with us, I suspected more on terms of adoption than fostering, and within days our routine was established. He slept on the end of our bed (or rather in the cavernous middle) and he edged towards the roaring fireplace, thinking himself so canny that we couldn't see him shuffling forwards. His presence was a boon to us all, and I regretted my previous denial of a real pet. Ollie, who'd grown up with a black Labrador, adored him and would whoosh the dog off for long walks after work, despite the darkening nights.

It had been my intention to slide into a self-induced coma, to ride out the weeks without actually living them. My affair lingered like an unfamiliar incense, a subtle but discernible change to the air. Ollie's anger was palpable, if contained, and once again I'd leave a room as he entered it. Soon, however, not content with his extensive solitary dog-walking, he took to joining Dougal and me each morning in the park before he opened up the shop. Entrapped by this move, I warily awaited his offensive, and while our conversation was perfunctory, about Sophie, her demeanour, her progress at school, I knew he was simply marking time until his thoughts on our future were ripe.

Indeed, one morning, he made for a bench and sat down, crossing his legs resolutely. Here we go, I thought, taking the far end of the bench. I watched Dougal tearing through the park with his friends, and I waited.

'I taught Sophie to ride a bike in this park,' he said finally.

'The pink one with raffia on its handlebars.'

'I was fit enough back then to jog alongside her. But she soon got the hang of it, made it to the far railings.'

'And then she looked back.'

This was Bond folklore.

'Then she looked back. Saw I wasn't holding on, and fell off.'

'Still has a scar on her shin.'

'It's very faint.'

I smiled to myself – always the last word.

A lengthy pause and then, 'We were happy enough back then, weren't we?'

So he'd opted for the philosophical.

I gazed over at the swings, saw myself pushing Sophie, every morning at 10am, and sank further back into those years of plastic toys and pink raffia. Forging pigs from play dough, their spiral tails rolled like string, pressing cubes into holes, inventing names for animals. Always educating, squeezing out food for my own brain where possible too, diverting the restless energy from career into child, into my project.

Soon I was securely domesticated. Should I have stayed on at work? Continued satisfying my soul? Would I have been a better mother? A better wife? I'd considered myself selfless as a stay-at-home mum, but surely one who lives vicariously through her offspring is selfish? Whatever, I would not have called myself happy.

I sighed. 'I just wanted to find *me* again.'

'So you had an affair?'

'You had one first.'

'Seriously? Tit for tat?'

'Gave me permission,' I shrugged.

He drew a deep breath and released it in one long sigh. 'I'm sorry.' The first time the words had sounded genuine. 'Guess I always thought you were happy. Never short of money, friends, holidays. And you were a great mum.'

Were. Not are.

'You were always smiling...' he added.

'She was always smiling. Maybe that should be my epitaph?'

'Well you were.'

'And you were always laughing. Public school guffaws born of fight or flight. They pinioned me to the home, which is where you wanted me, didn't you? To ease your daily existence.'

'You *wanted* to stay at home.'

'I wanted to do it right, but that doesn't mean it was easy! And I certainly didn't want to become the little wife.'

I felt his searching gaze and was grateful to see Dougal lolloping towards us. Ball time. I stood and chucked it as far as I could, bending to repeat the game, until finally he flopped onto the grass, chin in paws. I sat back down.

'Do you want a divorce?' said Ollie.

So there we were, teetering on the brink of separation. Twenty years together, so much shared history; we were interwoven, interoperable, how could we trammel that to dust? And the prospect of single life chilled me now I knew what was out there; to start again in the frozen wastes, to be buffeted from one man to the next by my own dissatisfaction.

'No,' I said. 'You?'

He shook his head. 'How about we give it a few months. See how we go?'

'OK,' I said, warmed by relief.

We sat on, both of us perhaps contemplating how those few months might pan out, and it struck me that once again we had come full circle. Was it that I wanted to stay? Or that I didn't want to leave?

It took me another couple of days to face Gabryel. Finally he had replied to my text with formal words that mirrored my own, requesting that we meet in his flat – possibly hopeful that the memory of our snatched interludes there might sway me from the decision we both knew I'd reached?

On the short Tube ride to Earl's Court I rehearsed my speech, and then took a slow, delaying stroll. Once, the sight of his Victorian terrace had brought such a thrill, but that day it induced only a sad conviction. This affair was over. Whether or not I were ultimately to stay with Ollie, I no longer wished to be with Gabryel, the two matters were now distinct, no longer convoluted. I rang the bell.

I climbed the many stairs up to his door. There he waited and our eyes met in sorrow. He had bought the usual bottle of Chilean Sauvignon Blanc.

'Would you like a glass?' he asked as I removed my coat. 'It is chilled.'

With a shake of my head I sat down gingerly on the edge of a wooden chair. I'd chosen a soft jersey dress of ruby red, both flattering and confidence-boosting – and would the subtext of scarlet woman also resonate?

'I will have a glass, myself.' He poured himself a tumbler, took a lengthy swig, walked to the bed opposite me and sat down.

We contemplated each other. He wore new jeans, and that white billowing shirt I loved so much. The familiar frisson skittered, and with it a momentary vision of me standing to slide the shirt up and over his head.

'I'm sorry,' I began. And was unable to say more.

'I understand,' he said softly, and gulped his wine.

The struggle to go on took me by surprise. 'I think I might have a glass after all.'

He stood and busied himself at the fridge.

'It's just that I can't go on living like this,' I said to his back. 'I need to try again with my husband, I hate myself for being a crappy role model for my daughter.'

He turned to hand me the glass, his smile gentle.

'Even if she has no idea about us,' I added.

He smoothed my chin, the touch of his fingers bringing further quivers.

'It is OK, Anna.'

'Up yours.' I raised my glass in a lame attempt at humour and knocked back the wine, an instant relaxant. 'I mean, I still adore you, it's not that I want to end it.'

He had sat back down, watching while I gabbled on.

'Just that it's not decent, is it?'

I fell quiet, looked into those grey Slav eyes, and they seared me, hungry like the wolf. One last time? Surely that couldn't hurt anyone? I put down my glass and stood up. He followed suit.

Fitting, is how I described it to myself afterwards. We thrashed and we lingered, we bit and we nuzzled, we thrust and we slowed down time. Throughout it all, I found myself creating memories, flashes of feeling, emotional and physical, which I would return to in later months. Years even. And, as we subsided, my whole being was swept by that poignant sensation. Of the end.

We lay panting on our backs, while I committed to memory the smell of his flesh, the feel of the candlewick bedspread, the white lamp shade. Sealed in time.

'Mr Wolf,' I murmured, after a long while, squeezing his hand. 'It's been a pleasure.'

'The pleasure was mine.' He squeezed back.

I slipped off the bed and into my clothes. Slowly, my eyes on his, I buttoned up my coat, then turned and left, a soft click of the door behind me. On the stairs, my heart soared with the exhilaration of our oneness, knowing that it would soon plummet into the sorrow of our parting. It began already on the pavement outside, mounting with each step I took away from us. Moment by moment it engulfed me, consumed me, yet on I walked.

At home, in the scalding shower, I allowed myself tears, refusing to emerge until they were spent. Finally cleansed of guilt, I conjured up some sense of determination that from then on life would proceed on a simpler footing. And yet the ending was wedged undigested in my chest, lodged there as if I'd eaten a horse.

Or a wolf even.

That evening, to evade Ollie's arrival home from work, I turned up early for visiting time and found Elizabeth sitting at Fred's bedside. Bristling, I considered an about-turn, but Fred had already spotted me, and I could not thwart his brightening face, so I shambled over and kissed his baggy cheek.

'Hello Fred.'

I struggled to shift the images of John Mills as the village idiot in the film *Ryan's Daughter*, so confused and searching was his expression. He seemed even unable to recall my name.

'Anna,' he said finally.

'Yes.' I pulled up a chair. 'Hello Elizabeth,' I added icily.

'Anna.' Trumping me, she folded her arms and sniffed.

'How are you, Fred?' I took his malfunctioning hand between mine and squeezed it.

'Righ' as rain. Can I go hom', Anna?' He flapped the drip at his other wrist. 'Why have they go' me trussed up t' this?'

His speech had not progressed at all, and I was fearful that this time it might never return. I smiled softly.

'It's to hydrate you. If you drink more water you won't need it. Remember?' I added, wincing at my question.

Elizabeth let out a snort. '*Remember*? He remembers very little now, don't you Father? You can barely remember me, can you?'

I glared at her. Perhaps he wants to forget you.

She started as if I'd said it out loud, and possibly I had.

'I was just explaining to him that I'm going to arrange for a period of convalescence.' She raised her voice. 'Wasn't I, Father? A convalescent home.'

'I'm no' deaf, woman.' Fred turned to the window, his hands balled into fists, knuckles whitening; the cry of the impotent.

I was able to summon a smile as he turned back to me, but his gaze lingered and I shook my head, smile crumpling; nothing I could do to save him.

'It will be marvellous for you, Father.' The lying bitch. 'You need looking after for a while longer, then we'll see how it goes.'

My fury mounted, a taut cable about to snap, and I stood up with a final squeeze of Fred's hand.

'I'll pop back tomorrow, Fred. Spend some time alone with you, OK?'

'OK, love.' His eyes beseeched me to stay.

'I'll bring the crossword.' Not that he seemed up to that anymore.

He nodded, his smile now resigned. 'Thans' for all you do fo' me, Anna.'

Ignoring the muffled shriek his gratitude brought from Elizabeth, I kissed his forehead and walked out of the bay to the desk in the corridor, where I asked the matron to continue taking good care of Fred. Then I punched my way through the swing doors and left the ward.

Downstairs, I mooched into the dreary café, threading my way among gowned patients and glum visitors, minds no doubt teeming with their own ordeals. I ordered a chocolate muffin with my tea and stuffed chunks into my mouth. The cable was now whipping inside me. Of course, Fred would have to go into a care home; ridiculous to have insisted that I could look after him, but the shock of his demise shrieked inside my head. Only weeks before he had been physically fit, so lucid, such an intellect.

I hadn't been sitting there long before I felt Elizabeth looming, her shrill voice eclipsing my mind's chatter. 'He is eighty-six years old and he's now had three strokes. What *precisely* do you feel I should do for him?'

I glanced up and heard myself actually growl. 'Treat him with dignity? Don't steal from him? Be less of a bitch? I don't know, what do you *feel* you should do?'

She sighed, that patronising look. 'Can I sit down?'

'No, you can fuck off.'

Silence descended upon the café. Around us people froze, I could feel their scrutiny, and she rose to it.

'Who do you think you are? Pushing your way into my father's life, taking over his affairs when it's absolutely none of your business!' Her cheeks glowed purple beneath the silver hair, reminding me of a mouldy plum.

'I am someone who cares deeply about your father. Convalescence? Be honest with the man. He's not stupid, he knows you're dumping him into a care home for good. You're already selling his house, for Christ's sake!'

'He'll be so much better off in a home, and I'll have peace of mind.'

'You'll have your hands washed of him, you mean.'

I lost it then, set about pulping what was left of my muffin, while she edged backwards, finger pointed.

'If you attempt to interfere in this process…'

'You'll what?' I stood and kicked back my chair. Sharp intakes of breath, even the odd giggle then. 'Clearly you know nothing about safeguards against the deprivation of liberty.'

Incredulous, she turned for the exit, clack clack on her kitten heels, so I grabbed my handbag and pursued her. Reaching her at the revolving doors, I forced my way into her segment and hissed at her.

'Safeguards to stop vile people like you from abusing their parents.'

Out on the other side she span around in self-defence. 'You. Are a mad woman. Completely unhinged!'

'You bet I am. You make sure you choose the Rambling Rose, or you'll see just how mad.'

'That one is far too expensive.'

I let out another growl – unhinged indeed – and she scurried off, leaving me seething in her wake. I made it to my car, tore at the door and slumped into the driver's seat. Unrecognisable to myself.

264

28

Keeping my soul at bay, I waited for the hollow days to take themselves forwards, hopeful that time would bring a clarity of its own. Fred lingered in his hospital bed and I visited him often. Scar and I were again meeting regularly for breakfast on Monday mornings, but I told her nothing of my affair or of the atmosphere at home, rather updating her on my business. I had begun trading.

Meanwhile, Ollie and I moonwalked on, without gravity yoking us to anything resembling our marriage. An advert I'd spotted for Chinese cooking sessions saw us standing side-by-side in a stranger's kitchen, creating dim sum. Somewhat surreal, but we had resolved to give ourselves a few months, and our attempt with the chopsticks brought us both a moment of genuine laughter.

While I thought of Gabryel often, I attempted no contact, and gradually I began to rediscover a certain compatibility with Ollie which the gentle life teased to the fore. Call it white noise rather than kinship, but I was becoming aware that my incongruence with Gabryel, set in sharp relief by our awkward time in France, had brought me a renewed appreciation of my husband.

In marriage, you assimilate the other, lose sight of their qualities – just as you do your own. Haven't we all developed some remarkable life skill which we take for granted, rate as humdrum, indeed barely notice, but which others marvel at? And so it is with a long term partner. They slip inside our consciousness, remaining latent unless we pluck them out to admire afresh. To appreciate anew.

At home, life was eased too by Dougal who had already become an invaluable family prop, each of us speaking to him in silly voices, or communicating via him.

'Will Mum let me stay out till 1am tonight, Dougal?' Sophie would chance regularly, playing motorbikes with his ears.

'Tell Sophie she can have till midnight,' I'd reply, with a tap to the dog's nose. 'And no later.'

Relaxing my grip on Sophie was a challenge akin to giving up the booze in January, the urge to nag a physical hankering deep within. She tended to meet up at the homes of her girlfriends before a night out, and that stung, because I'd hoped that our house would be the trendy hub where they would want to hang out. That I might be hovering on the fringes, a popular mum. But who wanted a tiger prowling at pre-party drinks?

Then it was the end of October, and Quiz Night at school, a skirmish I had in the past steadfastly evaded. The very words *Quiz Night* brought a shudder – Ollie and I might squabble, may even argue the rest of the team down, and that would not do for the reputation of Chiswick's affable wine merchant. Sadly, that autumn however, I did not heed my instinct and submitted to his proposal for another foray into mutual socialising.

Earlier that afternoon, Fred had finally gone into a care home. *Unhinged?* That evening, I may have concurred with Elizabeth. She'd already returned to France, leaving me, the mad woman, to welcome Fred in the ambulance which would deliver him from hospital. Preposterous of a daughter not to be present at such a life changing moment for her father, but at least the woman had chosen the Rambling Rose.

Awaiting his arrival in reception, I'd sunk into one of the fuchsia sofas and covertly sussed the place out. First and foremost, it didn't smell. I cringed at the memory of other care homes, where the acrid stench had hit on entry and clung for the whole tour. The atmosphere too was vibrant, with much coming and going through the reception area. Visitors could let themselves in at will with a touch pad code, thus showing up impromptu, and keeping useful tabs on the staff (who all seemed bright and breezy). A plate of iced cakes sat beside a coffee machine, two budgies, aptly named Rosie and Rambles, cheeped in a cage, and the hair salon beside reception was painted a cheerful pink. Not that Fred would have much call for a shampoo and set.

They'd wheeled him out of the ambulance, a man much diminished both in stature and spirit. While his face and speech had both marginally recovered, I had not yet seen him use his left arm again, and that hand lay palm down on his lap, covered protectively by his right one.

'Where am I?' Little boy lost, he gazed around the foyer and then up at me, breaking my heart.

Gently I settled him into his south-facing bedroom which overlooked the garden and was lit with the hues of a golden afternoon.

'Season of mists and mellow fruitfulness,' I murmured, failing to draw his eye onto the vista from his new home.

I'd unpacked his belongings – meticulously selected – and a framed photo of Dougal was already up on the wall alongside the pressed wedding bouquet of peonies. His mantel clock sat on the sideboard, albeit silently – they'd asked me to disable its alarming chimes.

'Am I goin' home soon, Anna?' He stared forlornly at the

window locks, at the red emergency call button dangling by the bed.

'You're here to get better, Fred.'

It killed me to respond obliquely.

Finally, he'd agreed to take a walk down to the communal living room, succumbing even to the wheeled walking frame with which the hospital had discharged him, using his right hand to lift his left onto the bar before setting off. The sight of his tiny shuffles along the carpet had pierced me, and I'd conjured up the pride of a bodyguard flanking the President as I took my own fairy steps alongside him. That afternoon it was the second People's Vote March in central London, but Brexit was now an alien concept to Fred – the transformation wrought in this man by a mere matter of weeks.

We found a 'nice chair' for him (what words I was using) and I unfurled his *Guardian* to the crossword. He looked around the room, taking in its residents one by one. Several were asleep, one woman sat repeating herself incessantly, while winding her long grey hair around her index finger, another was being transferred into a wheelchair via a mechanical hoist.

'Grea' big muddle puddle,' he mumbled.

The chap sitting beside him seemed delighted with the new arrival, calling out the odd crossword answer, while Fred remained silent, unable or unwilling to join in. Eventually, however, he had let out a grunt, even allowing the man a sideways glance. That had lightened my departure somewhat.

I was still reassuring myself with this memory as, with confident swaggers, Ollie and I entered the brightly lit dining hall of Sophie's school. We found our names on the board and wandered between the tables towards the back.

'Shit.' I stopped in my tracks.

'What?' Ollie's sociable smile wavered.

'Jack's parents.'

'On our table?'

'Yup.'

'What the *fuck*?'

We walked on as if towards the gallows and took seats on the far side of the round table. But Candice Mattison had clearly clocked our names and she was up and around, doling out such intimate embraces that I nearly shoved her off me. That's where Jack gets his confidence from then, I thought, visualising her sprawling across the floor, stilettoes flailing, dress tearing.

'We've never met, but I do so feel as if I *know* you already,' she said, beckoning her husband, who despite our four months as the parents of Jack's girlfriend, I knew only from his garden design website. 'Come on, Gordon, let's move beside the Bonds.'

I watched in horror as the Scotsman, tanned and muscle-bound from his work, stood and made his way, not towards her, but around the other side of the table to sit beside me. The woman was already seated at Ollie's side, pinning us in as if we were at a bloody wedding. When he spoke, I flinched from the pewter eyes which were so familiar to me, and an icy shiver rippled my back. Was Jack there too? Sophie was waitressing to raise funds for her World Challenge trip to Asia before university, and I'd blithely assumed this would be for the girls only, but a frantic glance around the hall and I spotted boys roaming about too. I sensed his presence, even if he appeared not to be among them.

Two other couples joined our table, including Bianca's parents, the mother distancing herself with a perfunctory hello, and soon we sat as a team of eight.

'What will our name be?' asked Jack's dad, or Gordon as he

was now known. 'How about *The Winning Team*?'

How trite.

Jack appeared then from behind us, a wodge of raffle tickets in hand. I speared him with hostile eyes and he looked down, his cheeks sudden smudges of red. That, I had once found endearing. Ollie, who had not encountered him since Sophie's party, had also tensed up. Having sold raffle tickets to everyone else on our table, the boy then attempted to glide behind our seats without offering us any, until his mother pounced.

'Jack. Say good evening to the Bonds.'

I fumbled in my handbag. 'We'll have two strips please.'

Ollie sat blankly, fists clenched, while Jack took my cash and dropped the tickets in front of me.

'Our kids,' said his mother, watching him stride off. 'Sophie's such a darling. We were sorry when they split up.'

'Were you?' My voice was tight but I held it together, reached for a sheet of pre-quiz word puzzles and attempted to study them.

'So fickle, teenagers today, aren't they?' she said. 'Bet she's moved onto the next one already, too?'

'She's certainly in demand.'

She has a broken heart, you idiot.

'Ah dingbats, let's have a wee lookie.' Gordon muscled into me, pencil poised.

Ollie's foot stubbed my ankle and I glanced at him. *Great idea this*, my eyes said. *Sorry*, is what his replied.

'Round one.' The speakers came to life. 'Geography. Who wants to play their joker?' The quizmaster was a parent, and some famous actor.

Card aloft, Gordon decided unilaterally that we would do just that, and Ollie bristled – he would have played it on sport, as would any self-respecting man, he told me later.

Sophie emerged in a group from the school kitchen with a tray of poppadoms and relishes. As she bent to place the dishes on our table, I caught sight of some red image in the dip of her cleavage. A heart? Surely not a tattoo? Annoyance prickled, which I swiftly quashed. As long as my daughter didn't end up in hospital for a third time that year, as long as she remained robust against that little shit, Jack, I must not let such trivia matter. I took another tiny sip of wine; I was pacing myself after my emotional afternoon with Fred.

'Question one.' The actor's luvvie voice. 'Where would you find the Sea of Tranquillity?'

All heads dipped inwards as if dancing the Hokey Cokey. 'On the moon,' we whispered.

Gordon, sole keeper of the pen, was already scribing, an irritating flourish.

'Question two. What is the deepest lake in the world?'

Gordon raised his chin to the men, ignoring we woman.

'Caspian Sea?' said Bianca's dad, clearly grateful to be consulted.

'Lake Baikal,' said Ollie, but Gordon was already writing Caspian Sea.

My husband threw me a boss-eyed look, which I returned with a smile of solidarity, nudging his balled-up fist with mine.

'Question three. What is the capital of Moldova?'

'Chisinau.' I half shouted the answer, lowering my voice to a hiss after much male tutting around me. 'It's Chisinau.'

'No, it's Kishinev.' Gordon was already writing it down.

I felt myself drawing to full height. 'No. It's Chisinau.'

'Kishinev,' he said, tongue between lips with boyish focus.

Glowering at the man, I felt Ollie's hand on my thigh, the weight of reason. 'She's right, it is Chisinau,' he said. 'I import wine from Moldova.'

Thank you, Ollie. My heart reached out to him. But Gordon ignored us both and slapped down the pencil.

'You've got it wrong.'

I flung a dismissive hand in the air and reached for my wine, my eye snagging on a gaggle of laughing youths lined up against the far wall, Jack among them. I stood and headed to the toilet.

'Little shite,' I muttered as I skimmed past him.

From then on I sulked, refusing to join in, savouring the awkward atmosphere I was creating; a masochism unknown to me. Occasionally I sought out Jack and contemplated him, this sunny, polite youth who had spent so much time among my family, bringing joy and purpose to us all. And then he'd sucked it all away, leaving us in more disarray than when he'd found us. It was as if he'd planned it, intended every move. Had he conned us all? Was he some kind of nutter?

At half time, Sophie and her clan returned with plates of curry. I peered into her cleavage, yes that seemed to be a heart – and indeed also a tattoo, but as long as there was no J at its centre then what matter? I poured myself more wine.

During the meal I ate head down, ignoring everyone. Gordon had opted for a frosty stance, pouring his laughter on the woman at his other side, but Ollie, with a sterling effort, was attentive both to me and to Candice, as he had come to call her. Clearly, he was the adult between us that night. For every mouthful of food, I took a sip of wine, an easy feat given that our table was smothered with bottles, so I poured and topped up, topped up and poured.

Unhinged? Feral would have been another word for it.

'So,' called the actor as plates were being cleared. 'Answers for the first five rounds, starting with Geography.'

Show-off cheers met the correct answer to question one, even though we had all known it to be the moon.

'Question two. The deepest lake in the world is Lake Baikal.'

'Yes!' I gave Ollie a hearty slap on the arm in reaction to the male silence on our table. 'Well done Ol.'

'Yes, well done, Ollie,' said Candice, her own hand resting lightly on his other arm.

Lay off him, I thought, surprised at my propriety, and took another hefty sip of wine.

'Question three.'

Ha, I thought, fingers drilling, I'd get the crappy Mattisons. 'The capital of Moldova is Kishinev.'

I exploded. 'No it's not! It's Chisinau!'

I felt those on nearby tables sway towards me, while Gordon Mattison was pulling a victory pump. 'Yess!' he cried, lest all other parents should think our team got it wrong.

Ollie placed a calming hand on mine, his affable smile embracing our table. 'Think it used to be that during communism, but it's changed now. Let's Google it.'

I had already pulled my phone out.

'Put that away,' hissed Gordon. 'You'll have us disqualified.'

'I doubt that very much, because he's giving the answers right now, isn't he? So… Chisinau, also known as Kishinev…' I beamed at the man.

'It's both,' I called to the quizmaster, who turned and held a theatrical hand out at me.

'Five points deducted for The Winning Team,' he cried. 'No phones allowed, on pain of death or five points off.'

When our table disbanded at the end of the evening, I was bright with alcohol, holding onto the back of my chair, possibly swaying. We had lost by six points. Gordon was the only one who was patently sulking, the others may have been graciously hiding it. Sloshed as I was, we all knew, however, that Ollie had been overruled on several of his correct answers, that he could have won us many more than the five points I had lost us.

'Good night, both.' Candice Mattison held up a hand rather than going in for the goodbye embrace. 'Keep in touch,' she added, unable to escape her middle-class manners.

'We won't,' I cried amiably, my own hand aloft to mirror hers.

'Anna!' Ollie sniggered, and our eyes met in a flash of amusement.

My hand tightly in his, we left the hall, two against the world. As it used to be.

Outside, the dark night swirled as if into a black hole, and while we waited for Sophie I sank back into the school railings, thankful for their solidity, for Ollie's arm around my shoulders.

'He was from Moldova,' I murmured.

'Guessed as much.'

When Sophie emerged through the school gate, she had done up a button on her shirt, and I couldn't resist it.

'Tattoo, Soph?'

Her eyes widened. 'No big deal. Everyone's got them.'

'It's cute,' I said.

Ollie knew when to remain silent. Or perhaps he was mulling over Moldova.

'Long as you didn't get a J inside it?'

'I'm not stupid, Mum.'

Her hand strayed in reflex to her top button.

29

On the wall outside Fred's bedroom there was a memory box, a small cupboard with a transparent door. Inside this I had placed familiar items – a photo of his late wife, Grace, one of their wedding day, a replica pipe and a packet of tobacco. The idea was that he would recall which room was his between the identical magnolia doors, and similar boxes lined the corridor to the communal living room.

Over the first few weeks, I made a point of matching the youthful faces in photos to the older versions now languishing in winged chairs, and learned the names of several residents. On each visit, I would aim to chat over some snippet of the outside world, tailoring it to what I knew of their interests – a football result, or a TV dance off. How had I never discovered the wonder of old people? The rich past, the bounty of experience, above all, the dry humour. And that stoic drive for self-reliance – a sore bend of the knees to pick a thread of lint up from the carpet, a painstaking reach to close an awkward window.

As for Fred's actual pipe, while the staff allowed him the pleasure of sucking on it, he was not permitted to light up inside the home. So, despite the November chill I would often wrap us both up warmly and lead him out to the garden, where we would sit by the fish pond and watch the leaves turn, then crisp, and fall. Inevitably, Fred would comment on the recent demise of the giant red carp, even though as the weeks went by it was no longer recent. Death, I reflected upon often, wondering if it was increasingly at the forefront of his mind.

Our crosswords were now plucked from a children's bumper puzzle book, and clues such as, *A yellow fruit, seven letters,* were of the norm. His response time was lengthening and I would have to nudge him with further pointers. Curiously, it was the more erudite prompts which clicked with him, such as, the EU once tried to ban bendy ones.

'Bananas,' he shouted.

Thus I enjoyed stimulating his mind, ever hoping for a glimmer of the old Fred to shine through.

One icy morning as we sat by the pond, the resident blackbird stuck its beak out from a dense evergreen bush and plucked at the red berries.

'Look at that cheeky chappie,' I said, delighted to raise a smile from Fred.

'Many berries, Anna. Means we're in for a cold win'er,' he said, as he always did when the bird appeared.

'Bet you're right there, Fred.'

We lapsed into a companionable silence and I hoped his mind was contemplating the blackbird, generating memories of those he used to feed in his own garden. Watching them that first time I had been bored, but I missed those days so badly.

After a while, he took a deep draught on his pipe.

'Anna?'

'Yes?' I smiled, held his gaze.

'When's Ma comin' hom'?'

'Ma?'

The panic rose and I glanced at the gardener who was sweeping leaves on the other side of the pond. Resting his arms on his brush, he listened in.

'Will she be home soon?'

'Your *Ma*?'

Fred nodded, pipe aloft awaiting a response, his now worried eyes searching mine. But I was speechless, it was the gardener who came to my rescue.

'Think she's on her way, Fred.'

I gawped at the man – I'd read much about this approach to dementia, to play along rather than potentially distress with the truth, but had never seen it in action – and he smiled at me with a comforting slow blink.

'Oh goo',' said Fred, face brightening. 'She's on her way.'

I nodded, and after a few beats said, 'She'll be here soon, I'm sure.'

'Yes.' He popped contentedly at his pipe.

My rock had left me for good. From that point on, however, I played along. Lying, fabricating, even at times instigating conversation about his childhood as if he were still living it – whatever was reassuring for him. Because my love for Fred knew no bounds.

At home, thank goodness, Dougal continued to regale us all.

'Do you think Dad will get me a MacBook Air for Christmas, Dougal?' was Sophie's running mantra.

'Do you think Sophie will get rid of that blue hair, Dougal?' Was Ollie's amused retort. Because that was another thing, the once platinum ombré fringes were now cobalt.

Heartened by the success of the tattoo, Sophie had also added to that collection, with tiny images at her ankle, the nape of her neck – and who knew where else? By success, I mean that Ollie too had not chastised her, though I still had not been able to ascertain if the heart contained a letter J.

We were all settling into a new regime where the tables were turning. Gone the days where Ollie or I would dictate our agenda, it was now she whose social life was the more vibrant, she who decided on the restaurant for a family night out. Constant requests for lifts of a weekend meant we would frequently refrain from drinking, awaiting the call for pick-up. Often Ollie and I, having spent a sober but amiable evening with the TV, would jokingly fight over it. That month, television loomed large in our lives, a friendly din against our quiet and gradual rapprochement. Ollie's foibles were again becoming background noise rather than irritations and our twenty years began enfolding us in their embrace once more. Quiz night had been a productive step forward, and was succeeded by salsa dancing, something we'd enjoyed many moons ago when we'd first met.

Sophie was also spending a chunk of her free time helping me set up *Forget-Me-Nots*, a name she had proudly come up with. I'd landed a grant specifically for social enterprises, also plundered my shares and savings, and our guest room was stacked high with stock, which we enjoyed sifting and packaging (Sophie never did query the whereabouts of that lilac sheepskin rug).

'Like playing shops when I was a kid,' she'd say, sitting cross-legged with me on the carpet, slicing open a box of ingenious clocks which prompted times for meals, medication and bed.

Initially, I'd decided to limit the scope of the business to West London and was garnering a team – of dog owners, artists, amateur actors, and local singers, many of whom had family members affected by dementia. I planned to build an agency, charge for their services on a sliding fee scale, and pay them by cross-subsidising from product profits. While the private care homes could afford the going rate, I wanted to embrace a much wider audience – dementia cafes, clubs for pensioners, individuals living at home too. And the state care homes would pay only a peppercorn fee.

As he did every year, Ollie took himself off to Beaujeu in France for the Beaujolais Nouveau festivities. The tradition embraced fireworks, dancing, and the first of the new wine released at one minute after midnight on the third Thursday of November, after which it would be drunk until dawn. Sometimes he'd drive there, returning with his van loaded for the renowned race to distribute the wine, but this year he had flown and was due back that Saturday afternoon.

In the late morning, Sophie came down to the kitchen and caught me in tears, a forlorn Dougal with his chin resting on my knees. Technically, my sadness was over the demise of the giant red carp, but in reality the decline was Fred's. Dementia was not only a disease of the memory, it could also rob people of their capacity to speak, to move, eventually even to breathe. During my visit the previous evening, I'd learnt that Fred was having difficulty swallowing, often coughing back liquids, and that they were now adding thickeners to his drinks to prevent him from choking. Dysphagia, one of the carers had called it, stirring a white powder into his evening glass of red wine. I'd watched Fred grimacing as he'd sipped the cloudy liquid, still swimming with globules. He'd fixed me with the eyes of a hangdog and said, 'I'm in God's waiting room, Anna.'

Another tear bubbled and Sophie slipped an arm around my shoulder. 'It's just a fish, Mum. Not as if it's Dougal.'

'You're right.' I coaxed the dog's paws up onto my lap and began to play motorbikes with his ears.

'Will Fred ever want Dougal back?'

I shook my head. 'He's ours forever now. Fred won't be

going home again.'

She brightened and I smiled at my daughter – well, eighty-six must seem ancient to any sixteen-year old, and she'd never actually met Fred.

'Fancy helping me add stock to the website?'

'Cool.' She gave my arm a final squeeze. 'I'll make coffee.'

We set ourselves up at the island and I brought up the website with its logo of delicate blue flowers, still enthralled that *Forget-Me-Nots* now actually existed as a social enterprise. We had taken a delivery of soft toys as realistic as pet dogs and cats, which many people with dementia found soothing to stroke on their laps, and we began adding to the products section of the website. A cosy, harmonious scene, chocolate biscuits and the mellow Tom Odell drifting from the speakers.

Then, for no doubt the fourth time that hour, Sophie checked her phone. She let out a howl and dropped it.

'Nooo!' She collapsed into sobs, hammer blows to my heart.

'What's wrong?' I reached for the phone and my blood ran cold.

Sophie stood naked. Behind her stood Jack, an arm slung across my daughter's breasts, a hand splayed at her crotch. Bizarrely, the first thing that struck me was relief at the size of his hand; nothing could be seen. It was as if she wore a human bikini.

'Give it to me.' She snatched the phone, her eyes despairing, and dropped it again. 'Bastard.'

'It's Snapchat, it disappears after a few seconds, doesn't it?'

Surely, I'd realised that so many seconds had been and gone?

She shook her head, now slumped between her hands. 'Not anymore. It's on his story, there for a whole day.'

Bastard indeed.

I placed a gentle hand on her head. 'You can't see anything, Soph.'

'He swore he wouldn't post them.'

'Them?'

She raised her flooded eyes to mine. 'There's worse than that. I'm sorry, Mum.'

'Right. His parents.' I reached for my own phone; Candice Mattison was still in my contacts. I jabbed at the screen and let myself out to the garden.

'This is Sophie Bond's mother,' I yelled when she answered.

A pause. 'Oh yes?'

'Your son has posted an obscene photo of my daughter on Snapchat.'

'Jack? I think you must be mistaken.'

'I have it right here. I insist you make him take it down. Now.'

'He's not here at the moment. Precisely what is this photo?'

'A disgusting image of my daughter naked.'

'Surely then the disgust lies with both parties?'

'Unless you get him to destroy these images immediately, I'm going to call the police.'

She sighed, as if I were a tiresome tradesman at her door. 'Let me see if I can contact him.'

'It's obvious you don't have a girl. Letting your son run around with his willy out, humiliating other women's daughters.'

'Enough.' She hung up.

I turned to see Sophie behind me on the patio. 'Will he do it, do you think?'

I took her in my arms. 'He will. Come on, it's freezing out here.'

Back inside the warm kitchen, we sat again at the island and

I pushed the plate of biscuits her way, but she shook her head

'When were these taken, Soph?'

'Last weekend.'

'So you're still seeing him?'

A nod. 'Dumped him last night.'

Hence this spiteful retaliation.

We lapsed into silence but my mind was shrieking. How had she gone back to the little shit? How had I not noticed? I should have told her the truth all those months back that he'd not kissed Bianca but had sex with her. I felt sick to my core.

'I found out that he cheated on me again,' she said finally.

Of course he had.

I slid my arms around her and pulled her close. I even suggested that I take a drive around Chiswick to find him; he always seemed to be somewhere on that bloody bike of his, but Sophie said no. She spent the rest of that day calling friends and scouring posts for any signs of the worst, while I checked in with her every thirty minutes. The image did disappear after a couple of hours but we were terrified of others that may be lingering. Twice I attempted to phone Jack's mother but both times she refused my call so I texted her relentlessly, my threats mounting. By evening, it seemed that no more images had been posted and we began to relax.

I'd considered putting Scar and Alex off for dinner, but Ollie was keen to ply his new Beaujolais, and Sophie wished to be alone in her room, so there seemed no point.

'Keys in,' said Alex, dropping his into the bowl beside mine with a prolonged kiss to my cheek.

You must be joking, I thought, there will be no flirting tonight.

Behind him, Scar, in a furry leopard print poncho, pressed

an icy cheek to mine, and I led them both to the kitchen and the well-timed pop of a red wine cork. Bottle aloft, Ollie, who knew nothing of the day's saga, let out one of his unprompted guffaws.

'Hey,' Scar said with a peck on his cheek.

'Hey.' He offered her a glass of wine

'It's cold,' said Alex, accepting his glass.

'You serve it chilled,' said Scar.

'Well remembered,' I said.

Ollie had asked me to prepare a starter of cold meats, and as we sampled the wine I offered little conversation, drifting in and out of the usual chatter with frequent checks on the venison casserole – and on my phone, which eventually I brought to the table, placing it rudely before me.

'Your twentieth coming up then?' Scar said once we were on the main course.

I smiled. 'You're on the ball tonight.'

'How are you celebrating?'

'Café on the River,' said Ollie, who'd had the grace to pick a new dining spot.

'Nice one, mate. Here's to you both.' Alex tipped his glass to ours.

'Our dearest friends,' said Scar, following suit.

A text pinged green. *I apologise for my son, he has removed all trace and deleted the images. He himself will be in touch with his own apologies.*

I shook my head at Scar's questioning frown. 'It's nothing,' I said, and forwarded the text to Sophie upstairs.

She responded with a series of heart emojis and, dipping out of dinner, I spent a good half hour hugging her back from the brink. She knew there would be screenshots, that at school there would be fallout, but she'd learn from it. Of course, Jack, the coward, never did text his apology, but I believe afterwards that she genuinely did consign him to the past.

Hers, I might add. Not mine.

30

Our twentieth wedding anniversary fell neatly on a Saturday. Sophie brought us breakfast in bed and we went for a walk as a family in Richmond Park. The Isabella Plantation had slunk from autumn opulence into winter barren, its trails scented with dank pine, but we were used to bleak anniversaries, not for us the woodland bluebells which marked so many marriages. In some ways, the gloom had served us well, given that we had lost our first baby just weeks after the wedding.

That evening, we took a cab to the Café on the River and were placed by a window, tiny white lights trickling at its pane. I looked across the cosy room, its clean lines and muted informality suited me well. Ollie knew the sommelier from old and we would be regaled with a series of sumptuous wines. Champagne first, naturally.

'To twenty years.' He raised his glass.

'Twenty years,' I said, chinking with him.

The phrase *Up Yours* did spring forth. Even if securely in my past, Gabryel was by no means a dim memory, and the thoughts brought a smile which I worked into a genuine one for Ollie. Neither he nor I would raise anything sticky or tricky that night, rather maintain the custom of recalling our wedding day – the weather, the church, the guests.

'Can you remember our first dance?' He reached for his

menu.

'Celine Dion, *My Heart Will Go On.*'

We'd seen the film *Titanic* together the evening he'd proposed. And he must have signalled, because the song itself drifted out over the speakers, volume raised slightly, just for us.

I smiled. 'Thank you. Thoughtful touch.'

He began to sing along, tone deaf as ever, and our eyes met in amusement.

'Can't believe I married you despite those dulcet tones.'

'Well you did,' he laughed. 'And I've been thinking. How about we renew our vows?'

It was my turn to laugh.

'I'm serious. Put it all behind us. Start afresh.'

'Hmm, not sure.' I laughed again.

Could he not remember how we used to mock such couples?

We savoured small plates scattered with tortellini and pine nuts, then larger ones of chargrilled monkfish, all accompanied by different wines. I brought up memories of our honeymoon in the Maldives and the morning we'd swum with dolphins. Only, we'd risen so late and the dolphins, having slept in the shallows, were by then so far out in the ocean that the skipper, fearful of sharks, had beckoned us back into the boat (and with me pregnant too).

At the end of the evening, nicely tipsy, we strolled along the river, a vista of stars and twinkling lights reflected in the water. We held hands, our voices low and languid, the occasional shared throaty laughter. It really was quite romantic; the night we would move on, I decided. Put it all behind us.

I had no inkling of what was to come.

Monday morning and Mum was arriving with Wayne in the

afternoon. They'd broken the trip up in Dubai to suss out potential sales opportunities for their trinkets, as I called them; the dolls, bowls, and primitive musical instruments made by Aboriginal hands and distributed far and wide by my altruistic mother. While out walking Dougal, I wondered again how she would take to him. She too had a fear of dogs, but had laughed during their Skype session when Dougal nosed the screen with a friendly woof.

The heating at school had packed in that day, so Sophie had returned home again and wanted to accompany me. Before collecting our visitors, she and I hopped by the care home, I wasn't sure how much opportunity I'd have to see Fred once they'd arrived, even though initially they would only stay for a short stint before visiting Scotland.

We let ourselves in with the touch pad code and found the residents in the communal living room playing *Pass the Beach Ball*. We stood on the fringes watching Fred give the inflatable a hearty right-handed thwack, eyes gleaming as he followed its progress, baying for another go. I loved hearing his earthy chuckles and laughed along. Afterwards, we approached him in his winged chair.

'Hello Fred,' I said. 'You're a dab hand at that game. Trounced the lot of them.'

He looked at me blankly. 'Who are you?'

A flush of heat and my insides squelched into the pit of my belly.

'I… I'm Anna.'

He was bewildered but trying so hard, searching my face as if in pain.

'I'm Anna, I'm your friend, Fred, I come to visit you. Nearly every day.'

'Will you ta' me ou' in the garden?'

We helped him to stand up at his walking frame, my daughter and I one on each arm. He shuffled out through the patio doors and sat down on the bench beside the fish pond, apparently immune to the freezing day.

'I'll fetch your coat, Fred.' I was thankful for the chance of a few minutes alone. 'Back in a tick, Soph.'

She smiled in empathy, fastening buttons and tightening her scarf.

Mind spinning like a top, I hurried down to Fred's room and took his winter coat from the wardrobe. Back in the corridor, a carer stopped me, the kindest one, my favourite.

'Are you alright, Anna?'

'Yes, I'm fine.'

'But... you're crying.'

'Am I?'

The woman pulled a tissue from her pocket and put a gentle hand to my shoulder, her face etched with concern. I hooked Fred's coat over my arm and blew my nose, wiped my eyes.

'He doesn't know who I am.'

'Ah,' she said.

'I... I can't believe it.'

She nodded. 'That's hard for you, love.'

'Will it come back?'

'It might. Sometimes it's a momentary lapse, sometimes a deterioration.'

I tucked the tissue up my sleeve. 'I'd better get his coat to him before he freezes to death.'

Outside, Fred was lighting his pipe, aided by Sophie who held the match steady.

'I also have a daugh'er,' he was saying to her.

'Beth,' I said, approaching them. 'She's called Beth, Fred.'

'Beth,' he said. 'Yes. Are you Beth?'

288

'No, I'm Anna.' I held out his coat. 'Here, let's put this on.'

His worried face was heart-rending as I carefully threaded his left arm inside one sleeve and waited for him to stick out the other arm as a child might.

'Beth's been very good t' me,' he said.

The house had been snapped up by property developers, its contents now emptied and flung, and Elizabeth had deigned to show her face at the care home just once in the seven weeks he'd been living there.

I smiled. 'Yes Fred, she has.'

'An' who are you?'

'I'm Anna.'

He nodded and popped at his pipe. What was happening in his mind?

I held his hand and we sat with him for a while, chatting about the winter jasmine which climbed the fence, but the shock was causing me to shiver more than the cold day required and we did not linger.

When we left the home, Sophie and I set off for the airport in silence.

'I'm sorry, Mum,' she said finally.

That brought fresh tears, blurring my vision.

'Thank you, darling,' I said, blinking them off. 'He's living his life out with dignity. It's a good home, isn't it?'

'Amazing. Budgies and a pub and everything.'

I smiled at her effort to cheer me.

'Oh damn,' I said, 'I've forgotten the flowers for Granny. Left them down in the cellar to keep them fresh. We'll have to zip past home and pick them up.' I glanced at the clock. 'We'll just about have time.'

There were never any spaces outside our house, so I pulled up and double parked.

Sophie also unclipped her seat belt. 'I need a pee, I'll come in too.'

'OK, let's be quick then.' I locked the car, hazard lights on, and we rushed up the front path.

When I look back, it does still seem surreal. I'm left with one overwhelming image. That of my best friend's crotch – I hadn't realised she shaved. At first, I hadn't caught it, even though she was sitting on our stairs legs akimbo, because my husband's head was in the way. But then, as he'd turned and stumbled down a stair or two, there it was, displayed in its resplendent glory. She seemed so shocked that it was a good few moments before she closed her legs on it.

I'm not sure now if it was I or Sophie who screamed first. Nor is it clear to me how many times my fists railed on Ollie, or what language streamed from me. Slut, slag, bastard. I think the bastard was Sophie addressing her father. Was it bizarre of us both to have continued on our mission? She to the toilet, I for the forgotten flowers. For us to have slammed the front door on the scene and got back in the car? To have set off once again for Heathrow? Well, a no show at the airport was not an option, and that's what we did, stunned to silence though we were.

By the end of the road, Sophie was weeping silently, but my state of shock was immobilising. Ollie and Scar? How was that even possible? In a frenzied quest for clues, I hurtled through our dinner parties, High Road Brasserie, even Sophie's sixteenth. Yes they'd been sitting on the bed together, but they were just mates, had always been just mates. The sheer cunning. Such lies from my husband, an excess of tenderness to mask the devil inside. Such subterfuge from my best friend, the times I'd confided in her about Ollie. Royally duped by them both.

My whole body was shaking. With a flimsy grip on the

wheel, I fumbled at the gearstick, foot loose on the pedals, and we hadn't gone that far before it happened. I vaguely remember passing the bike, or maybe I've planted the memory. Whatever, there was a cyclist on the road. I think Sophie might even have said something, a name, but I really cannot for the life of me recall her words. I was transfixed by the spectacle on our stairs.

We reached the lights just as they were turning green, but the car in front was indicating right. That I remember. It nudged forwards a yard or so, then sat waiting to turn. That I can also still recall. And, after a nifty swerve around the car, I myself was able to turn left.

Sophie did scream then. A blood-curdling howl. The bicycle rode into the car, striking my wing all of a clatter, and then it dropped, rider with it. I braked.

'Mum!' Sophie opened her door and almost fell out of the car. She sank below the window, out of my vision, shrieking incessantly.

I sat for a moment, trying to make sense of what had happened, hands shuddering at the wheel. Then I pulled on the handbrake, turned off the engine and climbed out of the car. A wobbly walk around the front of the bonnet and I collapsed, catatonic, to the tarmac. Like a puppet on chopped strings.

Jack lay motionless before me, his left arm skewed at a bizarre angle. I held my breath and searched the boy for any sign of his own.

31

Afterwards, they all said he should have been wearing a helmet. Despite the hullaballoo from his parents, I was not prosecuted, because I had not been driving dangerously, had been manoeuvring slowly. And he had ridden into me. Thus spoke a fortuitous witness who'd been walking his dog. Of course I was mortified, crippled by shock, but there was no cycle lane, and he should have hung back rather than attempt to undertake me. I know my Highway Code. Do not overtake where you may come into conflict with other road users, it says. Filtering on the left-hand side should only be done when the traffic is completely stationary. It says that too, or something along those lines. And, like they all said, he should have been wearing a helmet.

I called my mother while completing the police report, and I asked her to stay at a hotel that night.

'Bit of a crisis,' I think I said, and there must have been a tremor because she asked no questions.

When Sophie and I finally returned home, Ollie had packed a bag and left, so I tucked my traumatised daughter up in bed, plonked Dougal on her duvet, shut myself in our darkening kitchen, and called the hospital.

Ollie I dealt with the next morning, a simple text with the word *divorce* bringing him to the house. I sat calmly at the island, coffee in hand, as he mooched into the kitchen, head bowed. A naughty boy awaiting punishment, the slouched shoulders, the hands hanging like plumb-lines – with ingenious calculation – I recognised his every angle. I slotted one hand into the other and gripped; he knew nothing of the accident and I didn't want him to think I was shaking because of him.

'Can't even look at me in the eye, can you?' I said.

When he did raise his eyes I caught the glimmer of hope and laughed.

'You must be fucking joking.'

'I'm sorry, Anna, really, it was just a fling.'

'With my best friend.' I forced a casual tone.

'I don't know why, she was there for me after…'

'Oh no you don't. This dates way back, I've been trying to work out when exactly. A quick poke at Sophie's party?'

'No!'

'On our bed? While I was downstairs?'

'I promise you. I needed to talk, and she was there, and she just,' he shook his head, 'lured me in.'

'With her Chanel perfume?' I started laughing then. 'How much *luring* did you need, Ol?'

'Honestly, it's over, I swear.'

'What astounds me is the level of cunning. Not only in the logistics. Long walks with Dougal was it? Fuck her on a park bench?'

'Anna –'

'But also in your manner. I have a theory, you see, that the intensity of your affection has been directly proportionate to the level of your deceit.'

'But I love you.'

'Ha!' A high pitched squeak. And I'd thought my madness spent.

'Anna…' he took a step towards me.

I held up my palm. 'We're done here.'

'But…'

'Collect your gear another day, Sophie's upstairs.'

A flick of my hand to say, and she wants nothing to do with you.

Scar I have never once spoken to since that day. She did email me, insinuated I was making a fuss about nothing, that they were merely *fun* buddies, crazy woman. I chose silence. She left Ollie high and dry, ditched him, and I was eventually calm enough to feel smug about that.

So much betrayal. Indeed, I kept my mother at bay, paying their hotel for several further nights, prolonging their Scottish holiday with the briefest of explanations. She knew me too well and would have unravelled the many threads, my own infidelity among them. Sophie and I spent one meagre afternoon with them, at a hotel restaurant on Christmas Day. We were both distraught about Ollie's affair with my best friend, I told Mum, too distressed to host lunch at home.

Contrary to my fears, one year on, and I'm enjoying being *out there* again – more like fecund soils than frozen wastes. Not sure I'll ever fall in love again. Only forty-six, as my friends tell me, but I'm content alone – and it's a matter of trust. I do miss Ollie actually, his humour, our sparring, and I still reflect often on what went wrong in our marriage. Was it a flimsy foundation? Boredom? Or simply that we caught a glimmer of permission to stray and both hoped we could step out and back in without hurt?

I miss our shared history. Our memory muscle too; so much of life performed together without conscious effort. We were so interwoven that threads of me were also stripped out when he'd gone, leaving gaps which could never be filled by anyone else. Most of all, I miss our bond over Sophie, those cords of love that led directly from our hearts to hers, pulsing with care and protection. Where they met within her heart there must have been some conduction, through his to mine, through mine to his. And whenever her heart constricted we were both jarred, not only by her emotion, but by each other's.

However, once again I am nigh on a confident woman. My office is a short walk from our new home, and I thrive on my capacity to run a business, a social enterprise no less – warm words those. I'm particularly proud of the services we provide to the state-run care homes, some of those places are lamentable. Something magical, Scar had once said. And to witness a spark in the eyes of an old lady with dementia when she's singing along to *You Are My Sunshine,* to unearth a glimmer of the woman she once was, well that is indeed a moment of magic.

Fred passed away this spring. One night in his sleep. He was nearly eighty-seven – and isn't that how we'd all like to go? During his last months he had the occasional lucid interlude, when he would examine my face and call me Anna, but usually he took me for Elizabeth. And I played along. After his funeral I planted two bushes in the care home garden, double headed peonies (Angel Cheeks) and a rosette rose (Wild Eve). Side by side, both a pale blush pink. Often of an afternoon I find myself scattering raisins on the lawn at home and taking a moment, silent and still, to watch the blackbirds swoop. I do miss him dreadfully.

Jack lived. The nerves in his left elbow were so damaged by the fall, however, that he nearly lost his arm. I did see him once, from afar, and it hangs more loosely than the other one; I'm told that he no longer plays tennis. It's a mark on my soul, a young man cut down in his prime. And how do I feel about it?

Ashamed. Stunned by the depths of my anger towards him, the frenzied manifestation of my over-protective mothering. As Sophie once said, tiger, helicopter, submarine – she invented that last one, of course, even if it too was spot on. But I'm only human. Aren't we all?

Chiswick, my once constant companion, is no longer my home. On my rare ventures back there, I am aware of the hand-over-mouth whispers, and I know that some people call me *that* woman. Sophie and I live with Dougal and Horace in a small terraced house in Brackenbury Village on the fringe of Hammersmith. Impossible for either of us to have remained in our old home, not after seeing that montage played out on our stairs, but I do miss Chiswick, its air steeped with Fuller's beer.

As for Sophie, well she is now immersed in her A levels. Part of me does wish she had stayed in the car that morning, that she had escaped a sight which will surely remain indelible, and yet it was so much simpler to extricate myself from Ollie given that she was a witness to the 'crime'. She suffered, I know. Still has nightmares. And I do wonder if the scars will remain. All men are bastards, I once joked with her, but of those she was closest to that summer, her first boyfriend and her father, well both of them were indeed bastards. She has only recently been willing to see Ollie again, tells me he has lost weight, baggy face, the sandy hair now salt and pepper.

Of my own affair I believe she knows nothing, and I am humbled. We are close again, she and I, but within a matter of months she'll be off travelling before university and I am preparing to shoot the arrow. There are nights when I awake drenched, my mind a-chattering. Would she know not to enter a cave of bats? Deadly diseases are caught from bat guano. Not to take a night bus in Thailand? Drivers notoriously fall asleep. Not to wear a long scarf in an open-top car in case it catches in the wheels? That could decapitate a person.

Thus far, we have never talked about that morning. We both succumbed to counselling, separately, and I imagine that she relived the scene of the accident just as I did. The aftermath played out in slow-motion, a gathering crowd, a screeching ambulance, her hysteria. And me, slumped inert in the road.

Young people are resilient, and one day we will discuss it, when she's older, much older. When we're more like equals. Sometimes I contemplate her while she's head down in her books, her silken hair falling about a face which is now that of a young woman, and so strikingly beautiful it tears at my heart. And I wonder.

In all honesty, I'm not sure whether she's aware – or whether she will ever figure it out. The trauma of that day has left me blank and my own recollection is hazy. Various scenarios play out – was there heavy traffic ahead? Roadworks?

Because the quickest route to the airport had been straight on. And I will have to live for the rest of my life wondering why I, on that particular day, had taken a left turn.

Acknowledgements

Once again, profound thanks to all at Blackbird, especially Stephanie Zia, the most supportive and caring editor one could wish for – and also the kindest friend. We Blackbird authors owe it all to her and our loyalty knows no bounds. Particular thanks to those who scrutinised early drafts of *Only Human*: Ruth Hunter, Cath Hurley, Wilma Ferguson, Barbara McKinlay, Susie Howells, Janet Daykin and Catherine Davidson. Thanks also to my other kindred souls at Writers at Work: Judith Evans, Jana Ferguson, Peggy Hannington, Joy Isaacs, Janice Rainsbury, Barry Walsh. Thanks to Helen Boyce of The Book Club (TBC on FB) for her remarkable assistance. And thank you to my parents, to whom *Only Human* is dedicated. As I write, Mum is 86 and living with dementia, and Dad is 87 and going strong – enjoying crosswords and feeding raisins to blackbirds. In this novel, there are traces of them both. For the original cover artwork, my special thanks go to Maddie, my not-too-tricky teen (though she tells me there is still time). And most of all, thanks to Nick, for everything really.

About the Author

Diane Chandler worked first as a political lobbyist in Brussels, and then at the European Commission for several years, where she managed overseas aid programmes in Ukraine just after the fall of communism. Ukraine became the subject for her first novel, *The Road To Donetsk* which won The People's Book Prize for Fiction 2016. Her second novel, *Moondance*, was informed by her personal experience of the emotional and physical impact of IVF. She hosted the Chiswick Buzz TV Book Club – *Words With Wine in W4* – during lockdown.

Keep up to date with all Diane Chandler news and new titles, join the Diane Chandler Mailing List

http://eepurl.com/9QUyn

(All email details securely managed at Mailchimp.com and never shared with third parties.).

Facebook: @DianeChandlerAuthor
Twitter: @Dchandlerauthor

Blackbird Digital Books
07816 491189
editor@blackbird-books.com
The #authorpower publishing company
Discovering outstanding authors
www.blackbird-books.com
@Blackbird_Bks

Blackbird